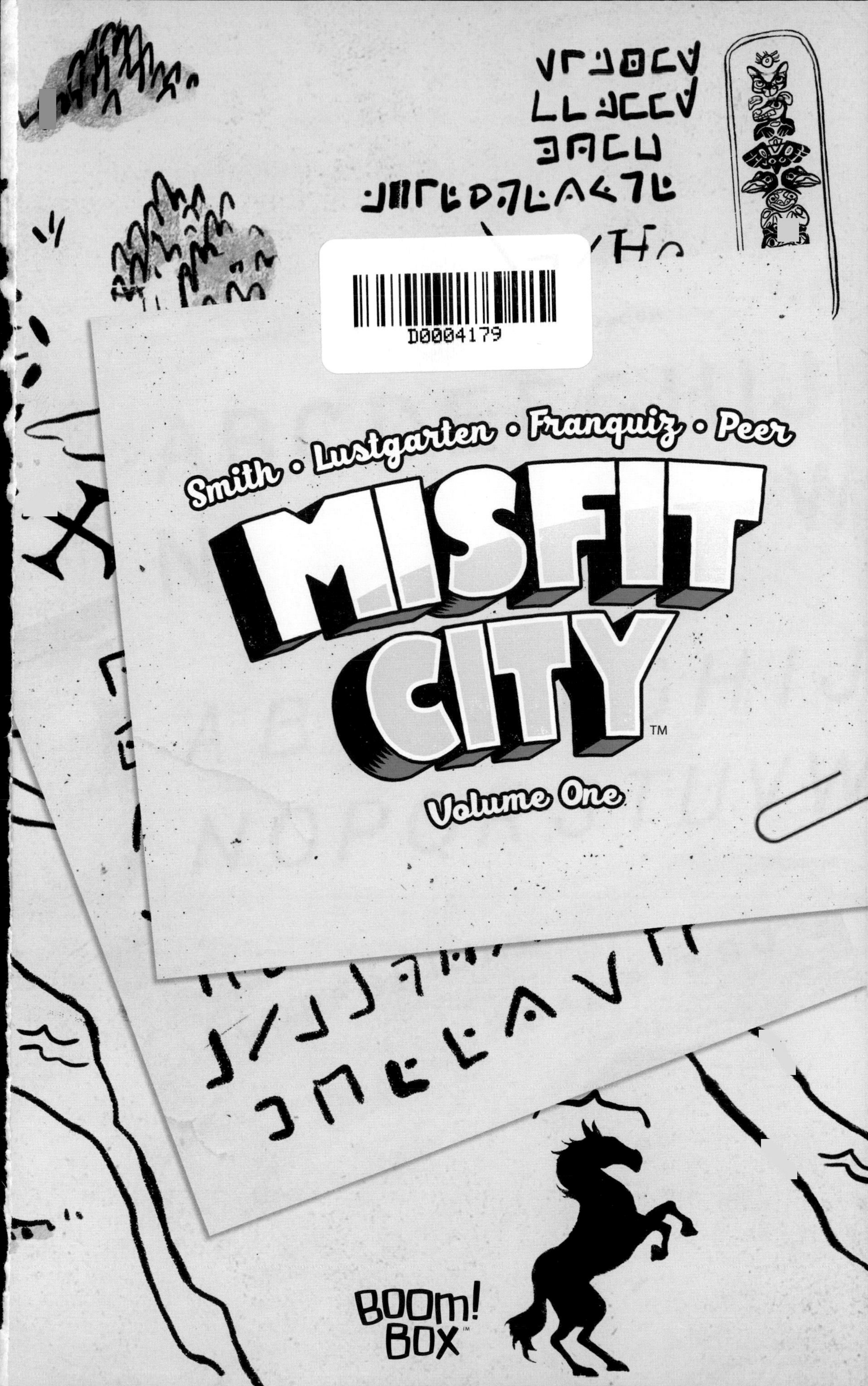
Smith • Lustgarten • Franquiz • Peer
MISFIT CITY™
Volume One
BOOM! BOX™

Ross Richie	CEO & Founder	Matthew Levine	Editor
Joy Huffman	CFO	Sophie Philips-Roberts	Assistant Editor
Matt Gagnon	Editor-in-Chief	Gavin Gronenthal	Assistant Editor
Filip Sablik	President, Publishing & Marketing	Michael Moccio	Assistant Editor
Stephen Christy	President, Development	Amanda LaFranco	Executive Assistant
Lance Kreiter	Vice President, Licensing & Merchandising	Jillian Crab	Design Coordinator
Phil Barbaro	Vice President, Finance & Human Resources	Michelle Ankley	Design Coordinator
Arune Singh	Vice President, Marketing	Kara Leopard	Production Designer
Bryce Carlson	Vice President, Editorial & Creative Strategy	Marie Krupina	Production Designer
Scott Newman	Manager, Production Design	Grace Park	Production Design Assistant
Kate Henning	Manager, Operations	Chelsea Roberts	Production Design Assistant
Spencer Simpson	Manager, Sales	Elizabeth Loughridge	Accounting Coordinator
Sierra Hahn	Executive Editor	Stephanie Hocutt	Social Media Coordinator
Jeanine Schaefer	Executive Editor	José Meza	Event Coordinator
Dafna Pleban	Senior Editor	Holly Aitchison	Operations Coordinator
Shannon Watters	Senior Editor	Megan Christopher	Operations Assistant
Eric Harburn	Senior Editor	Rodrigo Hernandez	Mailroom Assistant
Whitney Leopard	Editor	Morgan Perry	Direct Market Representative
Cameron Chittock	Editor	Cat O'Grady	Marketing Assistant
Chris Rosa	Editor	Breanna Sarpy	Executive Assistant

BOOM! BOX™

MISFIT CITY Volume One, December 2018. Published by BOOM! Box, a division of Boom Entertainment, Inc. Misfit City is ™ & © 2018 Kiwi Loves You, Inc. and Kurt Lustgarten. Originally published in single magazine form as MISFIT CITY No. 1-4. ™ & © 2017 Kiwi Loves You, Inc. and Kurt Lustgarten. All rights reserved. BOOM! Box™ and the BOOM! Box logo are trademarks of Boom Entertainment, Inc., registered in various countries and categories. All characters, events, and institutions depicted herein are fictional. Any similarity between any of the names, characters, persons, events, and/or institutions in this publication to actual names, characters, and persons, whether living or dead, events, and/or institutions is unintended and purely coincidental. BOOM! Box does not read or accept unsolicited submissions of ideas, stories, or artwork.

BOOM! Studios, 5670 Wilshire Boulevard, Suite 400, Los Angeles, CA 90036-5679. Printed in China. Second Printing.

ISBN: 978-1-68415-027-4, eISBN: 978-161-398-704-9

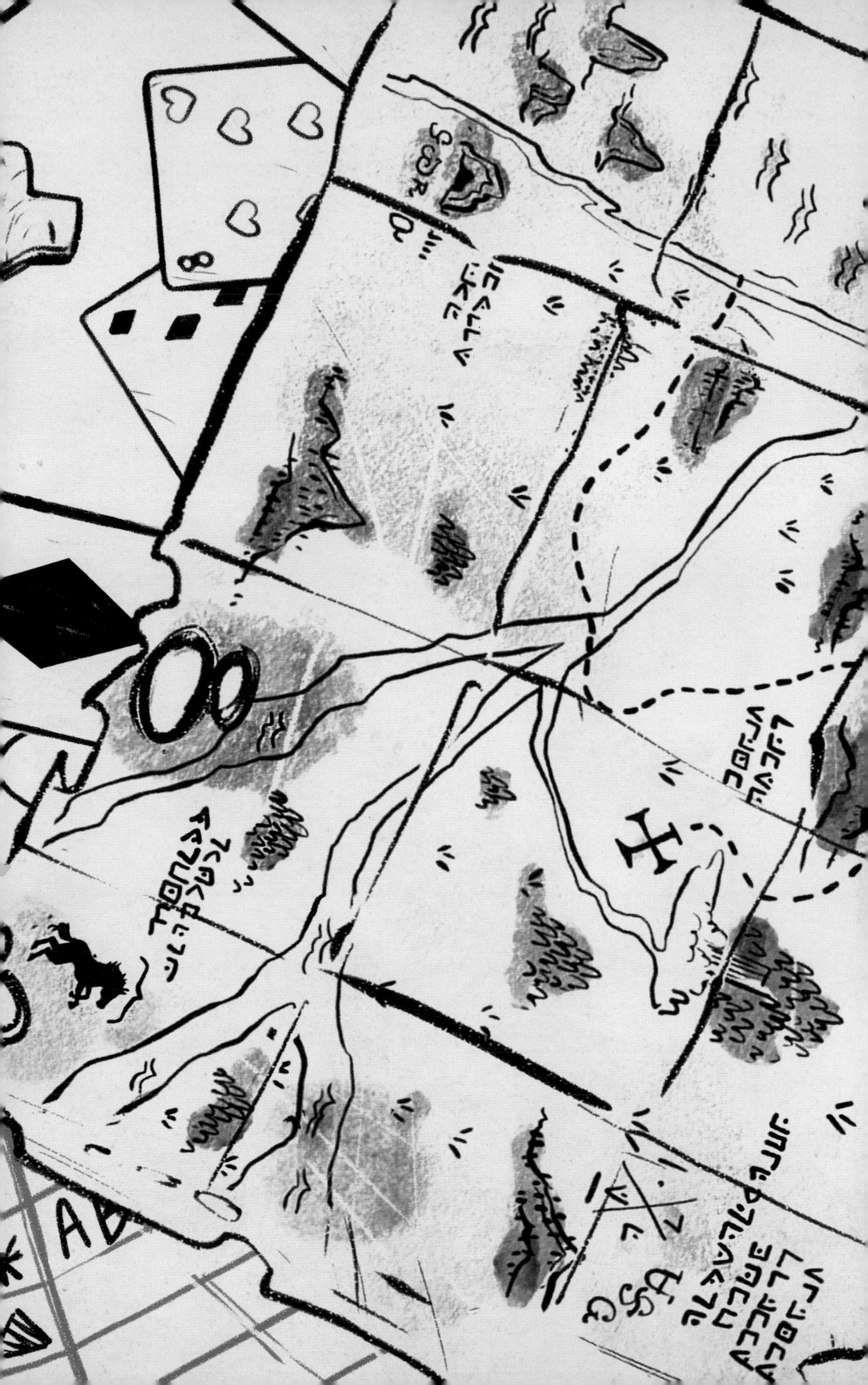

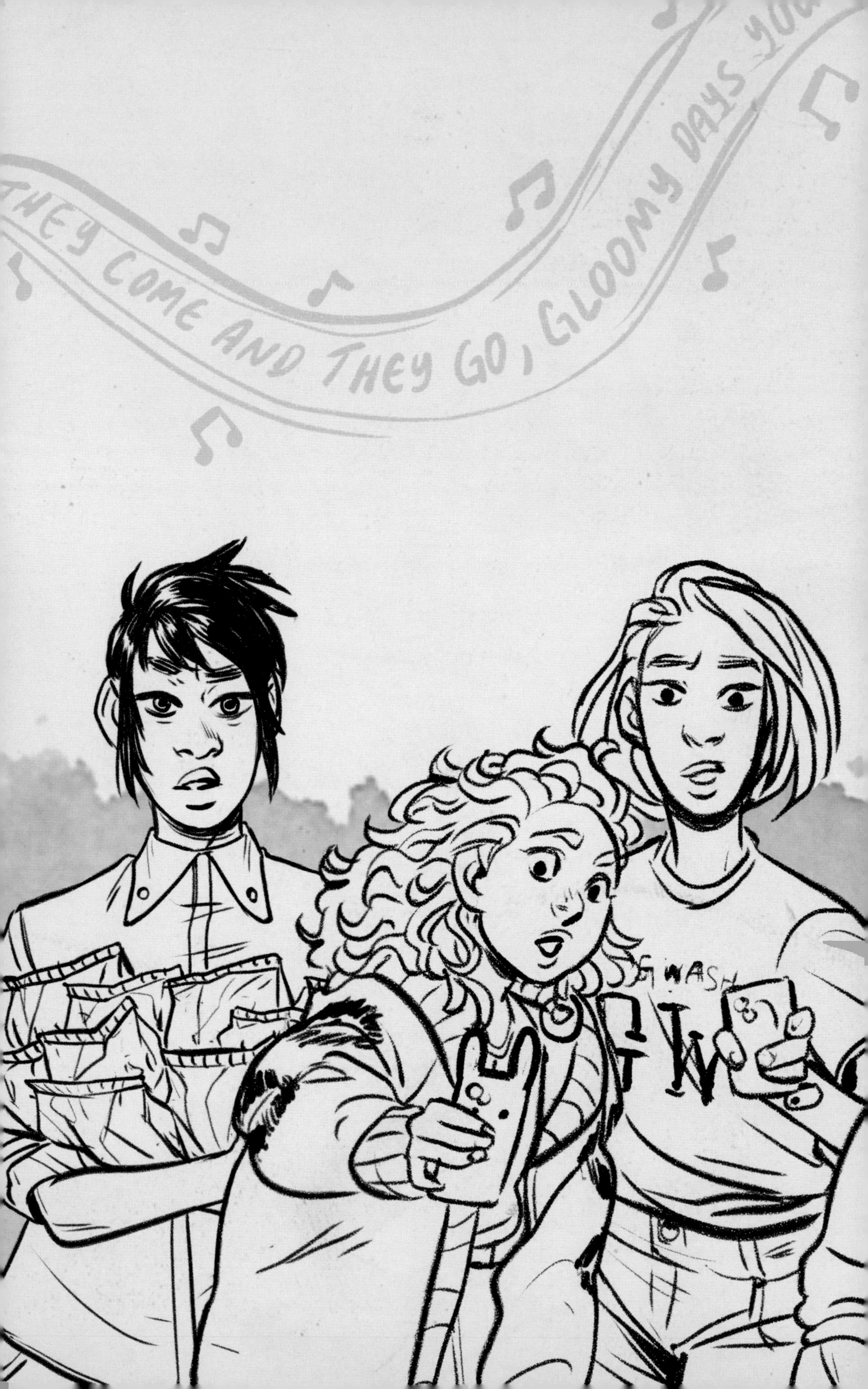
HEY COME AND THEY GO, GLOOMY DAYS YOU

Created and Written by
Kirsten 'Kiwi' Smith & Kurt Lustgarten

Illustrated by
Naomi Franquiz

Colored by
Brittany Peer

Lettered by
Jim Campbell

Cover by
Naomi Franquiz
Colors by **Brittany Peer**

Designer **Marie Krupina**
Logo Design **Kelsey Dietrich**
Assistant Editor **Sophie Philips-Roberts**
Editor **Shannon Watters**

CHAPTER
I

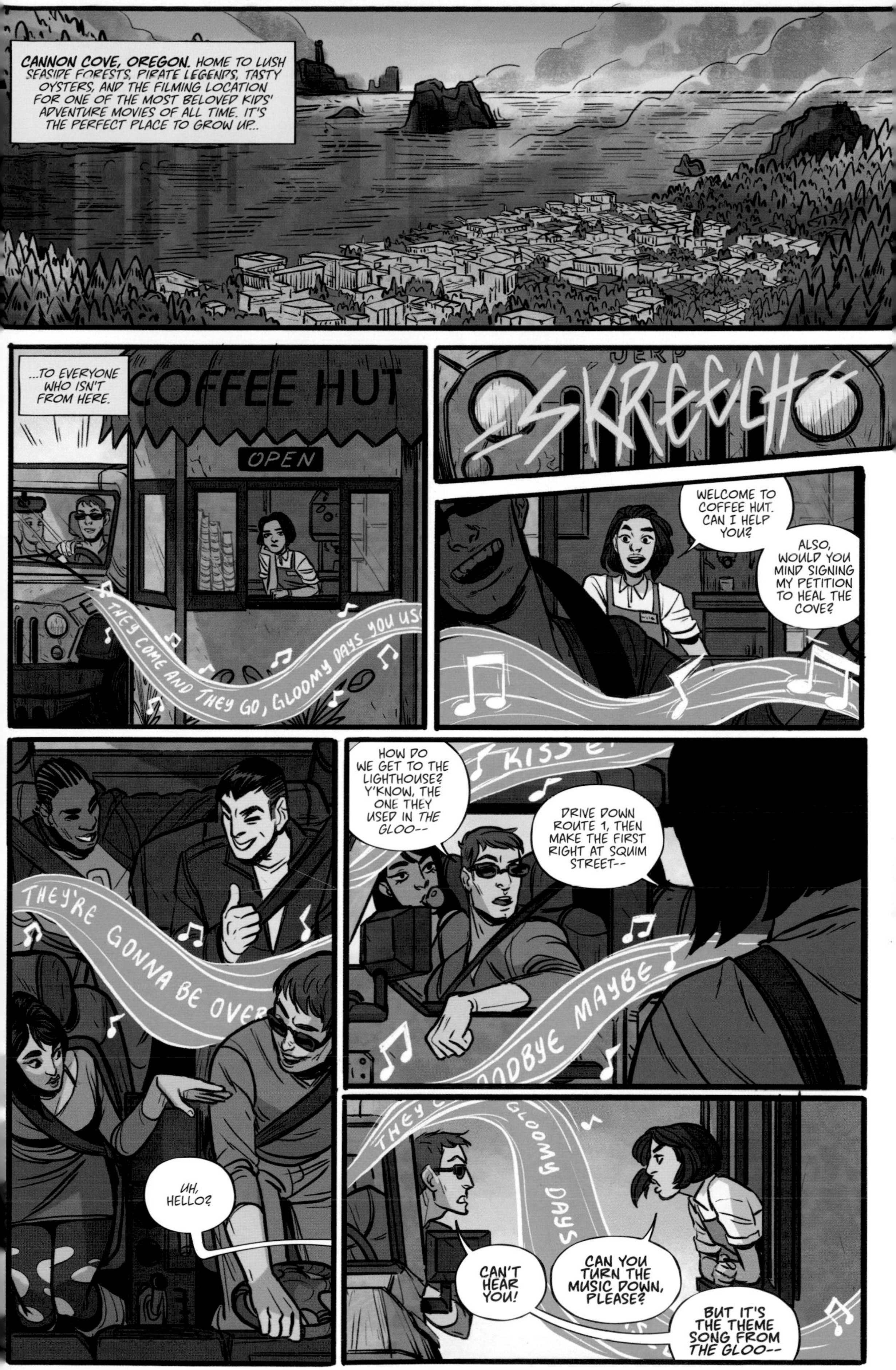
CANNON COVE, OREGON. HOME TO LUSH SEASIDE FORESTS, PIRATE LEGENDS, TASTY OYSTERS, AND THE FILMING LOCATION FOR ONE OF THE MOST BELOVED KIDS' ADVENTURE MOVIES OF ALL TIME. IT'S THE PERFECT PLACE TO GROW UP...
...TO EVERYONE WHO ISN'T FROM HERE.
COFFEE HUT
OPEN
THEY COME AND THEY GO, GLOOMY DAYS YOU USE
SKREECH
WELCOME TO COFFEE HUT. CAN I HELP YOU?
ALSO, WOULD YOU MIND SIGNING MY PETITION TO HEAL THE COVE?
THEY'RE GONNA BE OVER
UH, HELLO?
KISS
HOW DO WE GET TO THE LIGHTHOUSE? Y'KNOW, THE ONE THEY USED IN THE GLOO--
DRIVE DOWN ROUTE 1, THEN MAKE THE FIRST RIGHT AT SQUIM STREET--
ODBYE MAYBE
GLOOMY DAYS
CAN'T HEAR YOU!
CAN YOU TURN THE MUSIC DOWN, PLEASE?
BUT IT'S THE THEME SONG FROM THE GLOO--

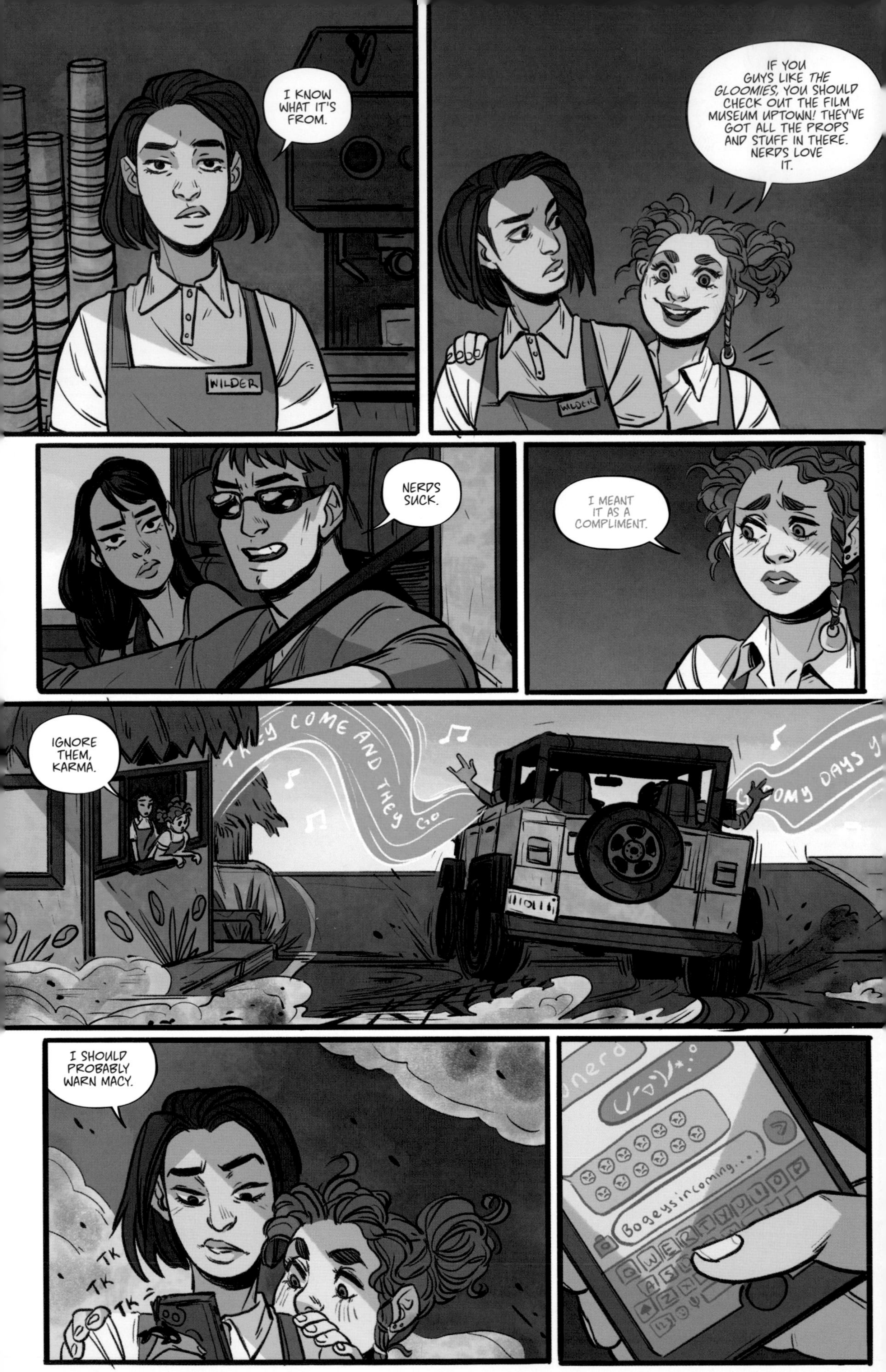
I KNOW WHAT IT'S FROM.
IF YOU GUYS LIKE *THE GLOOMIES*, YOU SHOULD CHECK OUT THE FILM MUSEUM UPTOWN! THEY'VE GOT ALL THE PROPS AND STUFF IN THERE. NERDS LOVE IT.
WILDER
NERDS SUCK.
I MEANT IT AS A COMPLIMENT.
IGNORE THEM, KARMA.
THEY COME AND THEY GO
GLOOMY DAYS
I SHOULD PROBABLY WARN MACY.
TK
TK
TK
Bogeys incoming....

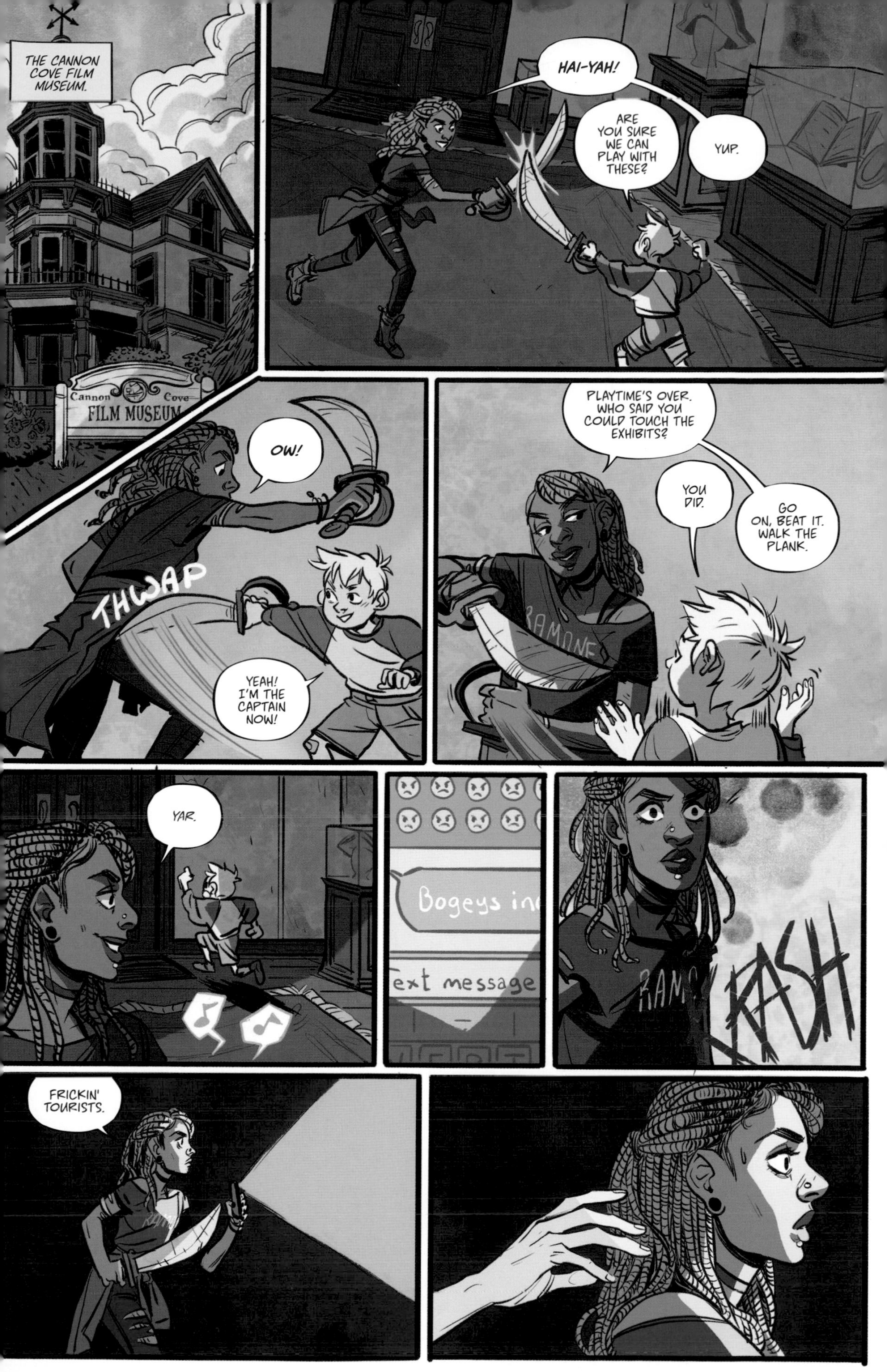
THE CANNON COVE FILM MUSEUM.
Cannon Cove FILM MUSEUM
HAI-YAH!
ARE YOU SURE WE CAN PLAY WITH THESE?
YUP.
OW!
THWAP
YEAH! I'M THE CAPTAIN NOW!
PLAYTIME'S OVER. WHO SAID YOU COULD TOUCH THE EXHIBITS?
YOU DID.
GO ON, BEAT IT. WALK THE PLANK.
RAMONE
YAR.
Bogeys in
Text message
KRASH
FRICKIN' TOURISTS.

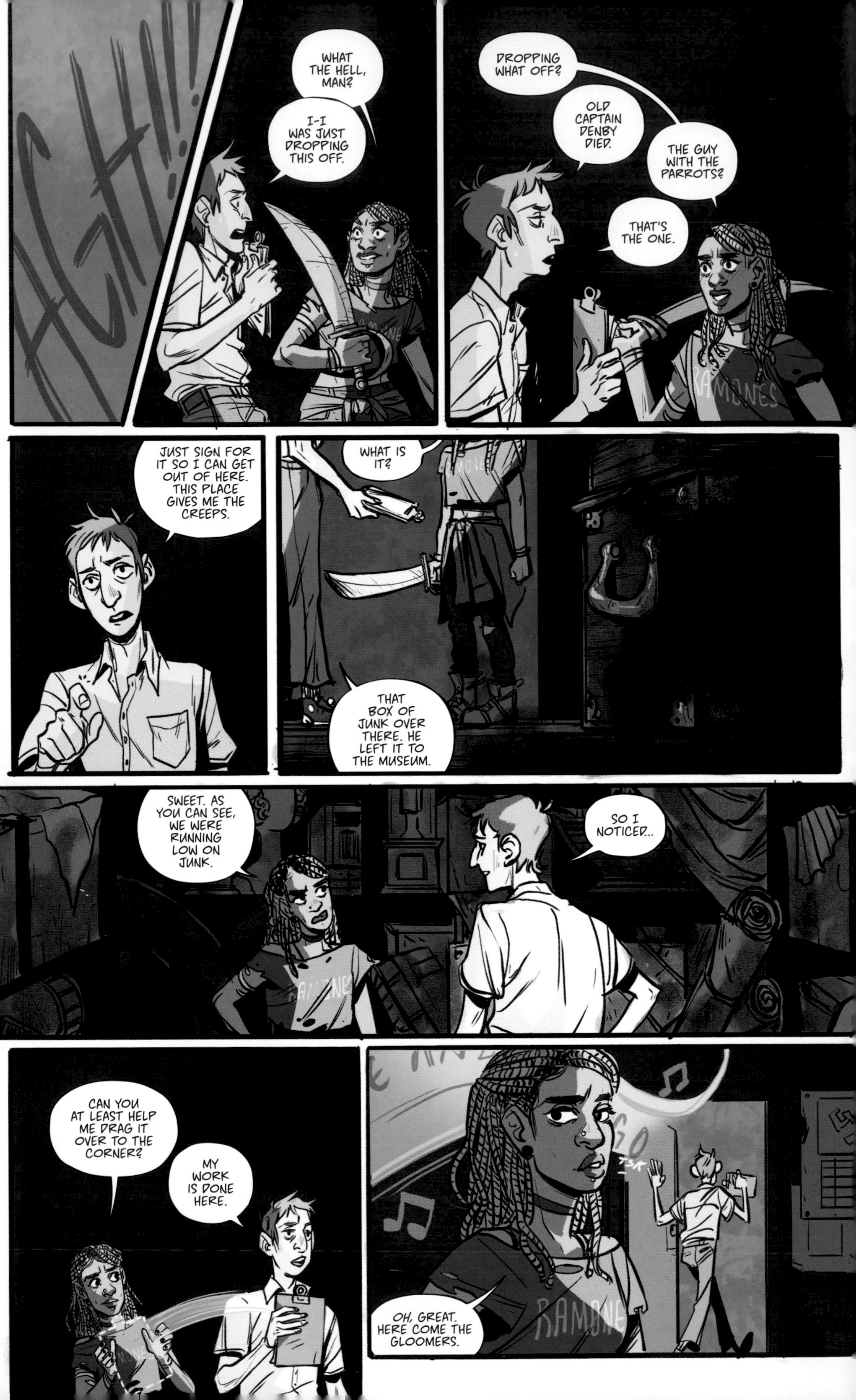
AAGH!!!
WHAT THE HELL, MAN?
I-I WAS JUST DROPPING THIS OFF.
DROPPING WHAT OFF?
OLD CAPTAIN DENBY DIED.
THE GUY WITH THE PARROTS?
THAT'S THE ONE.
RAMONES
JUST SIGN FOR IT SO I CAN GET OUT OF HERE. THIS PLACE GIVES ME THE CREEPS.
WHAT IS IT?
THAT BOX OF JUNK OVER THERE. HE LEFT IT TO THE MUSEUM.
SWEET. AS YOU CAN SEE, WE WERE RUNNING LOW ON JUNK.
SO I NOTICED...
CAN YOU AT LEAST HELP ME DRAG IT OVER TO THE CORNER?
MY WORK IS DONE HERE.
TSK
OH, GREAT. HERE COME THE GLOOMERS.

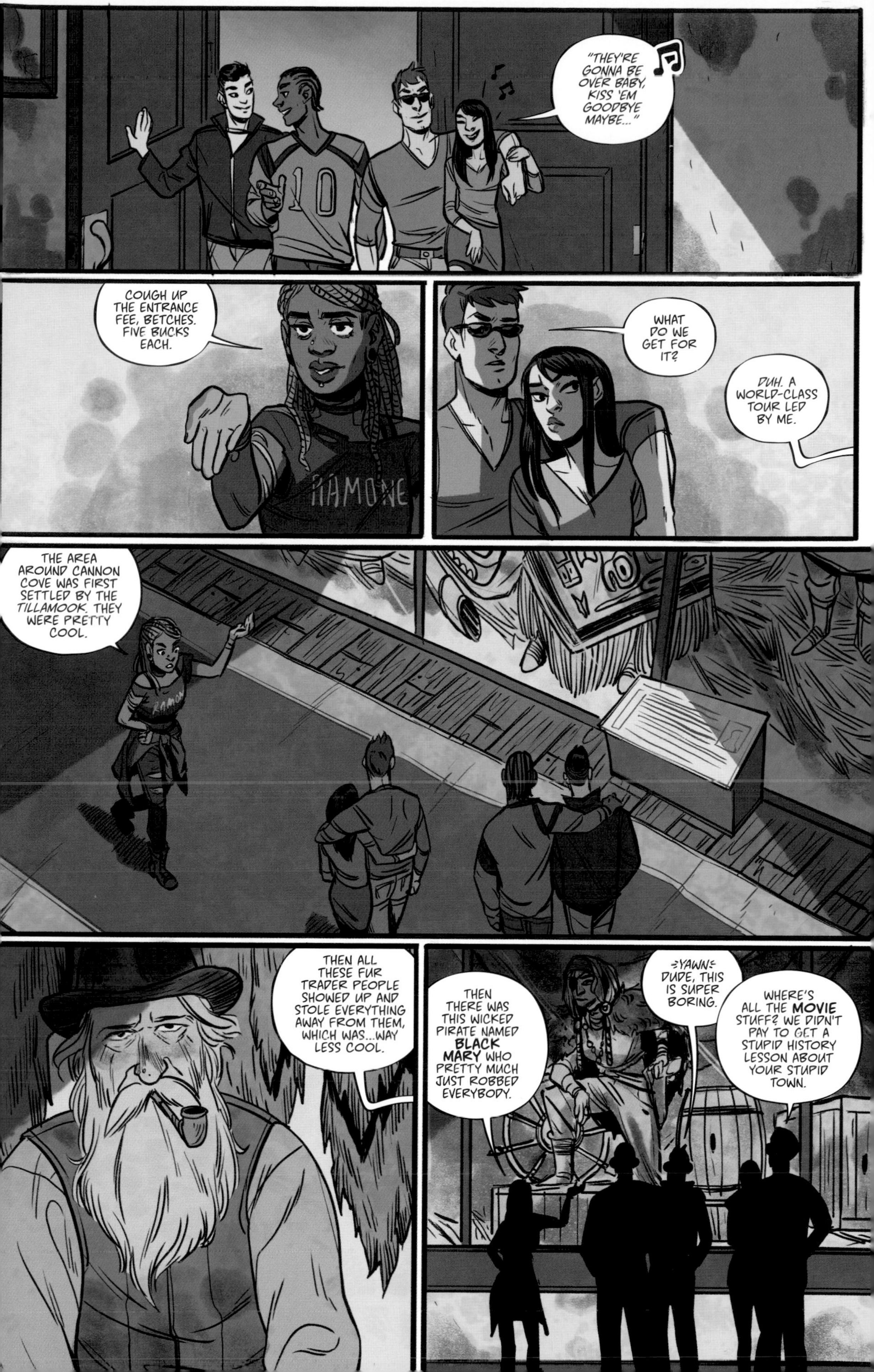
"THEY'RE GONNA BE OVER BABY, KISS 'EM GOODBYE MAYBE..."
COUGH UP THE ENTRANCE FEE, BETCHES. FIVE BUCKS EACH.
RAMONE
WHAT DO WE GET FOR IT?
DUH. A WORLD-CLASS TOUR LED BY ME.
THE AREA AROUND CANNON COVE WAS FIRST SETTLED BY THE *TILLAMOOK*. THEY WERE PRETTY COOL.
RAMONE
THEN ALL THESE FUR TRADER PEOPLE SHOWED UP AND STOLE EVERYTHING AWAY FROM THEM, WHICH WAS...WAY LESS COOL.
THEN THERE WAS THIS WICKED PIRATE NAMED **BLACK MARY** WHO PRETTY MUCH JUST ROBBED EVERYBODY.
YAWN DUDE, THIS IS SUPER BORING.
WHERE'S ALL THE **MOVIE** STUFF? WE DIDN'T PAY TO GET A STUPID HISTORY LESSON ABOUT YOUR STUPID TOWN.

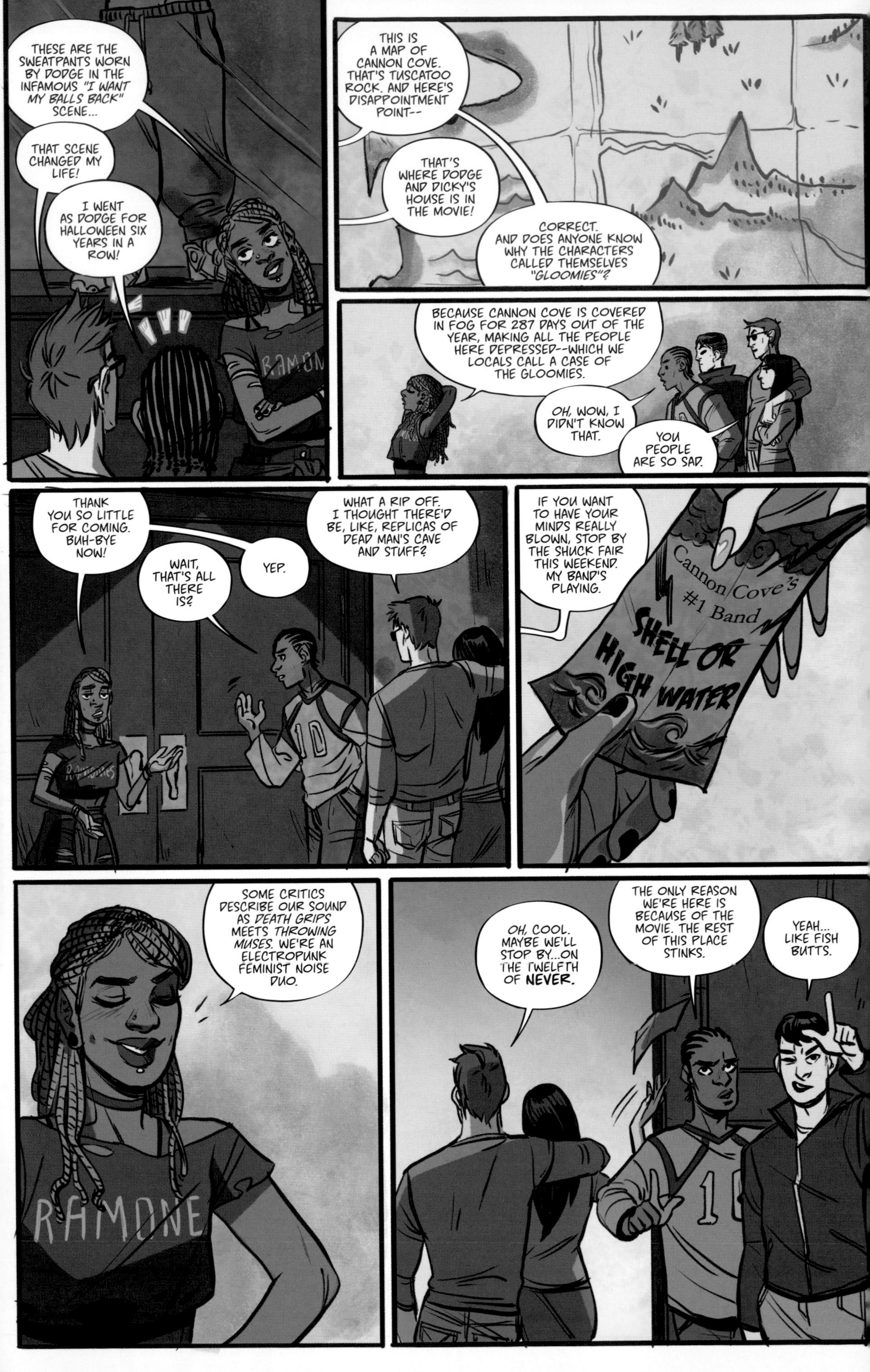
THESE ARE THE SWEATPANTS WORN BY DODGE IN THE INFAMOUS "I WANT MY BALLS BACK" SCENE...
THAT SCENE CHANGED MY LIFE!
I WENT AS DODGE FOR HALLOWEEN SIX YEARS IN A ROW!
RAMON
THIS IS A MAP OF CANNON COVE. THAT'S TUSCATOO ROCK. AND HERE'S DISAPPOINTMENT POINT--
THAT'S WHERE DODGE AND DICKY'S HOUSE IS IN THE MOVIE!
CORRECT. AND DOES ANYONE KNOW WHY THE CHARACTERS CALLED THEMSELVES "GLOOMIES"?
BECAUSE CANNON COVE IS COVERED IN FOG FOR 287 DAYS OUT OF THE YEAR, MAKING ALL THE PEOPLE HERE DEPRESSED--WHICH WE LOCALS CALL A CASE OF THE GLOOMIES.
OH, WOW, I DIDN'T KNOW THAT.
YOU PEOPLE ARE SO SAD.
THANK YOU SO LITTLE FOR COMING. BUH-BYE NOW!
WAIT, THAT'S ALL THERE IS?
YEP.
WHAT A RIP OFF. I THOUGHT THERE'D BE, LIKE, REPLICAS OF DEAD MAN'S CAVE AND STUFF?
10
IF YOU WANT TO HAVE YOUR MINDS REALLY BLOWN, STOP BY THE SHUCK FAIR THIS WEEKEND. MY BAND'S PLAYING.
Cannon Cove's #1 Band
SHELL OR HIGH WATER
SOME CRITICS DESCRIBE OUR SOUND AS *DEATH GRIPS* MEETS *THROWING MUSES*. WE'RE AN ELECTROPUNK FEMINIST NOISE DUO.
RAMONE
OH, COOL. MAYBE WE'LL STOP BY...ON THE TWELFTH OF **NEVER.**
THE ONLY REASON WE'RE HERE IS BECAUSE OF THE MOVIE. THE REST OF THIS PLACE STINKS.
YEAH... LIKE FISH BUTTS.

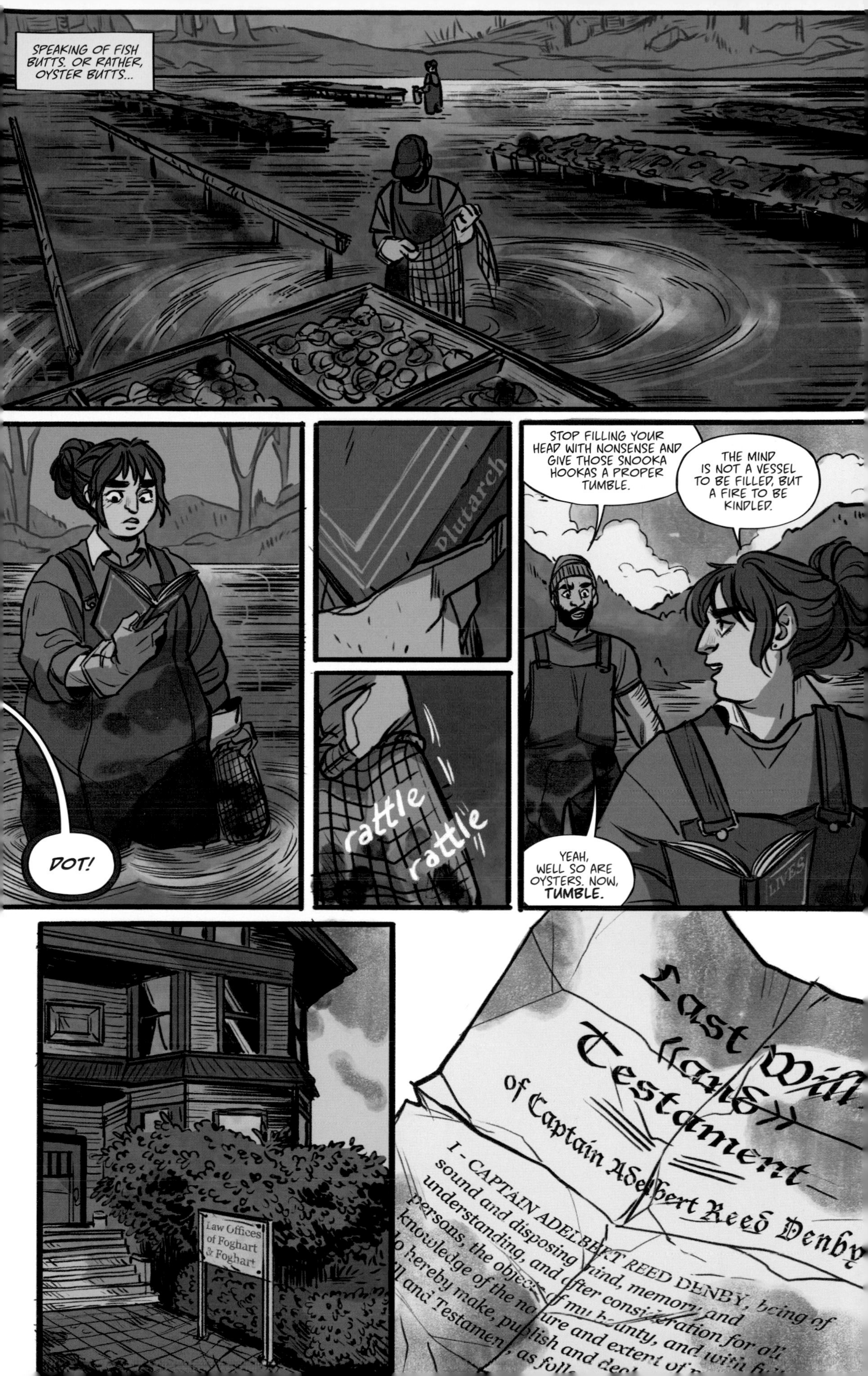
SPEAKING OF FISH BUTTS. OR RATHER, OYSTER BUTTS...
DOT!
plutarch
rattle
rattle
STOP FILLING YOUR HEAD WITH NONSENSE AND GIVE THOSE SNOOKA HOOKAS A PROPER TUMBLE.
THE MIND IS NOT A VESSEL TO BE FILLED, BUT A FIRE TO BE KINDLED.
YEAH, WELL SO ARE OYSTERS. NOW, **TUMBLE.**
LIVES
Law Offices of Foghart & Foghart
Last Will and Testament
of Captain Adelbert Reed Denby
I - CAPTAIN ADELBERT REED DENBY, being of
sound and disposing mind, memory and
understanding, and after consideration for all
persons, the objects of my bounty, and with full
knowledge of the nature and extent of
do hereby make, publish and decl
ll and Testamen, as foll

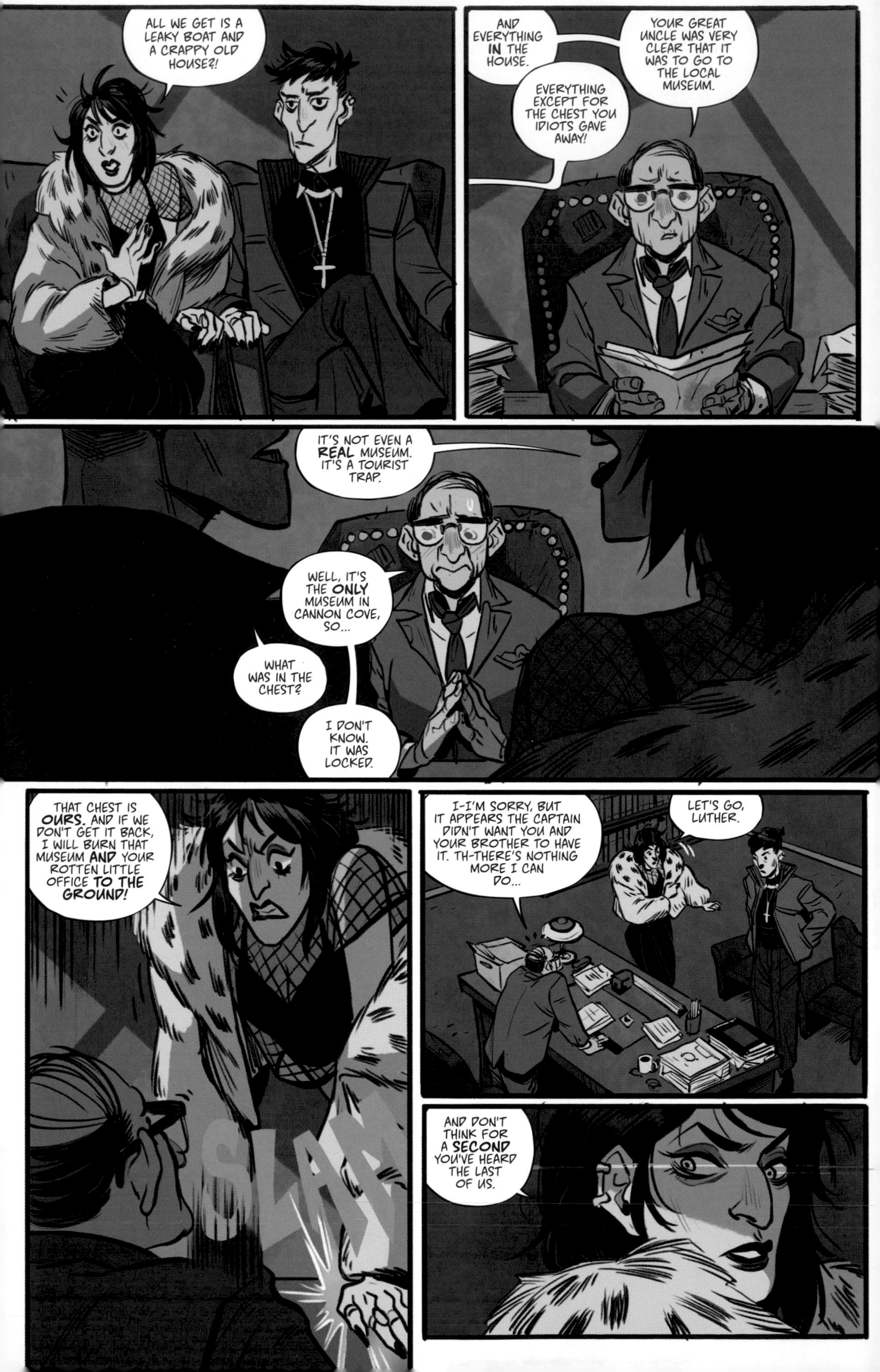
ALL WE GET IS A LEAKY BOAT AND A CRAPPY OLD HOUSE?!
AND EVERYTHING **IN** THE HOUSE.
YOUR GREAT UNCLE WAS VERY CLEAR THAT IT WAS TO GO TO THE LOCAL MUSEUM.
EVERYTHING EXCEPT FOR THE CHEST YOU IDIOTS GAVE AWAY!
IT'S NOT EVEN A **REAL** MUSEUM. IT'S A TOURIST TRAP.
WELL, IT'S THE **ONLY** MUSEUM IN CANNON COVE, SO...
WHAT WAS IN THE CHEST?
I DON'T KNOW. IT WAS LOCKED.
THAT CHEST IS **OURS.** AND IF WE DON'T GET IT BACK, I WILL BURN THAT MUSEUM **AND** YOUR ROTTEN LITTLE OFFICE **TO THE GROUND!**
SLAM
I-I'M SORRY, BUT IT APPEARS THE CAPTAIN DIDN'T WANT YOU AND YOUR BROTHER TO HAVE IT. TH-THERE'S NOTHING MORE I CAN DO...
LET'S GO, LUTHER.
AND DON'T THINK FOR A **SECOND** YOU'VE HEARD THE LAST OF US.

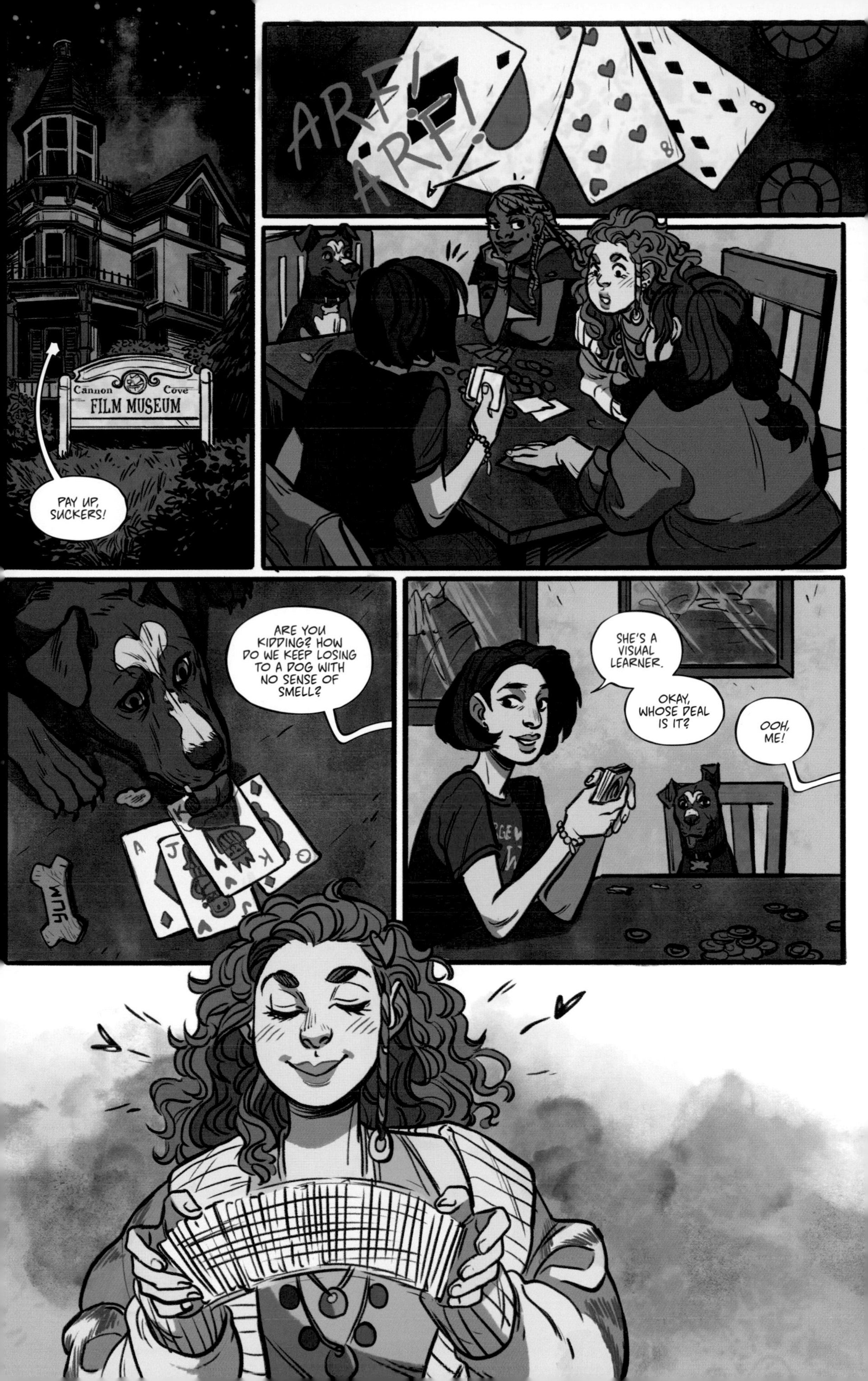
Cannon Cove
FILM MUSEUM
PAY UP, SUCKERS!
ARF! ARF!
ARE YOU KIDDING? HOW DO WE KEEP LOSING TO A DOG WITH NO SENSE OF SMELL?
YUM
SHE'S A VISUAL LEARNER.
OKAY, WHOSE DEAL IS IT?
OOH, ME!

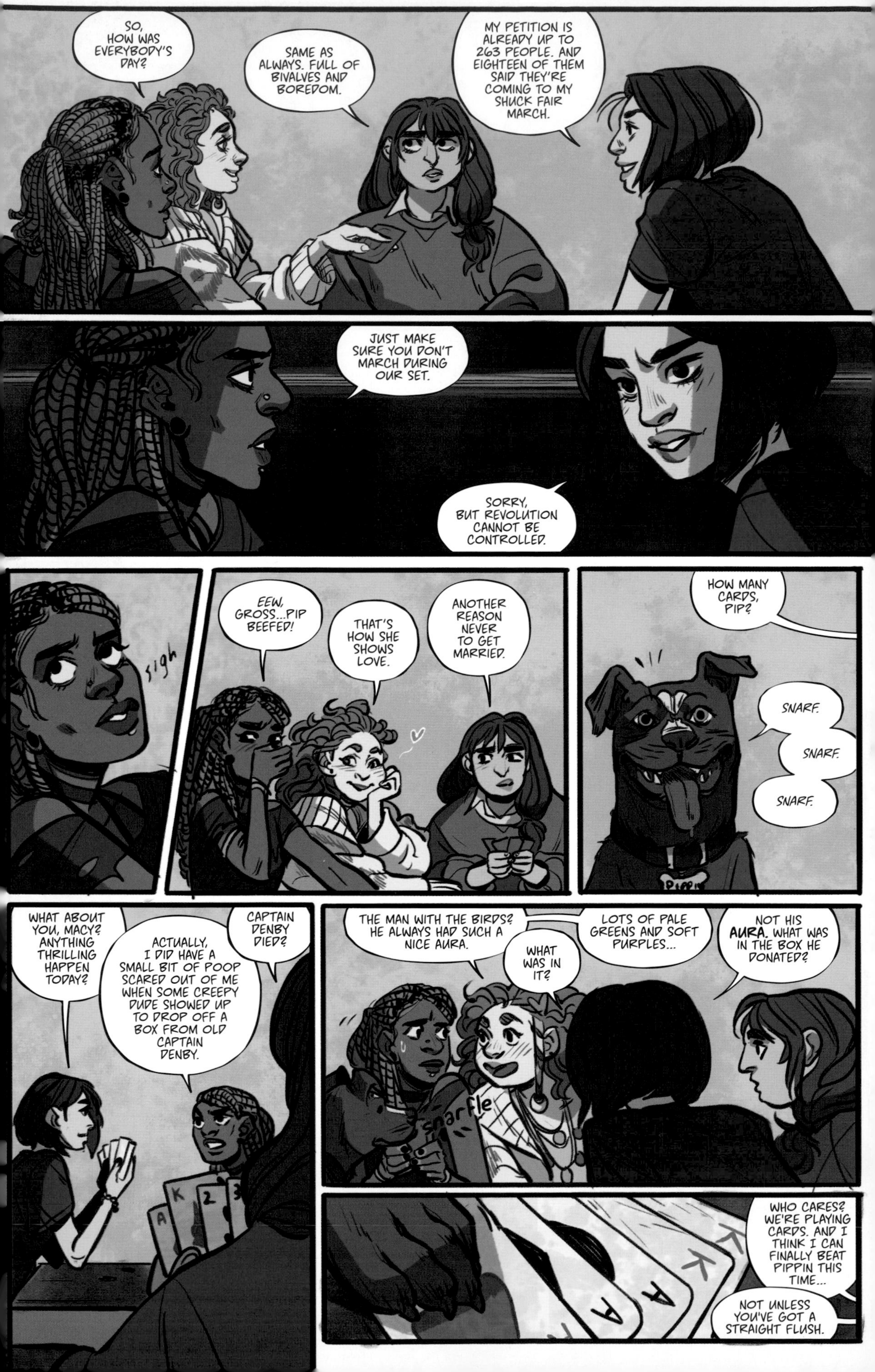
SO, HOW WAS EVERYBODY'S DAY?
SAME AS ALWAYS. FULL OF BIVALVES AND BOREDOM.
MY PETITION IS ALREADY UP TO 263 PEOPLE. AND EIGHTEEN OF THEM SAID THEY'RE COMING TO MY SHUCK FAIR MARCH.
JUST MAKE SURE YOU DON'T MARCH DURING OUR SET.
SORRY, BUT REVOLUTION CANNOT BE CONTROLLED.
sigh
EEW, GROSS...PIP BEEFED!
THAT'S HOW SHE SHOWS LOVE.
ANOTHER REASON NEVER TO GET MARRIED.
HOW MANY CARDS, PIP?
SNARF.
SNARF.
SNARF.
WHAT ABOUT YOU, MACY? ANYTHING THRILLING HAPPEN TODAY?
ACTUALLY, I DID HAVE A SMALL BIT OF POOP SCARED OUT OF ME WHEN SOME CREEPY DUDE SHOWED UP TO DROP OFF A BOX FROM OLD CAPTAIN DENBY.
CAPTAIN DENBY DIED?
THE MAN WITH THE BIRDS? HE ALWAYS HAD SUCH A NICE AURA.
LOTS OF PALE GREENS AND SOFT PURPLES...
WHAT WAS IN IT?
NOT HIS **AURA**. WHAT WAS IN THE BOX HE DONATED?
snarfle
WHO CARES? WE'RE PLAYING CARDS. AND I THINK I CAN FINALLY BEAT PIPPIN THIS TIME...
NOT UNLESS YOU'VE GOT A STRAIGHT FLUSH.

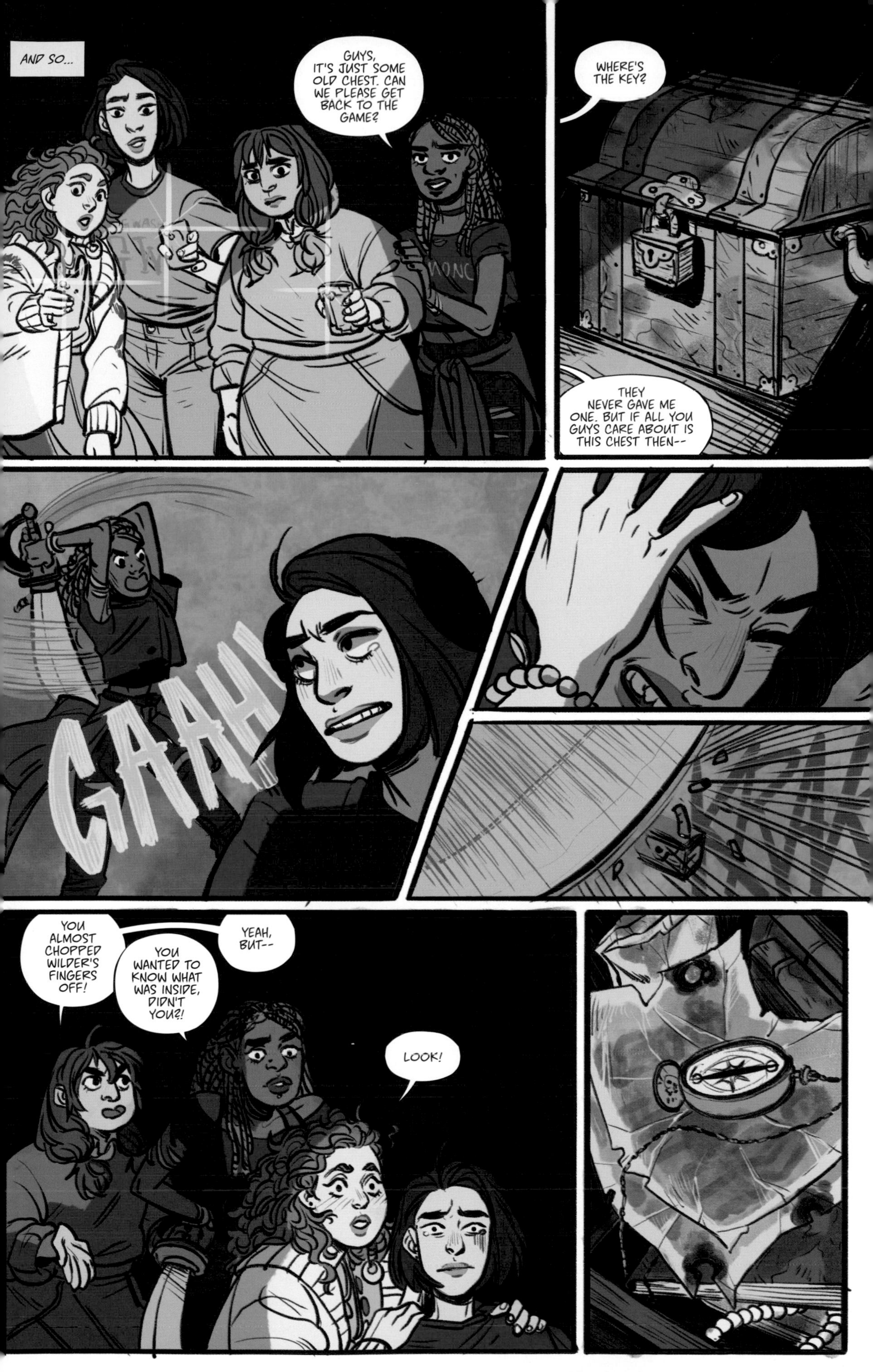

AND SO...
GUYS, IT'S JUST SOME OLD CHEST. CAN WE PLEASE GET BACK TO THE GAME?
WHERE'S THE KEY?
THEY NEVER GAVE ME ONE. BUT IF ALL YOU GUYS CARE ABOUT IS THIS CHEST THEN--
GAAH
YOU ALMOST CHOPPED WILDER'S FINGERS OFF!
YOU WANTED TO KNOW WHAT WAS INSIDE, DIDN'T YOU?!
YEAH, BUT--
LOOK!

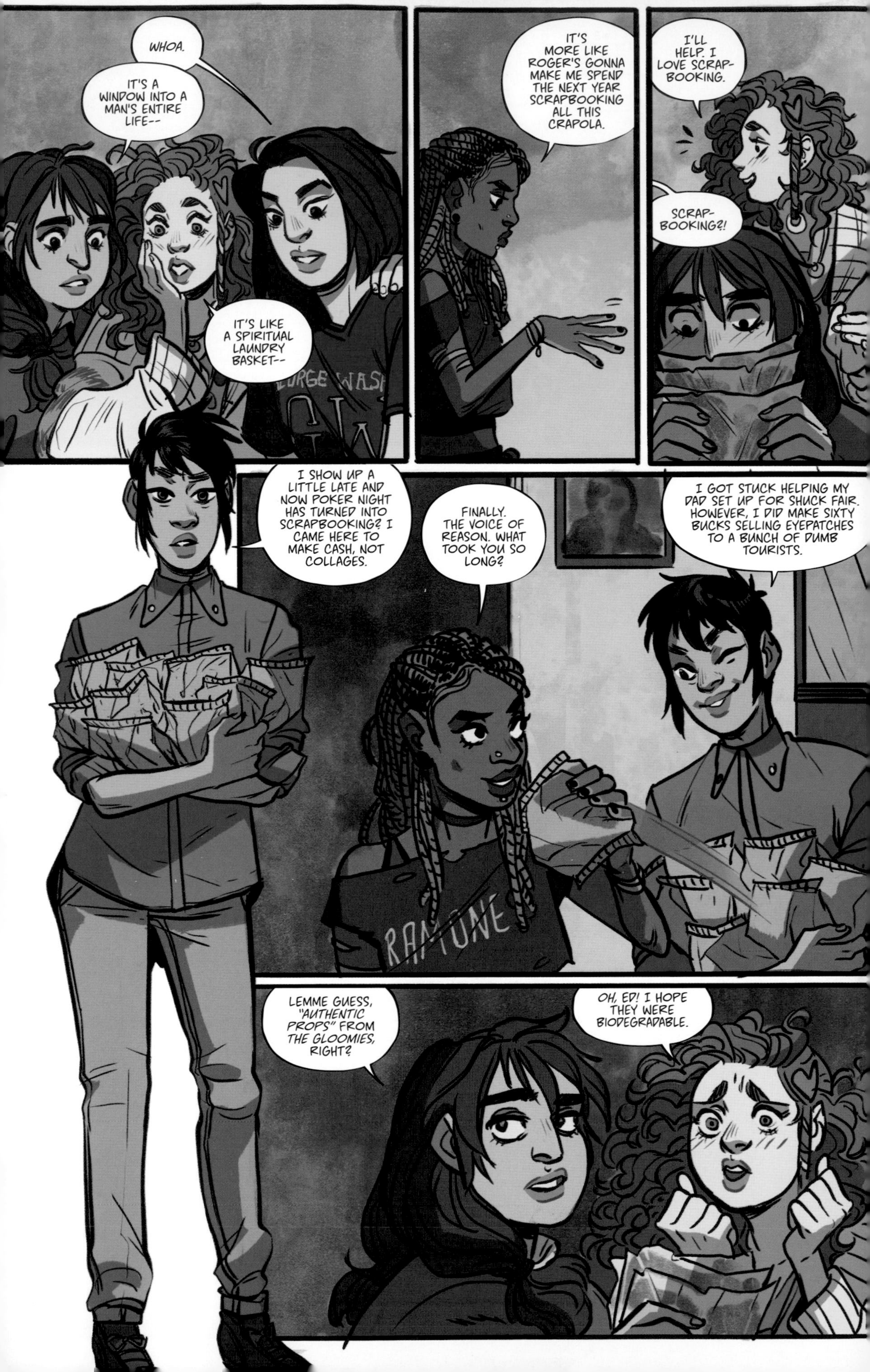
WHOA.
IT'S A WINDOW INTO A MAN'S ENTIRE LIFE--
IT'S LIKE A SPIRITUAL LAUNDRY BASKET--
IT'S MORE LIKE ROGER'S GONNA MAKE ME SPEND THE NEXT YEAR SCRAPBOOKING ALL THIS CRAPOLA.
I'LL HELP. I LOVE SCRAP-BOOKING.
SCRAP-BOOKING?!
I SHOW UP A LITTLE LATE AND NOW POKER NIGHT HAS TURNED INTO SCRAPBOOKING? I CAME HERE TO MAKE CASH, NOT COLLAGES.
FINALLY. THE VOICE OF REASON. WHAT TOOK YOU SO LONG?
I GOT STUCK HELPING MY DAD SET UP FOR SHUCK FAIR. HOWEVER, I DID MAKE SIXTY BUCKS SELLING EYEPATCHES TO A BUNCH OF DUMB TOURISTS.
LEMME GUESS, "AUTHENTIC PROPS" FROM THE GLOOMIES, RIGHT?
OH, ED! I HOPE THEY WERE BIODEGRADABLE.

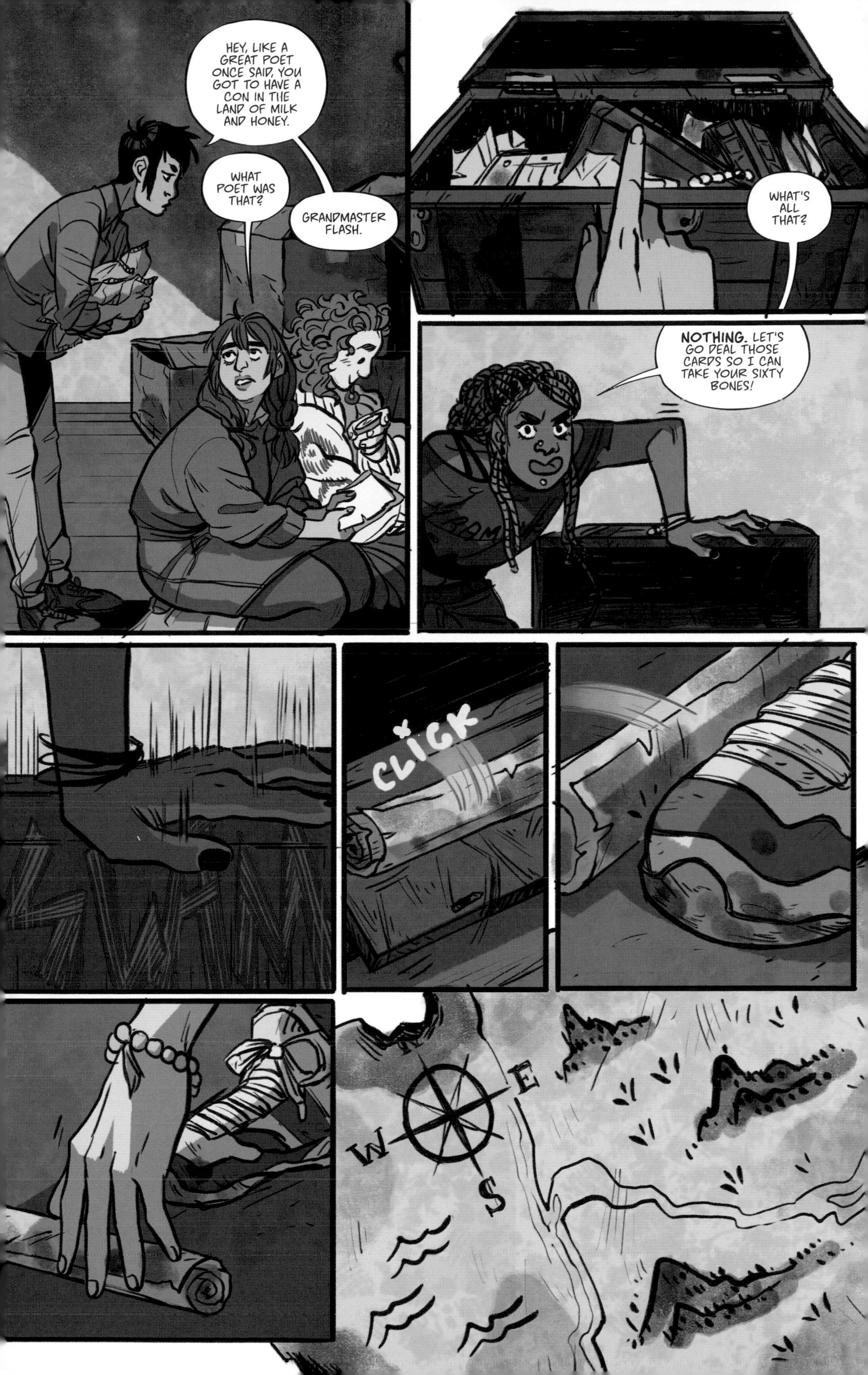
HEY, LIKE A GREAT POET ONCE SAID, YOU GOT TO HAVE A CON IN THE LAND OF MILK AND HONEY.
WHAT POET WAS THAT?
GRANDMASTER FLASH.
WHAT'S ALL THAT?
NOTHING. LET'S GO DEAL THOSE CARDS SO I CAN TAKE YOUR SIXTY BONES!
CLICK
W
E
S

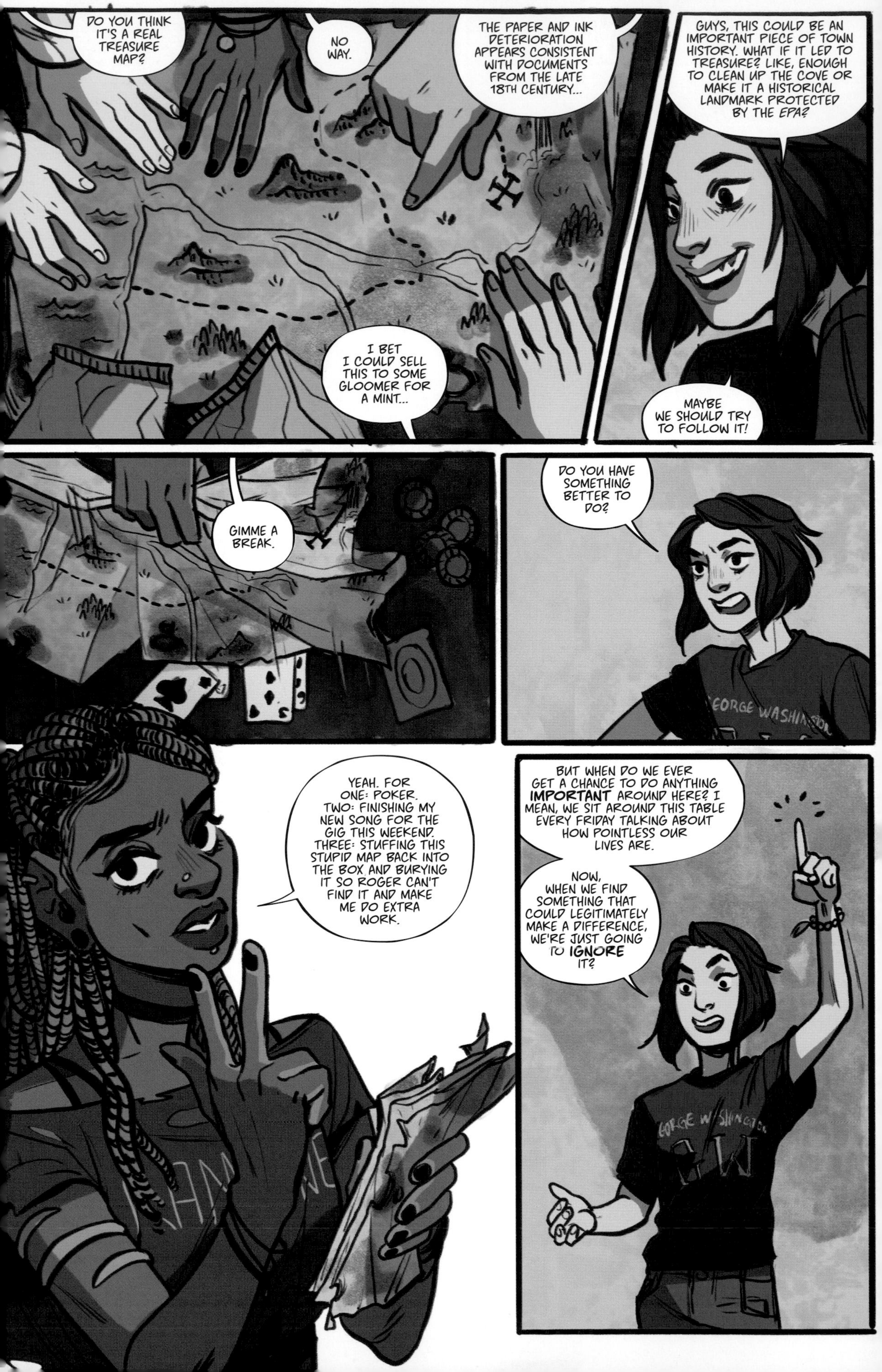
DO YOU THINK IT'S A REAL TREASURE MAP?
NO WAY.
THE PAPER AND INK DETERIORATION APPEARS CONSISTENT WITH DOCUMENTS FROM THE LATE 18TH CENTURY...
I BET I COULD SELL THIS TO SOME GLOOMER FOR A MINT...
GUYS, THIS COULD BE AN IMPORTANT PIECE OF TOWN HISTORY. WHAT IF IT LED TO TREASURE? LIKE, ENOUGH TO CLEAN UP THE COVE OR MAKE IT A HISTORICAL LANDMARK PROTECTED BY THE EPA?
MAYBE WE SHOULD TRY TO FOLLOW IT!
GIMME A BREAK.
DO YOU HAVE SOMETHING BETTER TO DO?
YEAH. FOR ONE: POKER. TWO: FINISHING MY NEW SONG FOR THE GIG THIS WEEKEND. THREE: STUFFING THIS STUPID MAP BACK INTO THE BOX AND BURYING IT SO ROGER CAN'T FIND IT AND MAKE ME DO EXTRA WORK.
BUT WHEN DO WE EVER GET A CHANCE TO DO ANYTHING **IMPORTANT** AROUND HERE? I MEAN, WE SIT AROUND THIS TABLE EVERY FRIDAY TALKING ABOUT HOW POINTLESS OUR LIVES ARE.
NOW, WHEN WE FIND SOMETHING THAT COULD LEGITIMATELY MAKE A DIFFERENCE, WE'RE JUST GOING TO **IGNORE** IT?

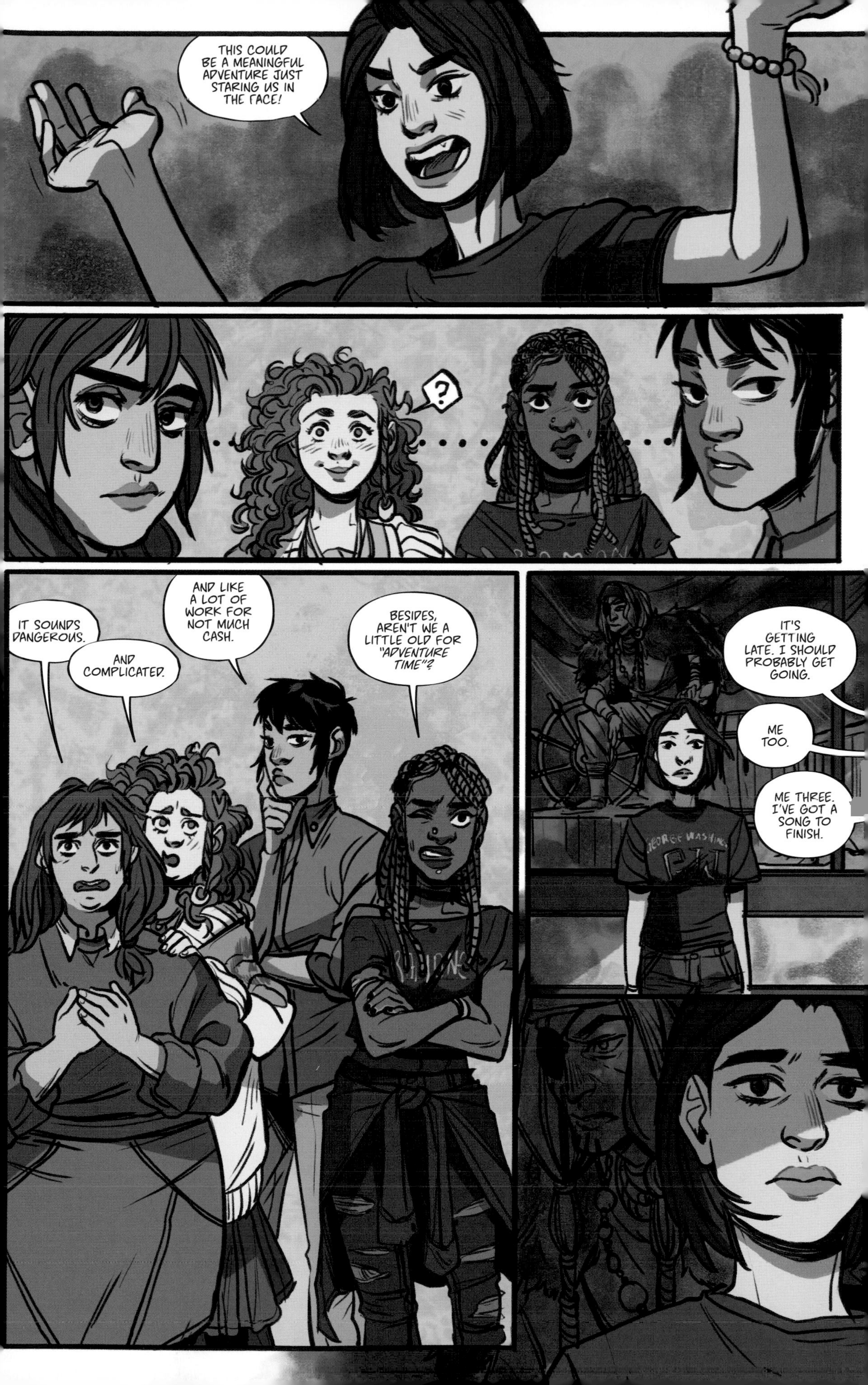
THIS COULD BE A MEANINGFUL ADVENTURE JUST STARING US IN THE FACE!
?
IT SOUNDS DANGEROUS.
AND COMPLICATED.
AND LIKE A LOT OF WORK FOR NOT MUCH CASH.
BESIDES, AREN'T WE A LITTLE OLD FOR "ADVENTURE TIME"?
IT'S GETTING LATE. I SHOULD PROBABLY GET GOING.
ME TOO.
ME THREE. I'VE GOT A SONG TO FINISH.

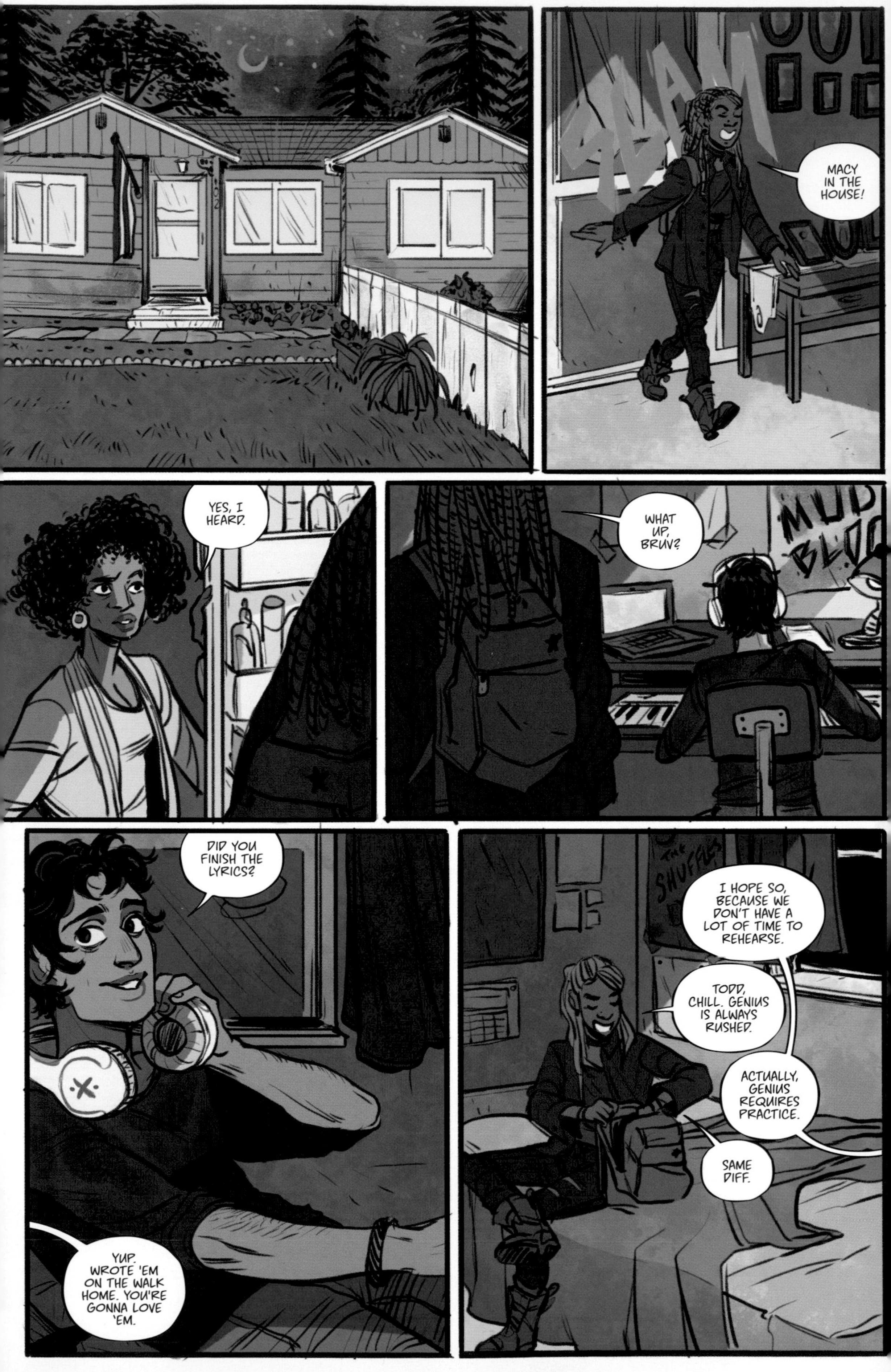
SLAM
MACY IN THE HOUSE!
YES, I HEARD.
WHAT UP, BRUV?
DID YOU FINISH THE LYRICS?
YUP. WROTE 'EM ON THE WALK HOME. YOU'RE GONNA LOVE 'EM.
I HOPE SO, BECAUSE WE DON'T HAVE A LOT OF TIME TO REHEARSE.
TODD, CHILL. GENIUS IS ALWAYS RUSHED.
ACTUALLY, GENIUS REQUIRES PRACTICE.
SAME DIFF.

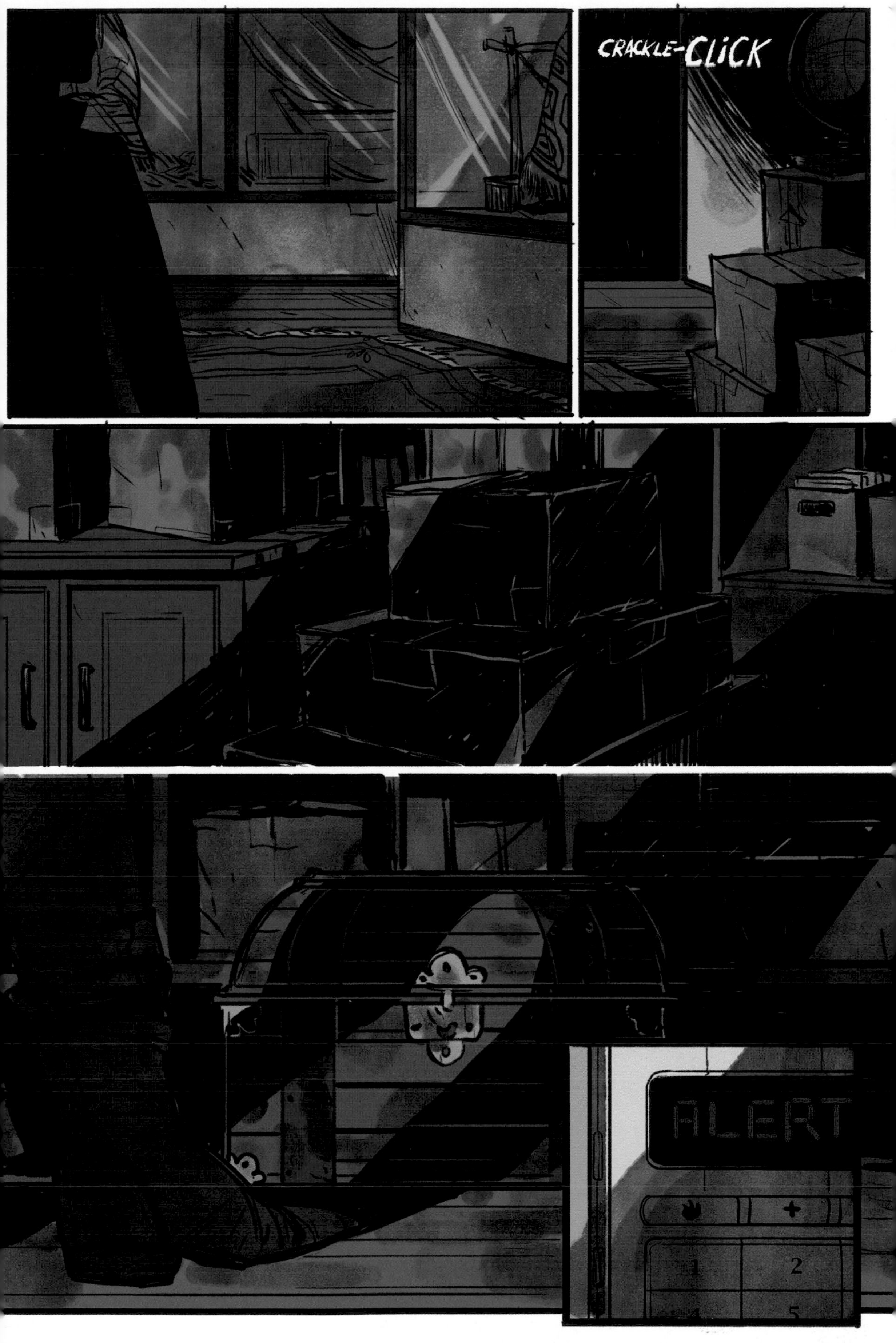
CRACKLE-CLICK
ALERT
1
2
5

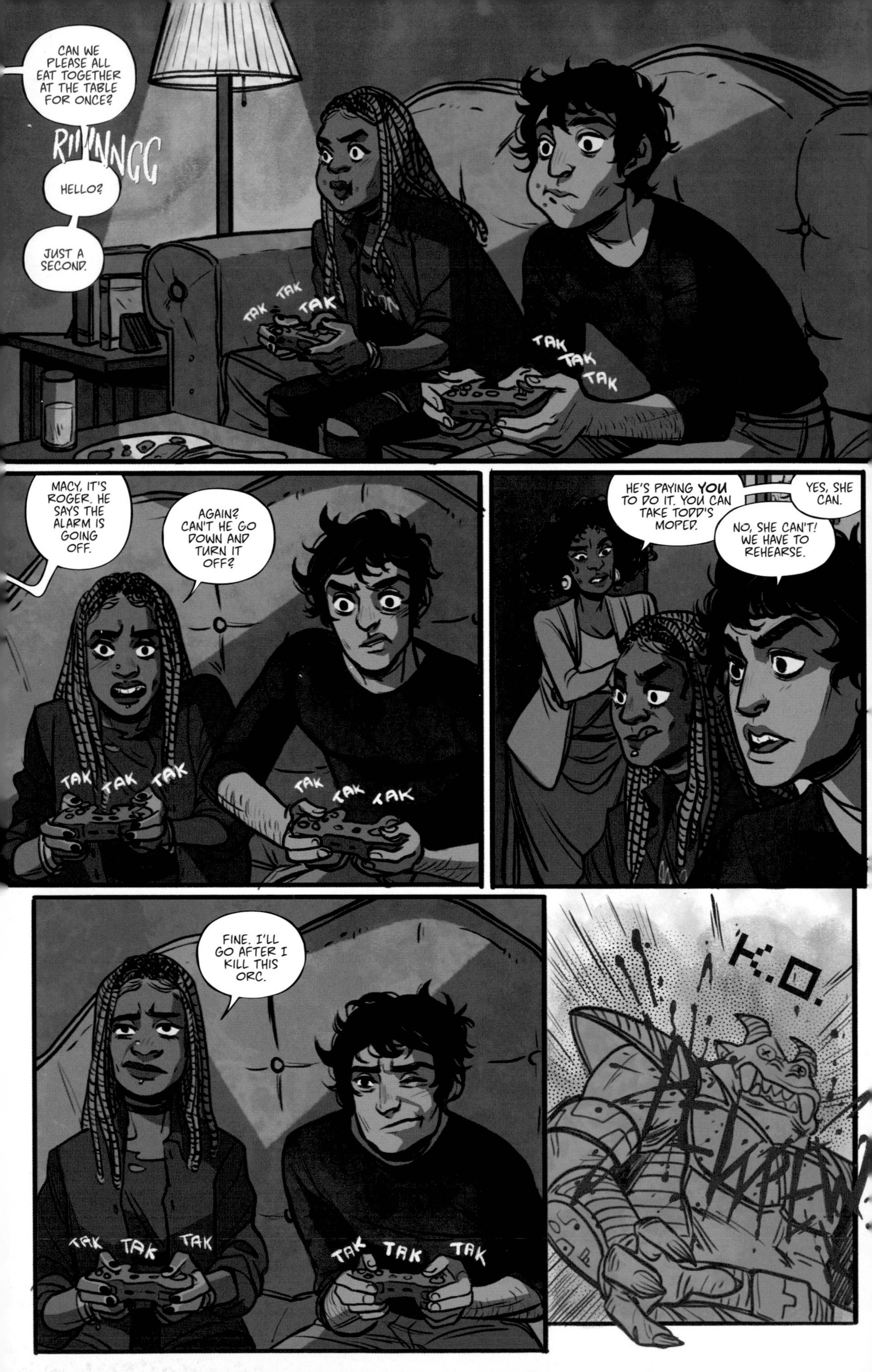
CAN WE PLEASE ALL EAT TOGETHER AT THE TABLE FOR ONCE?
RIIINNGG
HELLO?
JUST A SECOND.
TAK TAK TAK
TAK TAK TAK
MACY, IT'S ROGER. HE SAYS THE ALARM IS GOING OFF.
AGAIN? CAN'T HE GO DOWN AND TURN IT OFF?
TAK TAK TAK
TAK TAK TAK
HE'S PAYING **YOU** TO DO IT. YOU CAN TAKE TODD'S MOPED.
YES, SHE CAN.
NO, SHE CAN'T! WE HAVE TO REHEARSE.
FINE. I'LL GO AFTER I KILL THIS ORC.
TAK TAK TAK
TAK TAK TAK
K.O.

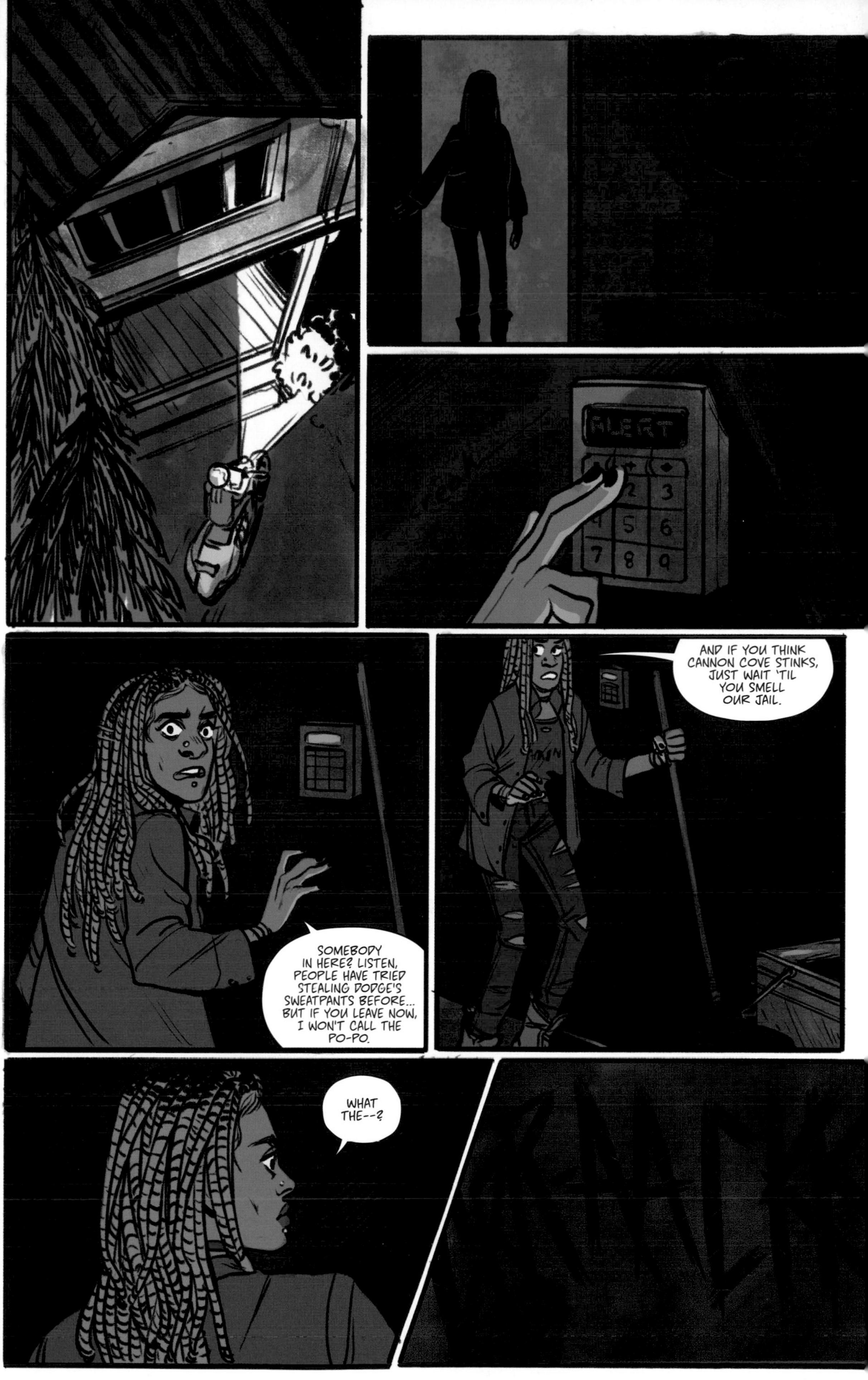
ALERT
SOMEBODY IN HERE? LISTEN, PEOPLE HAVE TRIED STEALING DODGE'S SWEATPANTS BEFORE... BUT IF YOU LEAVE NOW, I WON'T CALL THE PO-PO.
AND IF YOU THINK CANNON COVE STINKS, JUST WAIT 'TIL YOU SMELL OUR JAIL.
WHAT THE--?

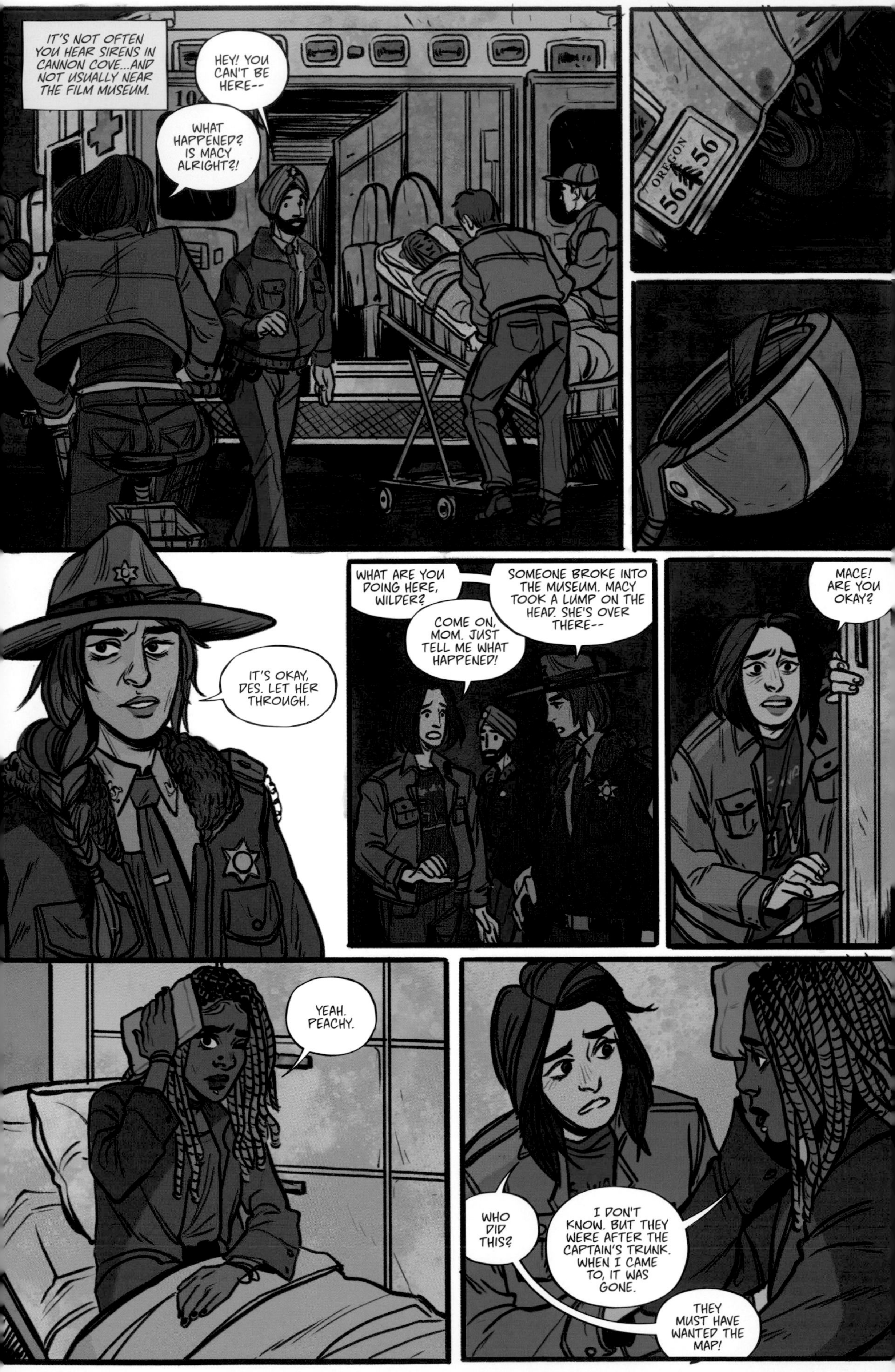
IT'S NOT OFTEN YOU HEAR SIRENS IN CANNON COVE...AND NOT USUALLY NEAR THE FILM MUSEUM.
HEY! YOU CAN'T BE HERE--
WHAT HAPPENED? IS MACY ALRIGHT?!
OREGON 56 56
IT'S OKAY, DES. LET HER THROUGH.
WHAT ARE YOU DOING HERE, WILDER?
SOMEONE BROKE INTO THE MUSEUM. MACY TOOK A LUMP ON THE HEAD. SHE'S OVER THERE--
COME ON, MOM. JUST TELL ME WHAT HAPPENED!
MACE! ARE YOU OKAY?
YEAH. PEACHY.
WHO DID THIS?
I DON'T KNOW. BUT THEY WERE AFTER THE CAPTAIN'S TRUNK. WHEN I CAME TO, IT WAS GONE.
THEY MUST HAVE WANTED THE MAP!

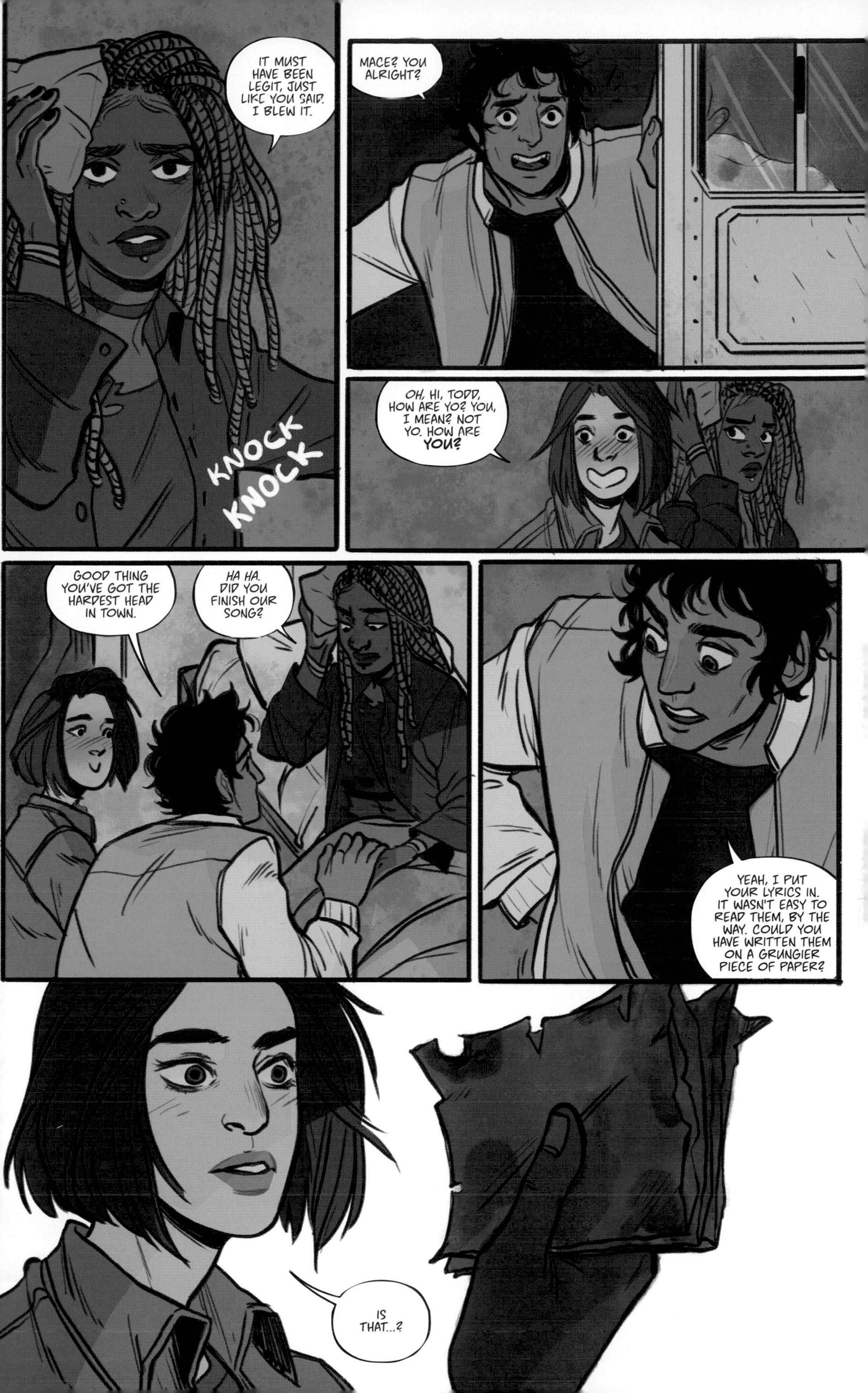
IT MUST HAVE BEEN LEGIT, JUST LIKE YOU SAID. I BLEW IT.
KNOCK KNOCK
MACE? YOU ALRIGHT?
OH, HI, TODD, HOW ARE YO? YOU, I MEAN? NOT YO. HOW ARE YOU?
GOOD THING YOU'VE GOT THE HARDEST HEAD IN TOWN.
HA HA. DID YOU FINISH OUR SONG?
YEAH, I PUT YOUR LYRICS IN. IT WASN'T EASY TO READ THEM, BY THE WAY. COULD YOU HAVE WRITTEN THEM ON A GRUNGIER PIECE OF PAPER?
IS THAT...?

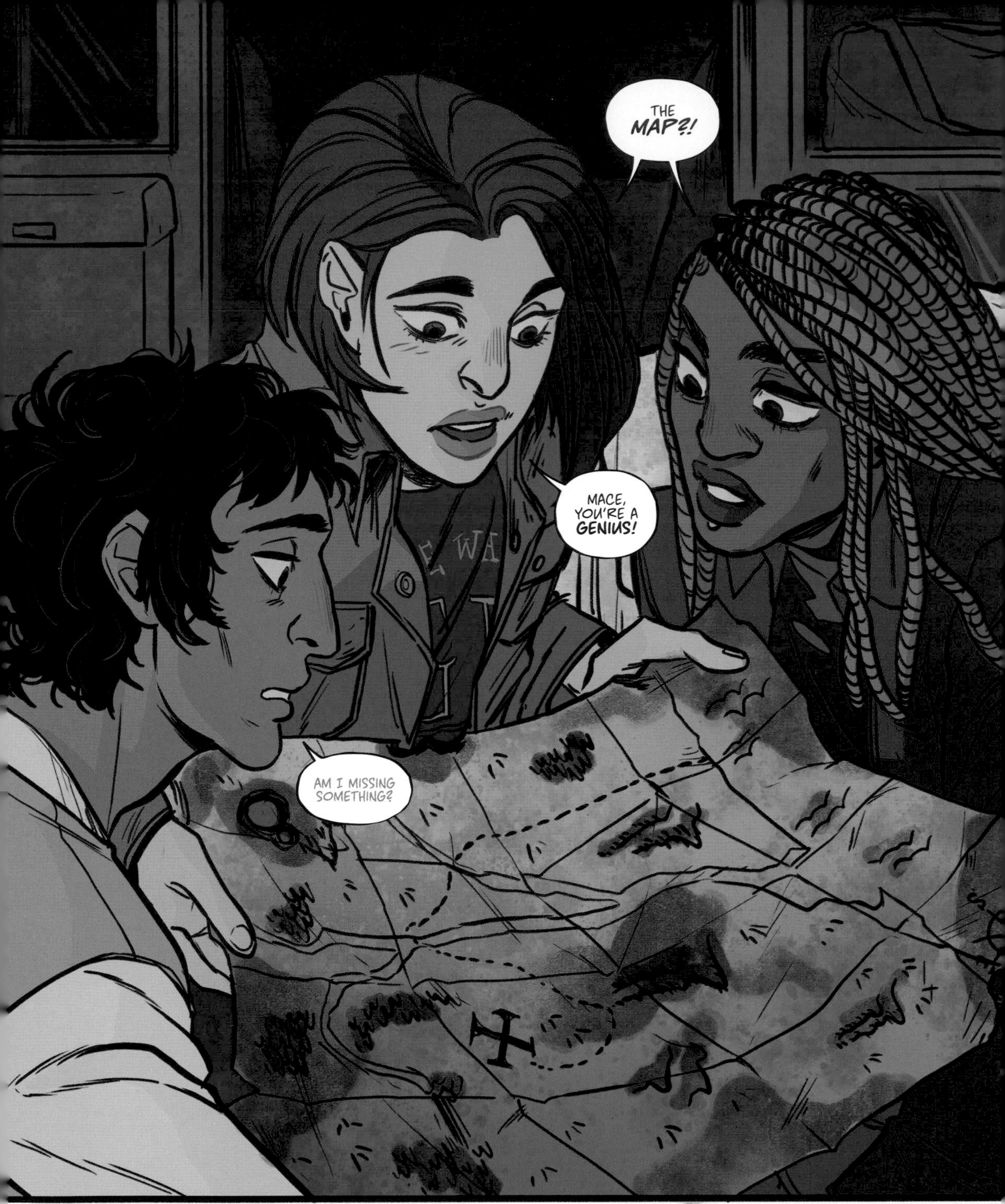
THE MAP?!
MACE, YOU'RE A GENIUS!
AM I MISSING SOMETHING?

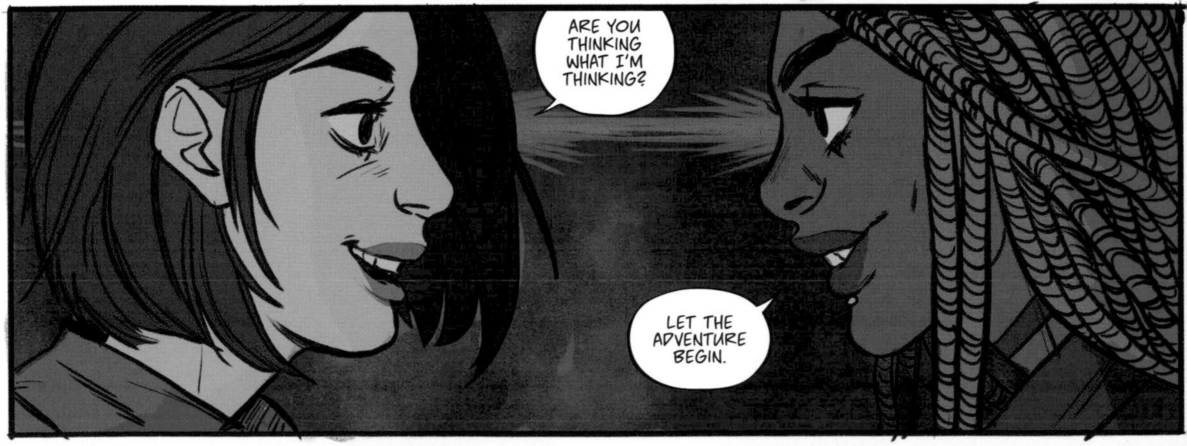
ARE YOU THINKING WHAT I'M THINKING?
LET THE ADVENTURE BEGIN.

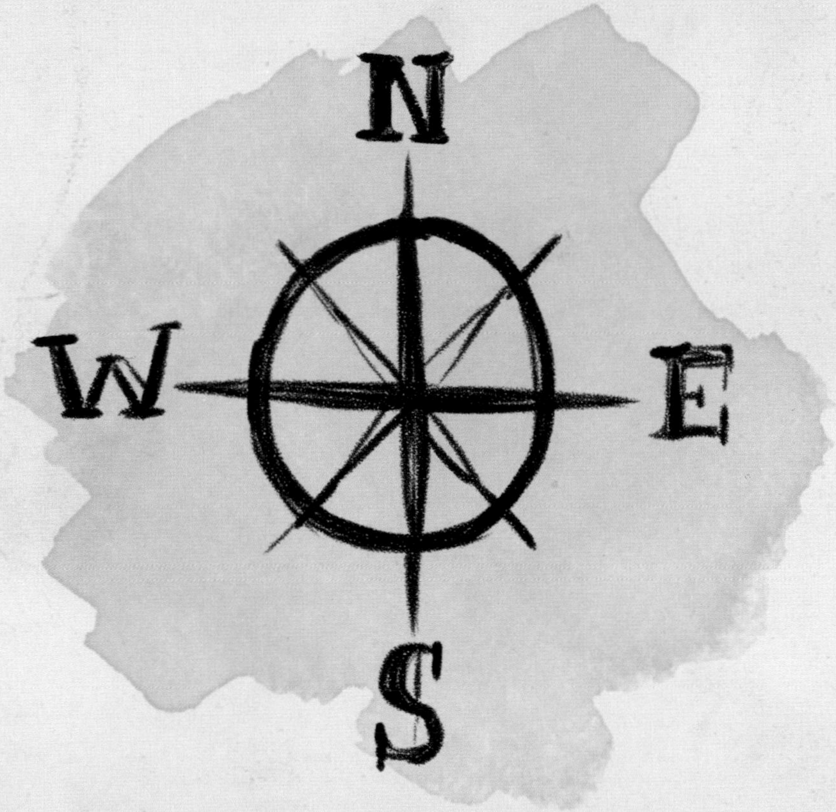
N
W
E
S

CHAPTER

II

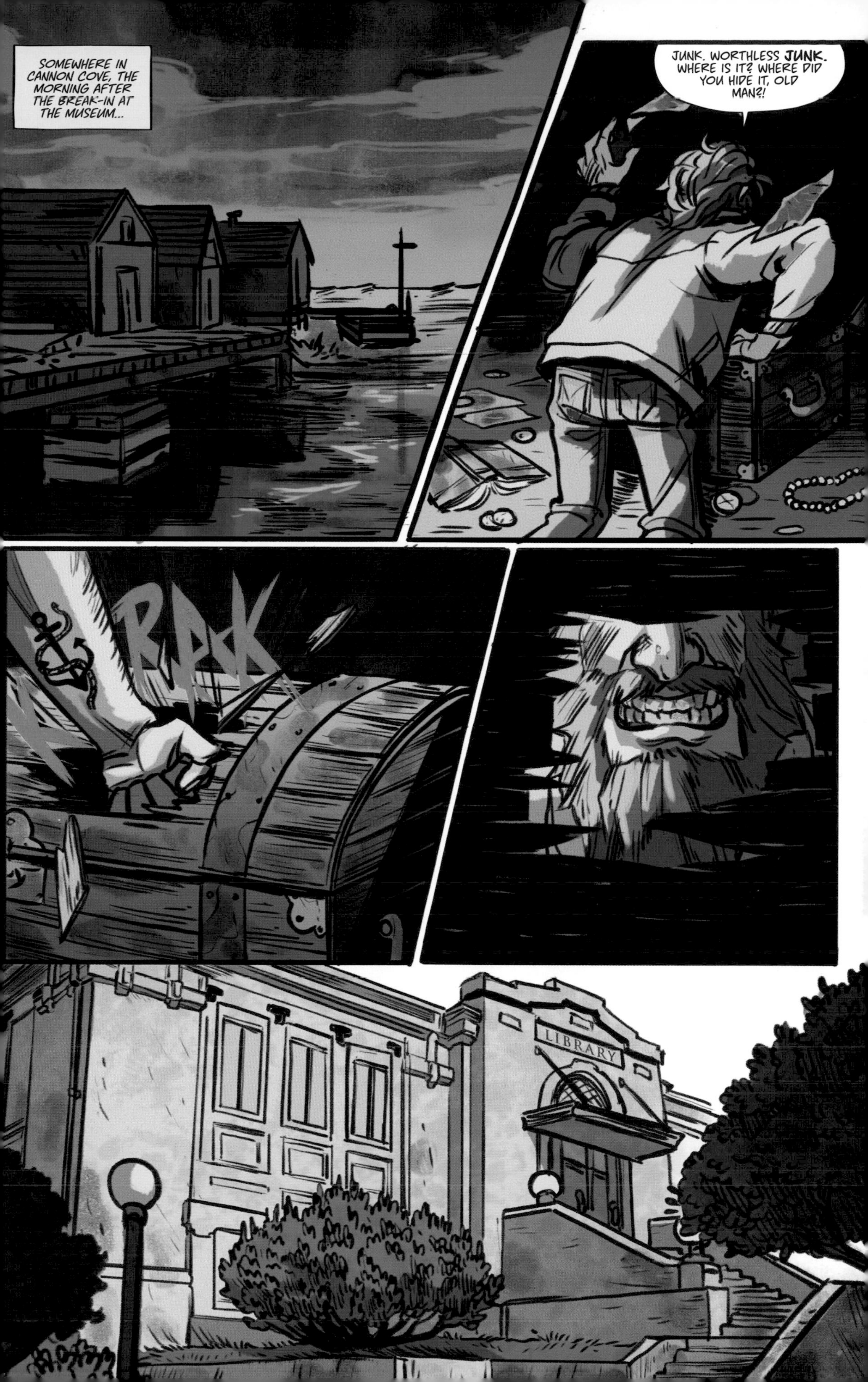
SOMEWHERE IN CANNON COVE, THE MORNING AFTER THE BREAK-IN AT THE MUSEUM...
JUNK. WORTHLESS JUNK. WHERE IS IT? WHERE DID YOU HIDE IT, OLD MAN?!
RAK
LIBRARY

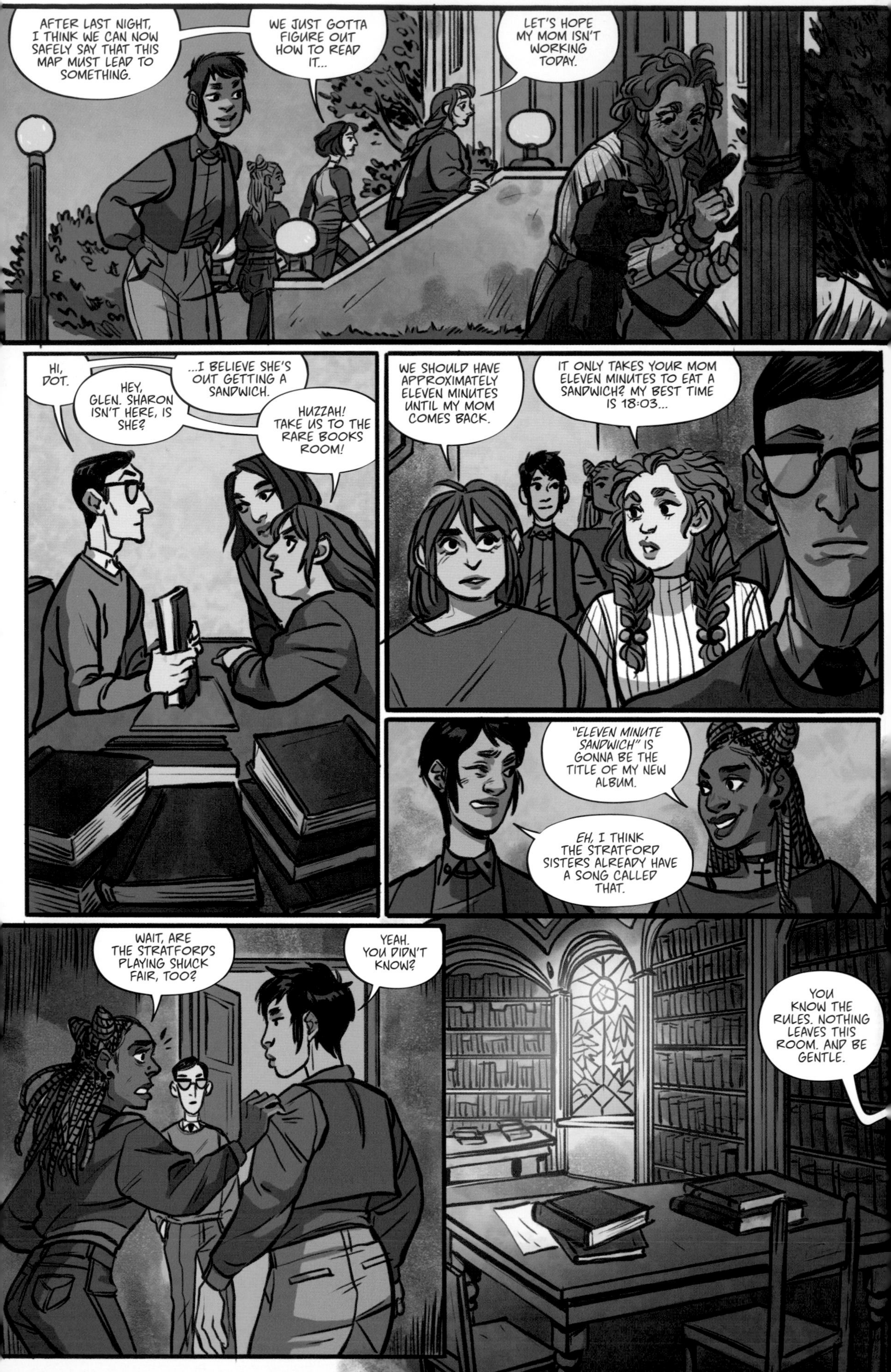
AFTER LAST NIGHT, I THINK WE CAN NOW SAFELY SAY THAT THIS MAP MUST LEAD TO SOMETHING.
WE JUST GOTTA FIGURE OUT HOW TO READ IT...
LET'S HOPE MY MOM ISN'T WORKING TODAY.
HI, DOT.
HEY, GLEN. SHARON ISN'T HERE, IS SHE?
...I BELIEVE SHE'S OUT GETTING A SANDWICH.
HUZZAH! TAKE US TO THE RARE BOOKS ROOM!
WE SHOULD HAVE APPROXIMATELY ELEVEN MINUTES UNTIL MY MOM COMES BACK.
IT ONLY TAKES YOUR MOM ELEVEN MINUTES TO EAT A SANDWICH? MY BEST TIME IS 18:03...
"ELEVEN MINUTE SANDWICH" IS GONNA BE THE TITLE OF MY NEW ALBUM.
EH, I THINK THE STRATFORD SISTERS ALREADY HAVE A SONG CALLED THAT.
WAIT, ARE THE STRATFORDS PLAYING SHUCK FAIR, TOO?
YEAH. YOU DIDN'T KNOW?
YOU KNOW THE RULES. NOTHING LEAVES THIS ROOM. AND BE GENTLE.

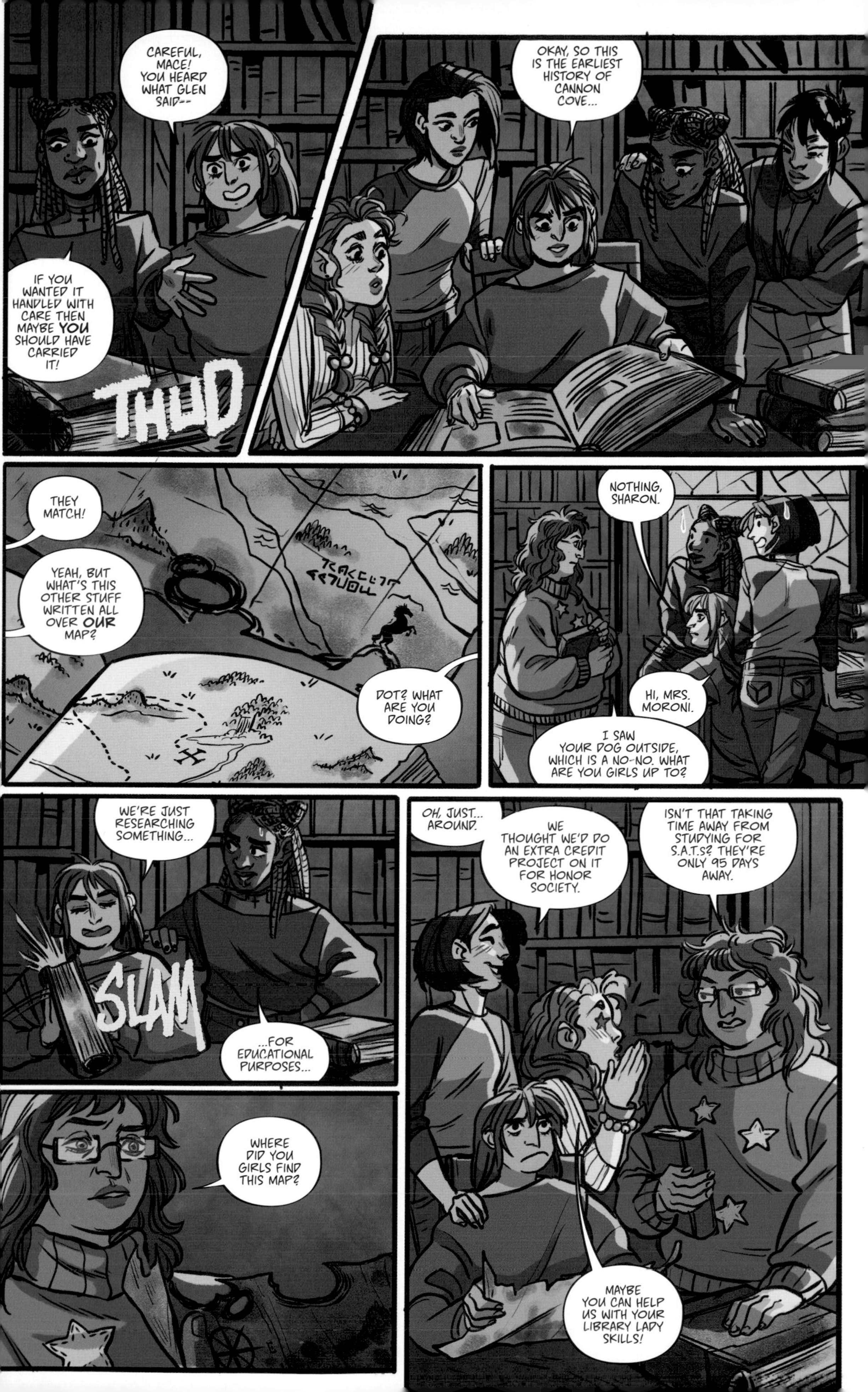
CAREFUL, MACE! YOU HEARD WHAT GLEN SAID--
IF YOU WANTED IT HANDLED WITH CARE THEN MAYBE **YOU** SHOULD HAVE CARRIED IT!
THUD
OKAY, SO THIS IS THE EARLIEST HISTORY OF CANNON COVE...
THEY MATCH!
YEAH, BUT WHAT'S THIS OTHER STUFF WRITTEN ALL OVER **OUR** MAP?
DOT? WHAT ARE YOU DOING?
NOTHING, SHARON.
HI, MRS. MORONI.
I SAW YOUR DOG OUTSIDE, WHICH IS A NO-NO. WHAT ARE YOU GIRLS UP TO?
WE'RE JUST RESEARCHING SOMETHING...
SLAM
...FOR EDUCATIONAL PURPOSES...
WHERE DID YOU GIRLS FIND THIS MAP?
OH, JUST... AROUND.
WE THOUGHT WE'D DO AN EXTRA CREDIT PROJECT ON IT FOR HONOR SOCIETY.
ISN'T THAT TAKING TIME AWAY FROM STUDYING FOR S.A.T.S? THEY'RE ONLY 95 DAYS AWAY.
MAYBE YOU CAN HELP US WITH YOUR LIBRARY LADY SKILLS!

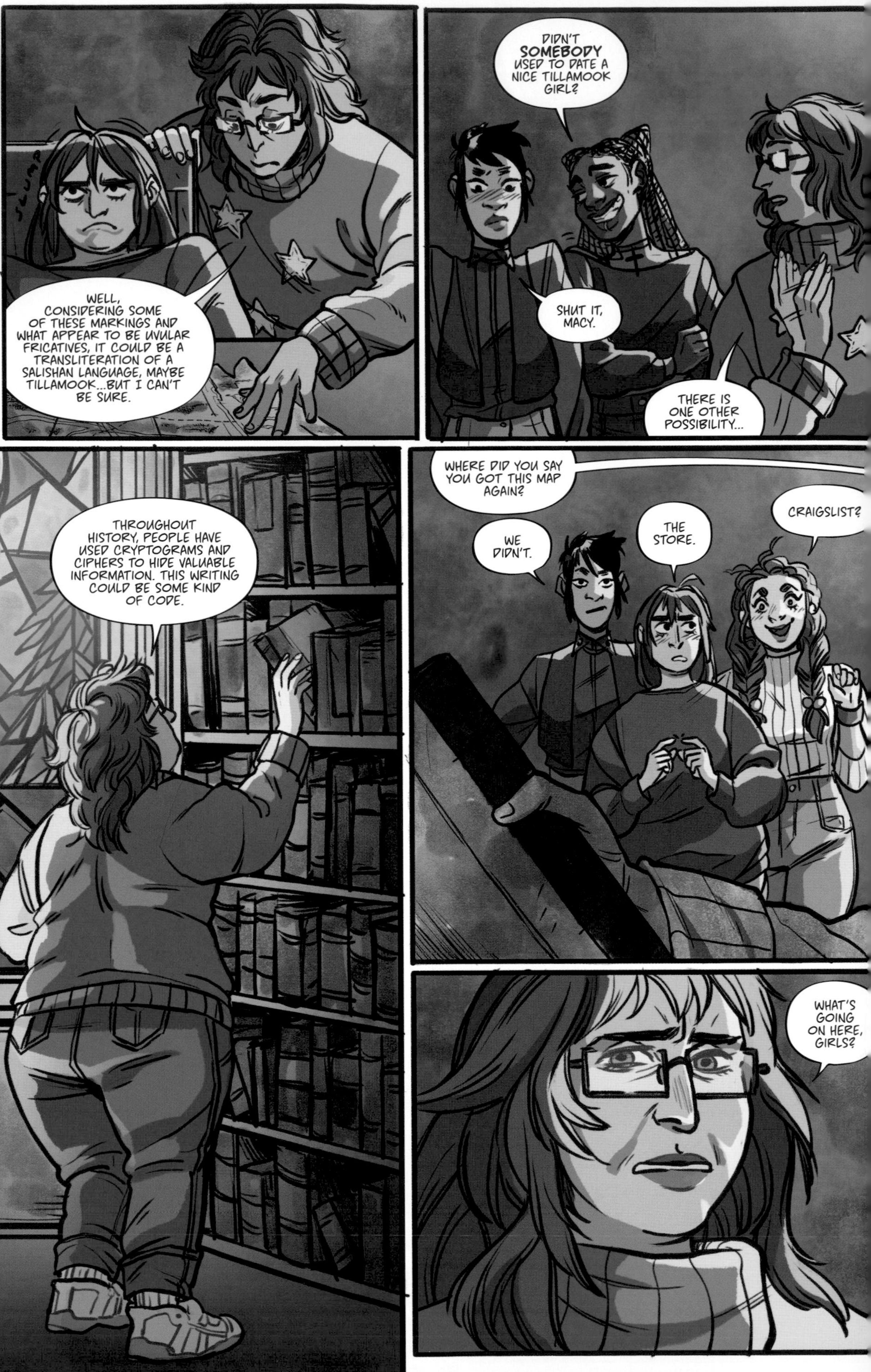
SLUMP
WELL, CONSIDERING SOME OF THESE MARKINGS AND WHAT APPEAR TO BE UVULAR FRICATIVES, IT COULD BE A TRANSLITERATION OF A SALISHAN LANGUAGE, MAYBE TILLAMOOK...BUT I CAN'T BE SURE.
DIDN'T SOMEBODY USED TO DATE A NICE TILLAMOOK GIRL?
SHUT IT, MACY.
THERE IS ONE OTHER POSSIBILITY...
THROUGHOUT HISTORY, PEOPLE HAVE USED CRYPTOGRAMS AND CIPHERS TO HIDE VALUABLE INFORMATION. THIS WRITING COULD BE SOME KIND OF CODE.
WHERE DID YOU SAY YOU GOT THIS MAP AGAIN?
WE DIDN'T.
THE STORE.
CRAIGSLIST?
WHAT'S GOING ON HERE, GIRLS?

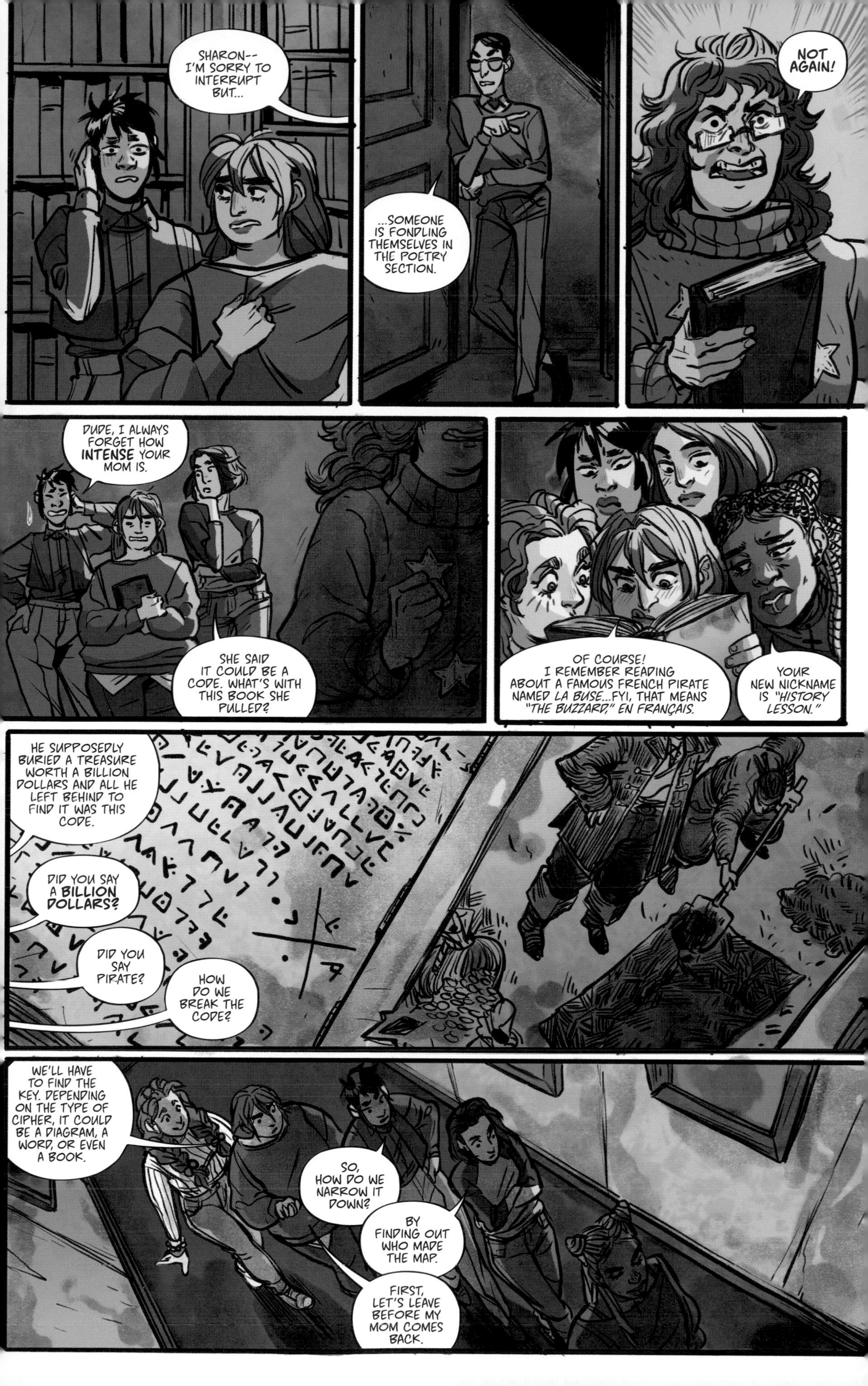
SHARON-- I'M SORRY TO INTERRUPT BUT...
...SOMEONE IS FONDLING THEMSELVES IN THE POETRY SECTION.
NOT AGAIN!
DUDE, I ALWAYS FORGET HOW **INTENSE** YOUR MOM IS.
SHE SAID IT COULD BE A CODE. WHAT'S WITH THIS BOOK SHE PULLED?
OF COURSE! I REMEMBER READING ABOUT A FAMOUS FRENCH PIRATE NAMED *LA BUSE*...FYI, THAT MEANS *"THE BUZZARD,"* EN FRANÇAIS.
YOUR NEW NICKNAME IS *"HISTORY LESSON."*
HE SUPPOSEDLY BURIED A TREASURE WORTH A BILLION DOLLARS AND ALL HE LEFT BEHIND TO FIND IT WAS THIS CODE.
DID YOU SAY A **BILLION DOLLARS?**
DID YOU SAY PIRATE?
HOW DO WE BREAK THE CODE?
WE'LL HAVE TO FIND THE KEY. DEPENDING ON THE TYPE OF CIPHER, IT COULD BE A DIAGRAM, A WORD, OR EVEN A BOOK.
SO, HOW DO WE NARROW IT DOWN?
BY FINDING OUT WHO MADE THE MAP.
FIRST, LET'S LEAVE BEFORE MY MOM COMES BACK.

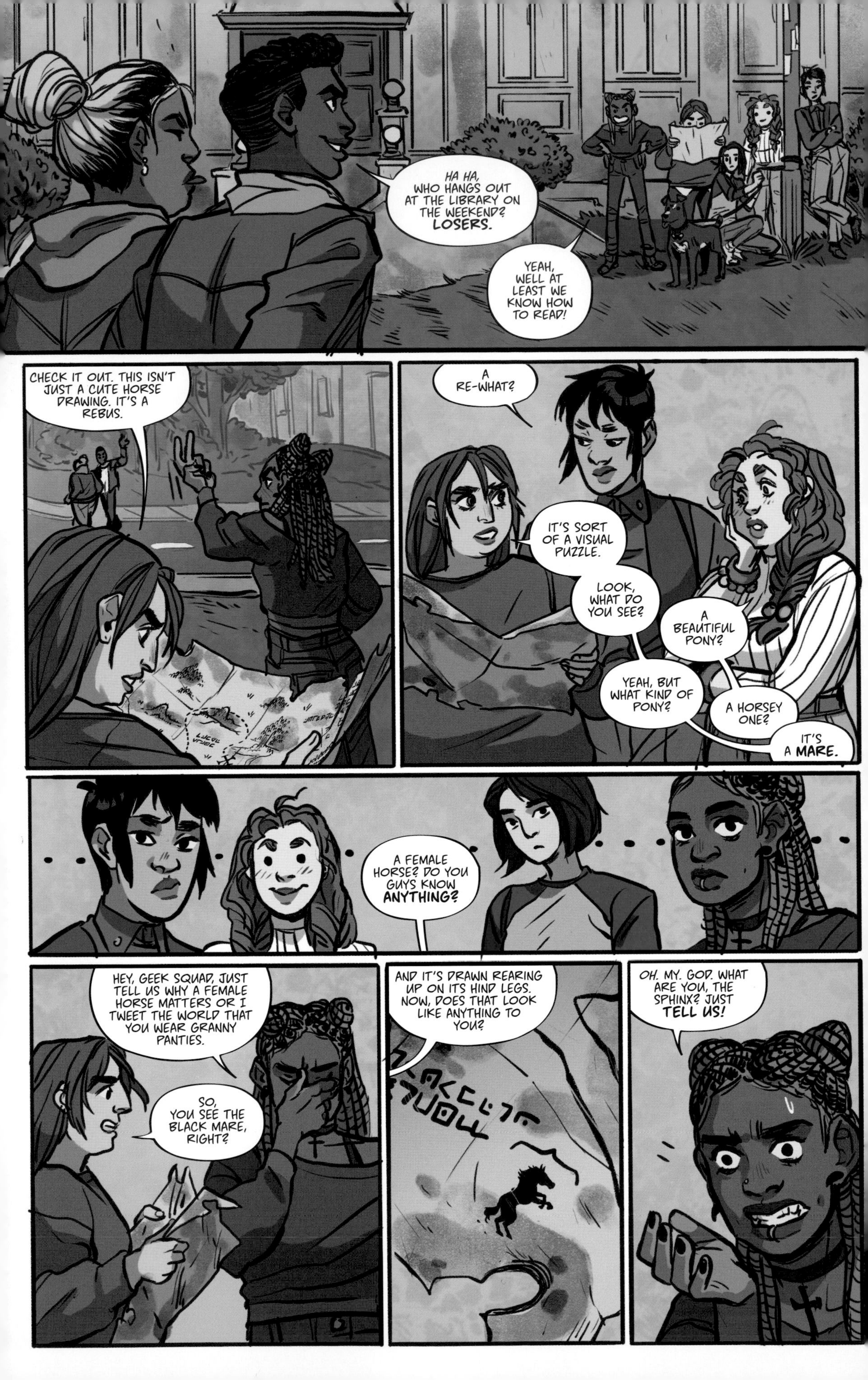
HA HA, WHO HANGS OUT AT THE LIBRARY ON THE WEEKEND? **LOSERS.**
YEAH, WELL AT LEAST WE KNOW HOW TO READ!
CHECK IT OUT. THIS ISN'T JUST A CUTE HORSE DRAWING. IT'S A REBUS.
A RE-WHAT?
IT'S SORT OF A VISUAL PUZZLE.
LOOK, WHAT DO YOU SEE?
A BEAUTIFUL PONY?
YEAH, BUT WHAT KIND OF PONY?
A HORSEY ONE?
IT'S A **MARE.**
A FEMALE HORSE? DO YOU GUYS KNOW **ANYTHING?**
HEY, GEEK SQUAD, JUST TELL US WHY A FEMALE HORSE MATTERS OR I TWEET THE WORLD THAT YOU WEAR GRANNY PANTIES.
SO, YOU SEE THE BLACK MARE, RIGHT?
AND IT'S DRAWN REARING UP ON ITS HIND LEGS. NOW, DOES THAT LOOK LIKE ANYTHING TO YOU?
OH. MY. GOD. WHAT ARE YOU, THE SPHINX? JUST **TELL US!**

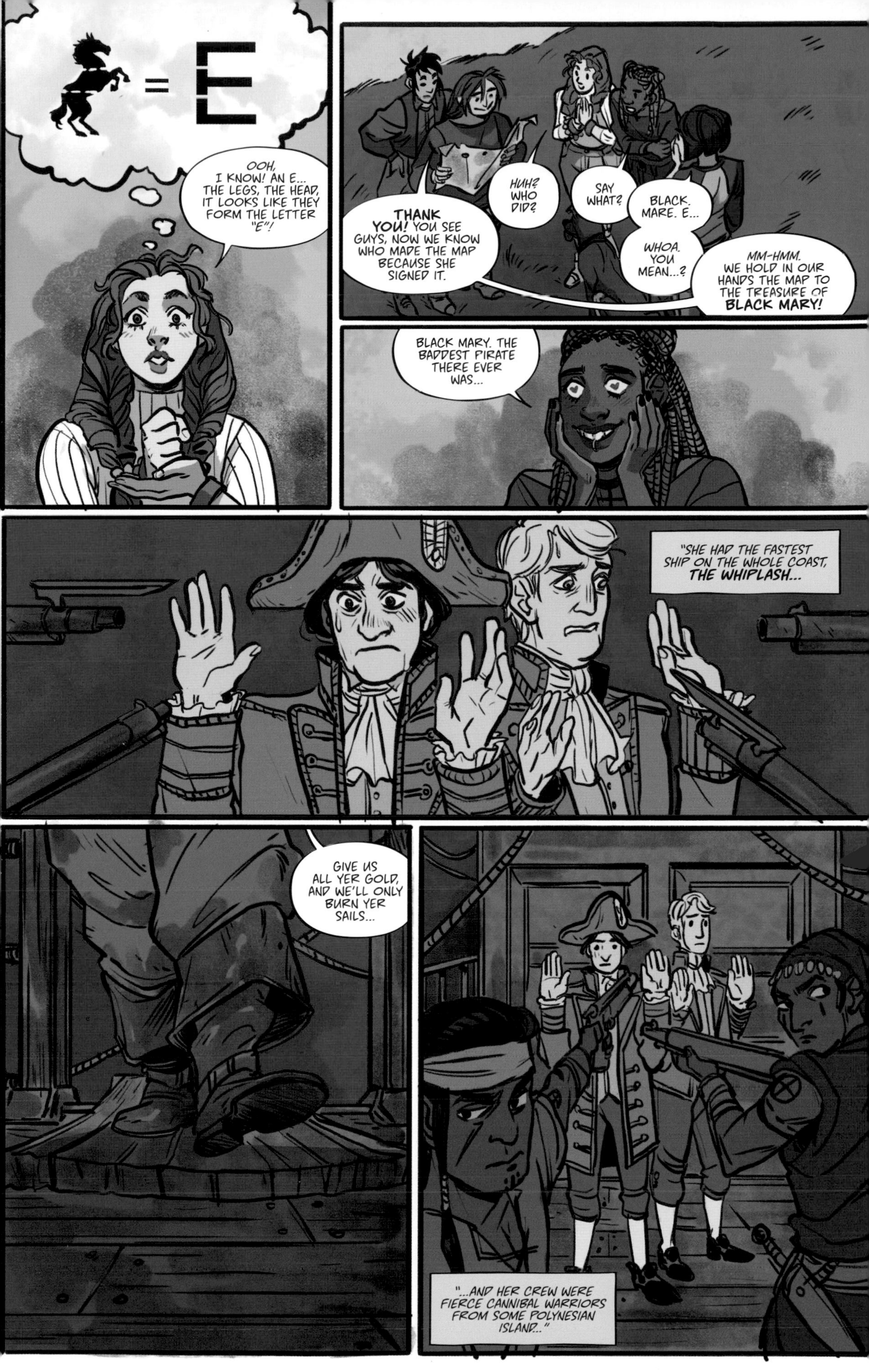

OOH, I KNOW! AN E... THE LEGS, THE HEAD, IT LOOKS LIKE THEY FORM THE LETTER "E"!
THANK YOU! YOU SEE GUYS, NOW WE KNOW WHO MADE THE MAP BECAUSE SHE SIGNED IT.
HUH? WHO DID?
SAY WHAT?
BLACK. MARE. E...
WHOA. YOU MEAN...?
MM-HMM. WE HOLD IN OUR HANDS THE MAP TO THE TREASURE OF BLACK MARY!
BLACK MARY. THE BADDEST PIRATE THERE EVER WAS...
"SHE HAD THE FASTEST SHIP ON THE WHOLE COAST, THE WHIPLASH...
GIVE US ALL YER GOLD, AND WE'LL ONLY BURN YER SAILS...
"...AND HER CREW WERE FIERCE CANNIBAL WARRIORS FROM SOME POLYNESIAN ISLAND..."

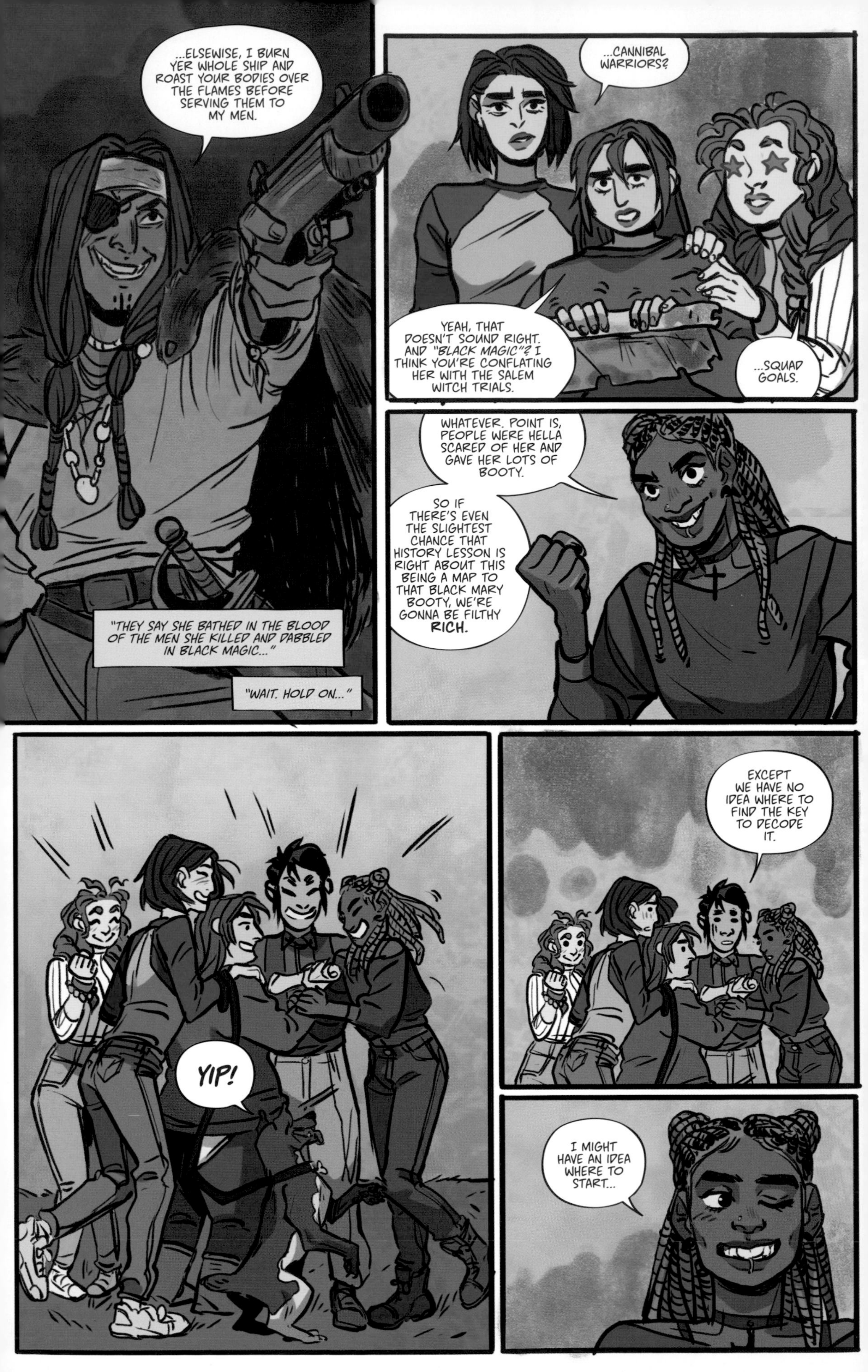
...ELSEWISE, I BURN YER WHOLE SHIP AND ROAST YOUR BODIES OVER THE FLAMES BEFORE SERVING THEM TO MY MEN.
"THEY SAY SHE BATHED IN THE BLOOD OF THE MEN SHE KILLED AND DABBLED IN BLACK MAGIC..."
"WAIT. HOLD ON..."
...CANNIBAL WARRIORS?
YEAH, THAT DOESN'T SOUND RIGHT. AND "BLACK MAGIC"? I THINK YOU'RE CONFLATING HER WITH THE SALEM WITCH TRIALS.
...SQUAD GOALS.
WHATEVER. POINT IS, PEOPLE WERE HELLA SCARED OF HER AND GAVE HER LOTS OF BOOTY.
SO IF THERE'S EVEN THE SLIGHTEST CHANCE THAT HISTORY LESSON IS RIGHT ABOUT THIS BEING A MAP TO THAT BLACK MARY BOOTY, WE'RE GONNA BE FILTHY RICH.
YIP!
EXCEPT WE HAVE NO IDEA WHERE TO FIND THE KEY TO DECODE IT.
I MIGHT HAVE AN IDEA WHERE TO START...

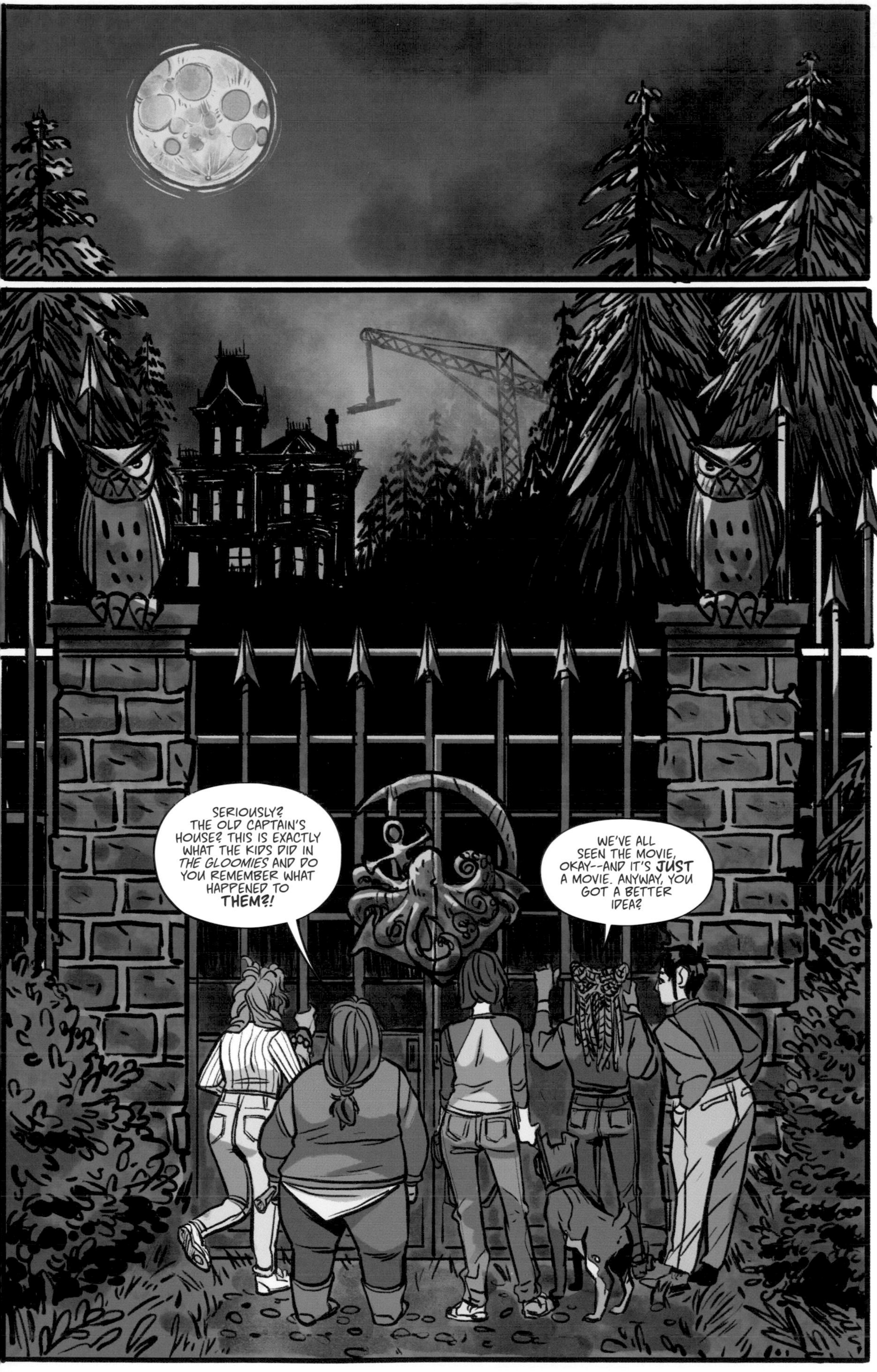
SERIOUSLY? THE OLD CAPTAIN'S HOUSE? THIS IS EXACTLY WHAT THE KIDS DID IN *THE GLOOMIES* AND DO YOU REMEMBER WHAT HAPPENED TO **THEM?!**
WE'VE ALL SEEN THE MOVIE, OKAY--AND IT'S **JUST** A MOVIE. ANYWAY, YOU GOT A BETTER IDEA?

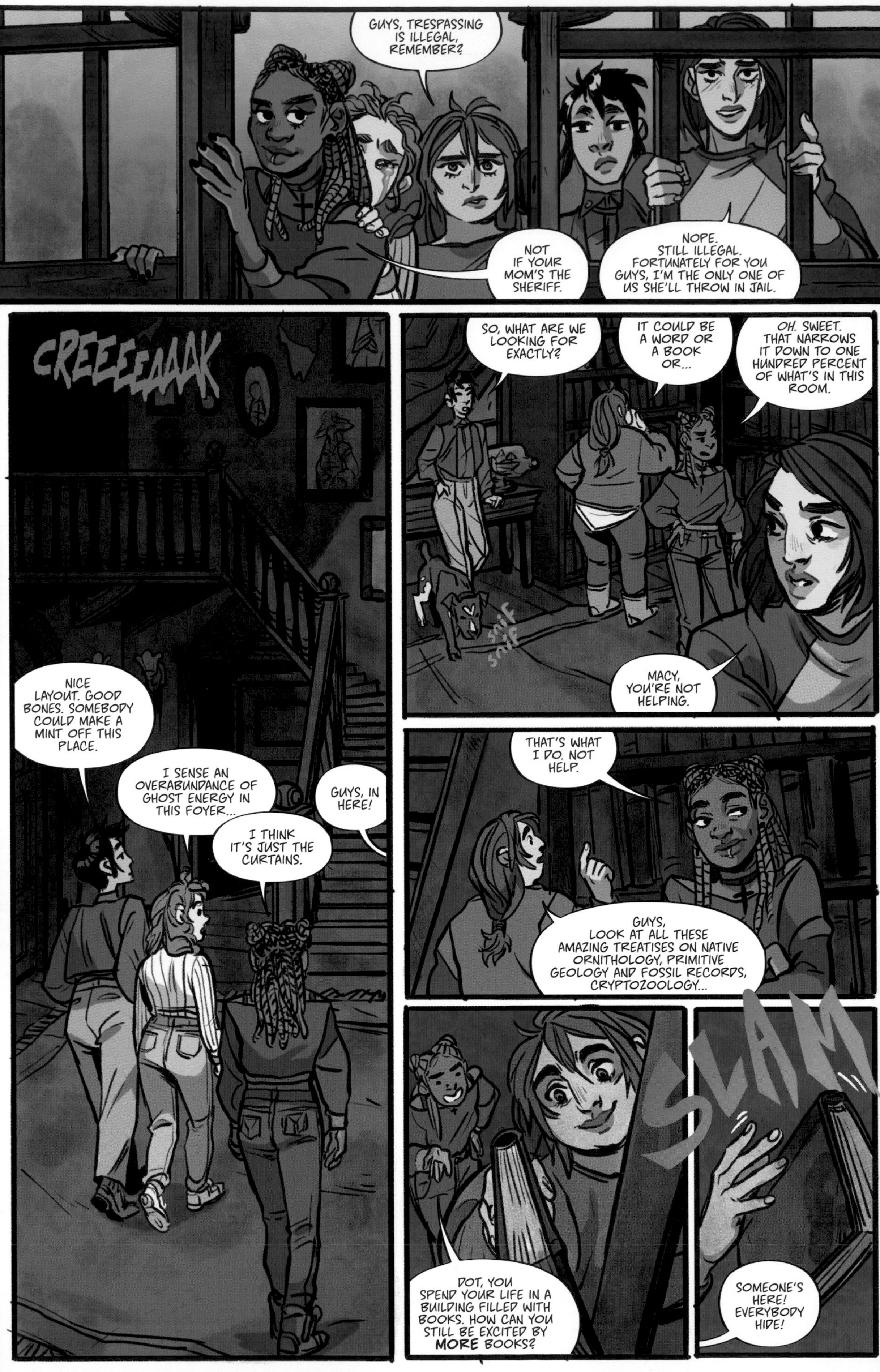

GUYS, TRESPASSING IS ILLEGAL, REMEMBER?
NOT IF YOUR MOM'S THE SHERIFF.
NOPE. STILL ILLEGAL. FORTUNATELY FOR YOU GUYS, I'M THE ONLY ONE OF US SHE'LL THROW IN JAIL.
CREEEEAAAK
NICE LAYOUT. GOOD BONES. SOMEBODY COULD MAKE A MINT OFF THIS PLACE.
I SENSE AN OVERABUNDANCE OF GHOST ENERGY IN THIS FOYER...
I THINK IT'S JUST THE CURTAINS.
GUYS, IN HERE!
SO, WHAT ARE WE LOOKING FOR EXACTLY?
IT COULD BE A WORD OR A BOOK OR...
OH. SWEET. THAT NARROWS IT DOWN TO ONE HUNDRED PERCENT OF WHAT'S IN THIS ROOM.
snif snif
MACY, YOU'RE NOT HELPING.
THAT'S WHAT I DO. NOT HELP.
GUYS, LOOK AT ALL THESE AMAZING TREATISES ON NATIVE ORNITHOLOGY, PRIMITIVE GEOLOGY AND FOSSIL RECORDS, CRYPTOZOOLOGY...
DOT, YOU SPEND YOUR LIFE IN A BUILDING FILLED WITH BOOKS. HOW CAN YOU STILL BE EXCITED BY **MORE** BOOKS?
SLAM
SOMEONE'S HERE! EVERYBODY HIDE!

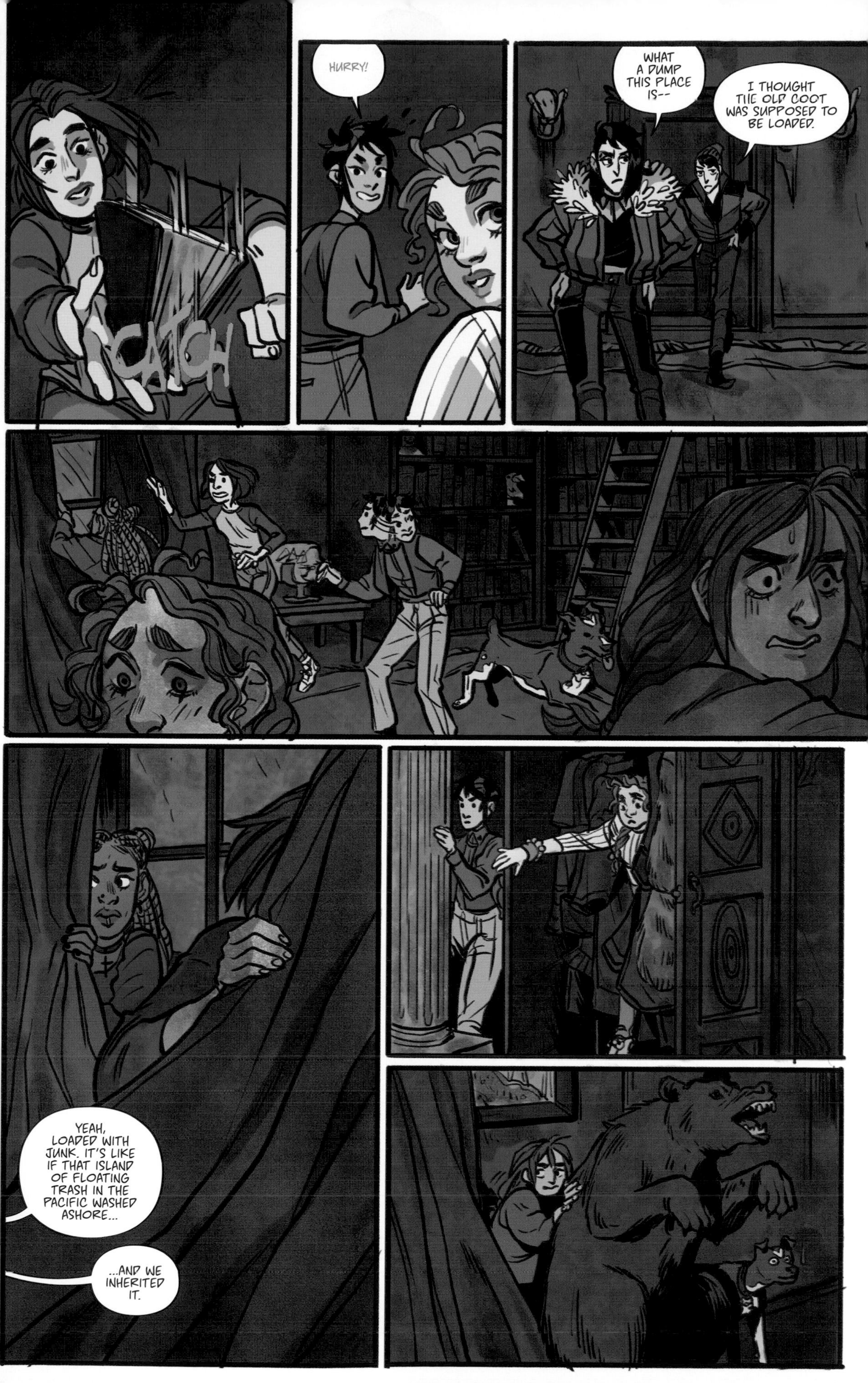
CATCH
HURRY!
WHAT A DUMP THIS PLACE IS--
I THOUGHT THE OLD COOT WAS SUPPOSED TO BE LOADED.
YEAH, LOADED WITH JUNK. IT'S LIKE IF THAT ISLAND OF FLOATING TRASH IN THE PACIFIC WASHED ASHORE...
...AND WE INHERITED IT.

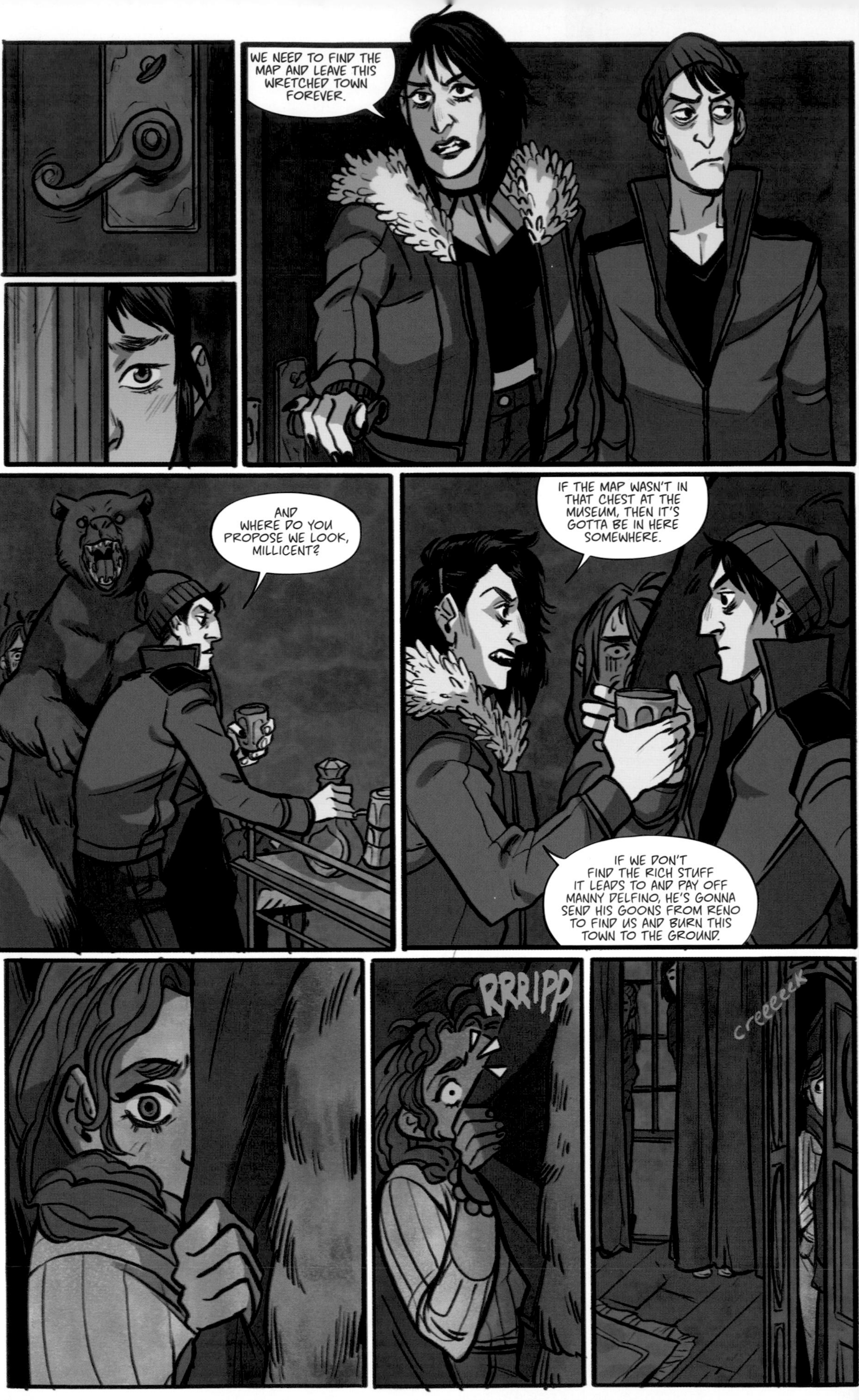
WE NEED TO FIND THE MAP AND LEAVE THIS WRETCHED TOWN FOREVER.
AND WHERE DO YOU PROPOSE WE LOOK, MILLICENT?
IF THE MAP WASN'T IN THAT CHEST AT THE MUSEUM, THEN IT'S GOTTA BE IN HERE SOMEWHERE.
IF WE DON'T FIND THE RICH STUFF IT LEADS TO AND PAY OFF MANNY DELFINO, HE'S GONNA SEND HIS GOONS FROM RENO TO FIND US AND BURN THIS TOWN TO THE GROUND.
RRRIPP
creeeek

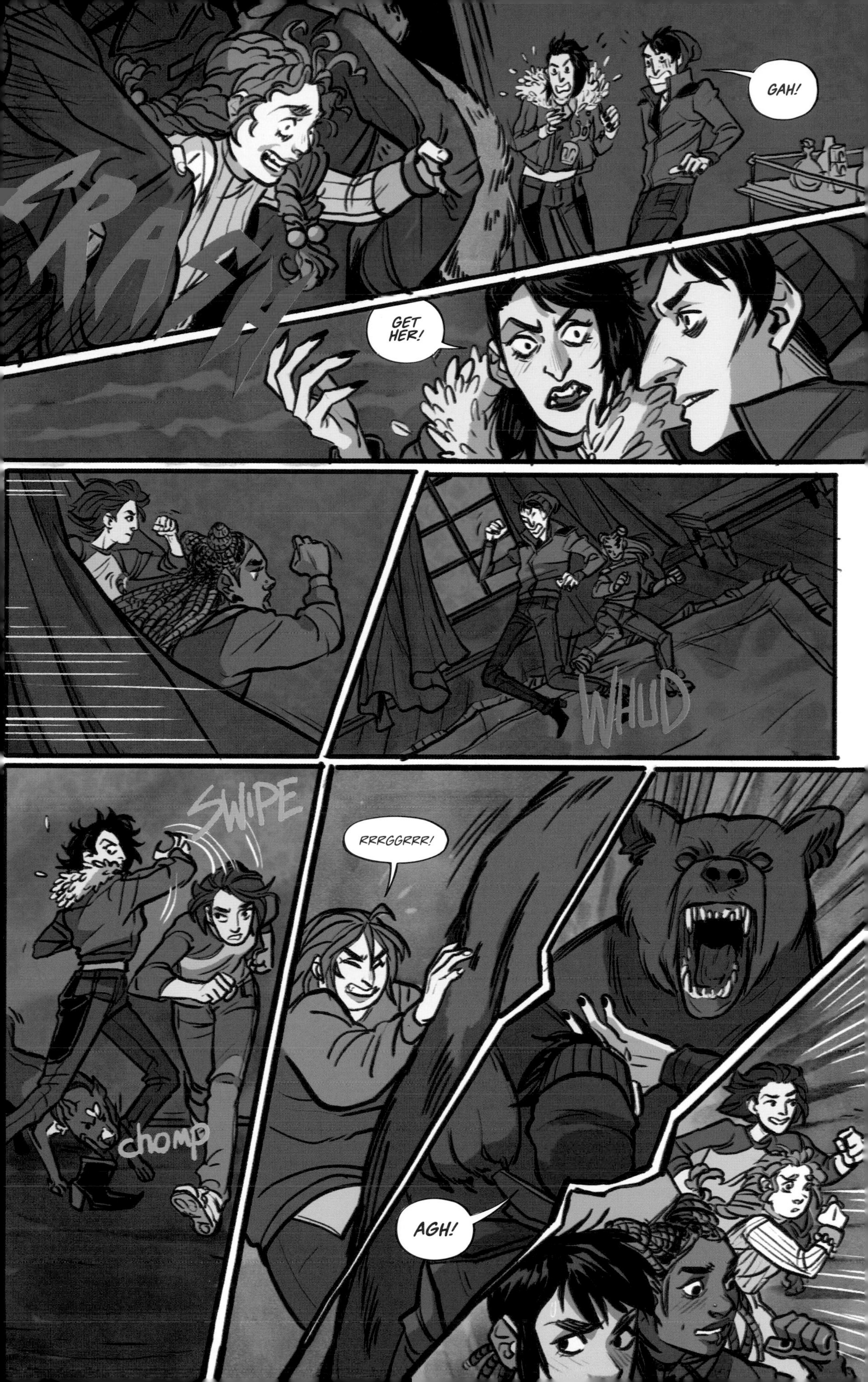
GAH!
CRASH
GET HER!
WHUD
SWIPE
chomp
RRRGGRRR!
AGH!

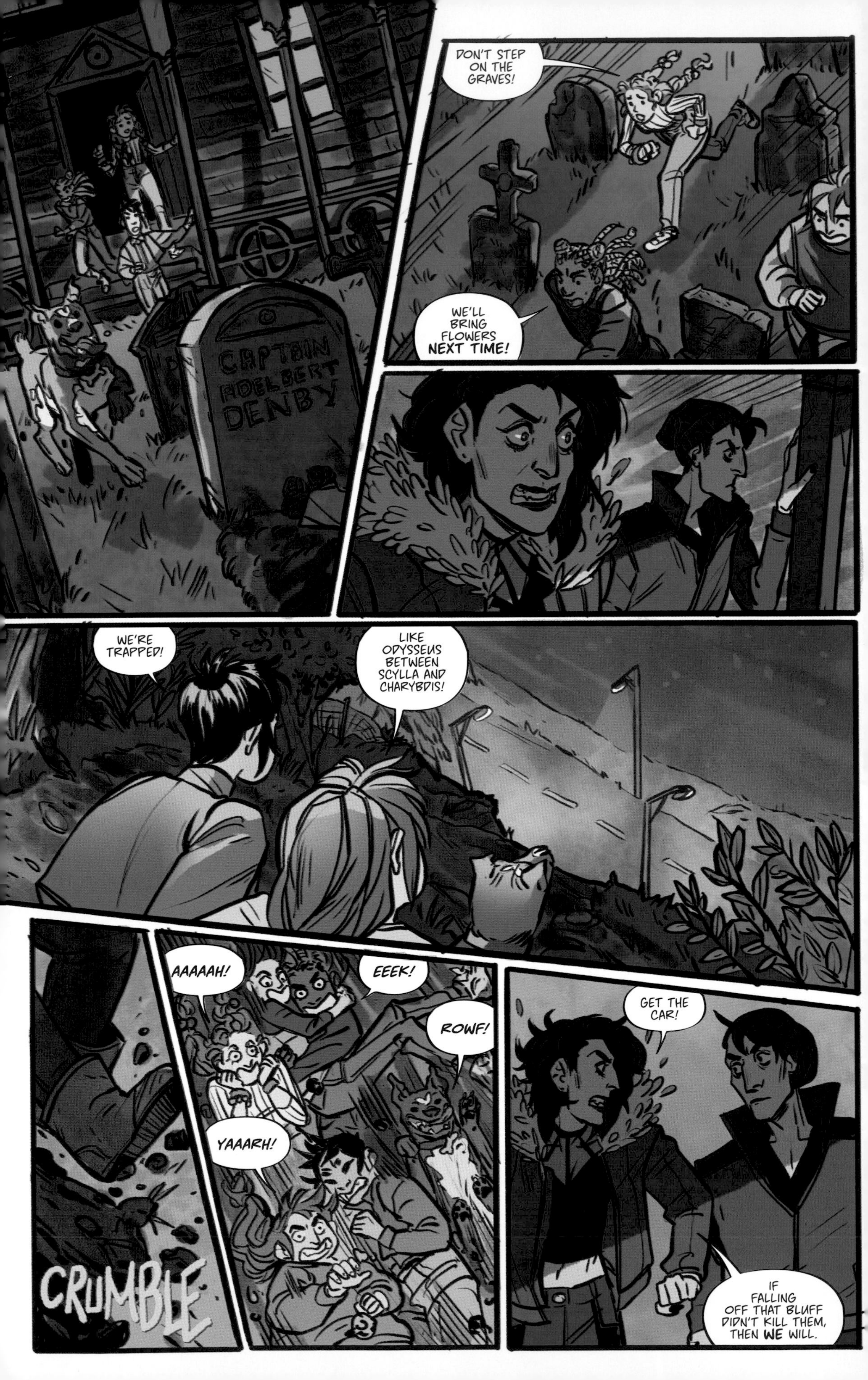
CAPTAIN ADELBERT DENBY
DON'T STEP ON THE GRAVES!
WE'LL BRING FLOWERS NEXT TIME!
WE'RE TRAPPED!
LIKE ODYSSEUS BETWEEN SCYLLA AND CHARYBDIS!
CRUMBLE
AAAAAH!
EEEK!
ROWF!
YAAARH!
GET THE CAR!
IF FALLING OFF THAT BLUFF DIDN'T KILL THEM, THEN WE WILL.

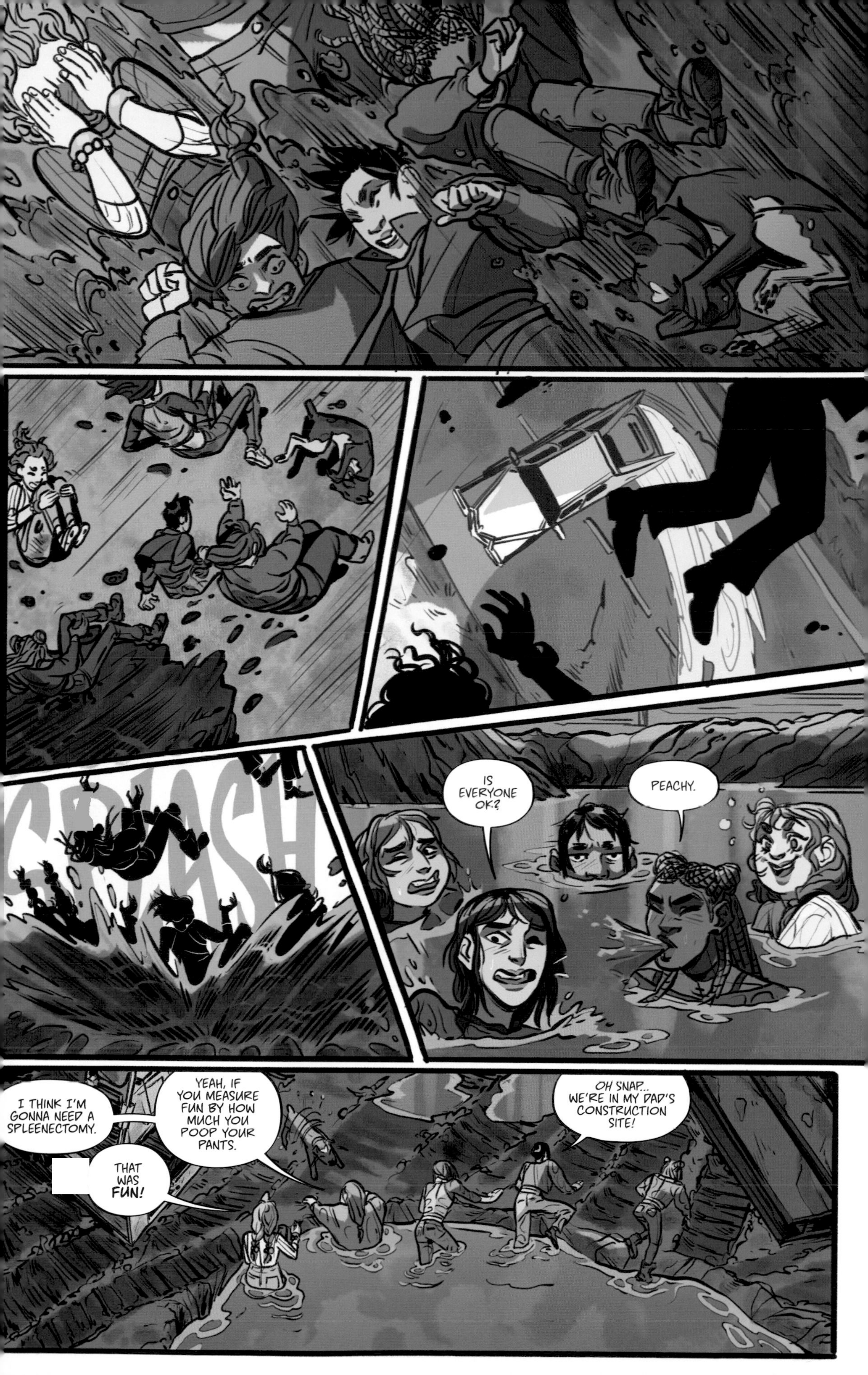
SPLASH!
IS EVERYONE OK?
PEACHY.
I THINK I'M GONNA NEED A SPLEENECTOMY.
THAT WAS **FUN!**
YEAH, IF YOU MEASURE FUN BY HOW MUCH YOU POOP YOUR PANTS.
OH SNAP... WE'RE IN MY DAD'S CONSTRUCTION SITE!

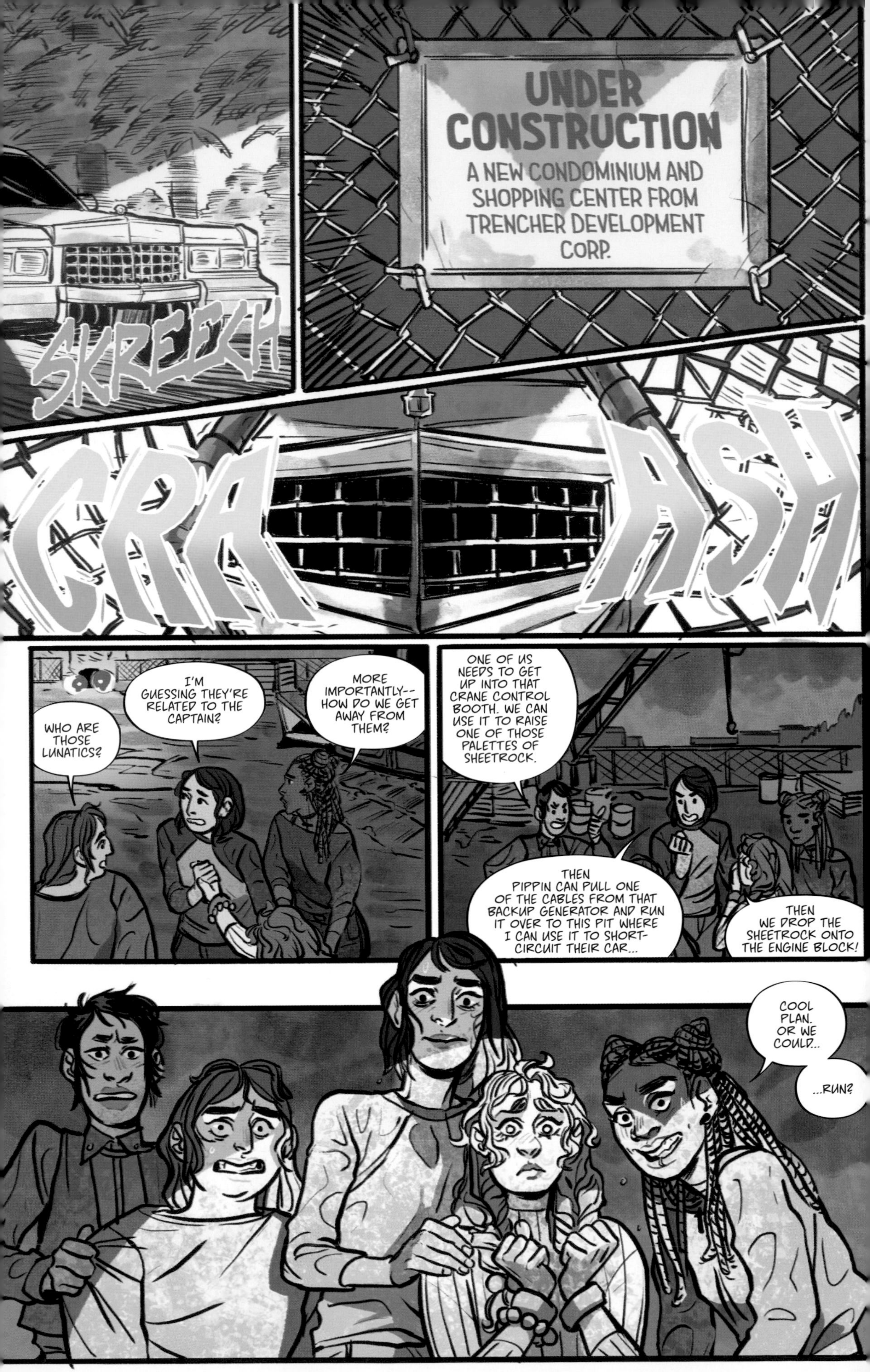
SKREECH
UNDER CONSTRUCTION
A NEW CONDOMINIUM AND SHOPPING CENTER FROM TRENCHER DEVELOPMENT CORP.
CRA ASH
WHO ARE THOSE LUNATICS?
I'M GUESSING THEY'RE RELATED TO THE CAPTAIN?
MORE IMPORTANTLY-- HOW DO WE GET AWAY FROM THEM?
ONE OF US NEEDS TO GET UP INTO THAT CRANE CONTROL BOOTH. WE CAN USE IT TO RAISE ONE OF THOSE PALETTES OF SHEETROCK.
THEN PIPPIN CAN PULL ONE OF THE CABLES FROM THAT BACKUP GENERATOR AND RUN IT OVER TO THIS PIT WHERE I CAN USE IT TO SHORT-CIRCUIT THEIR CAR...
THEN WE DROP THE SHEETROCK ONTO THE ENGINE BLOCK!
COOL PLAN. OR WE COULD...
...RUN?

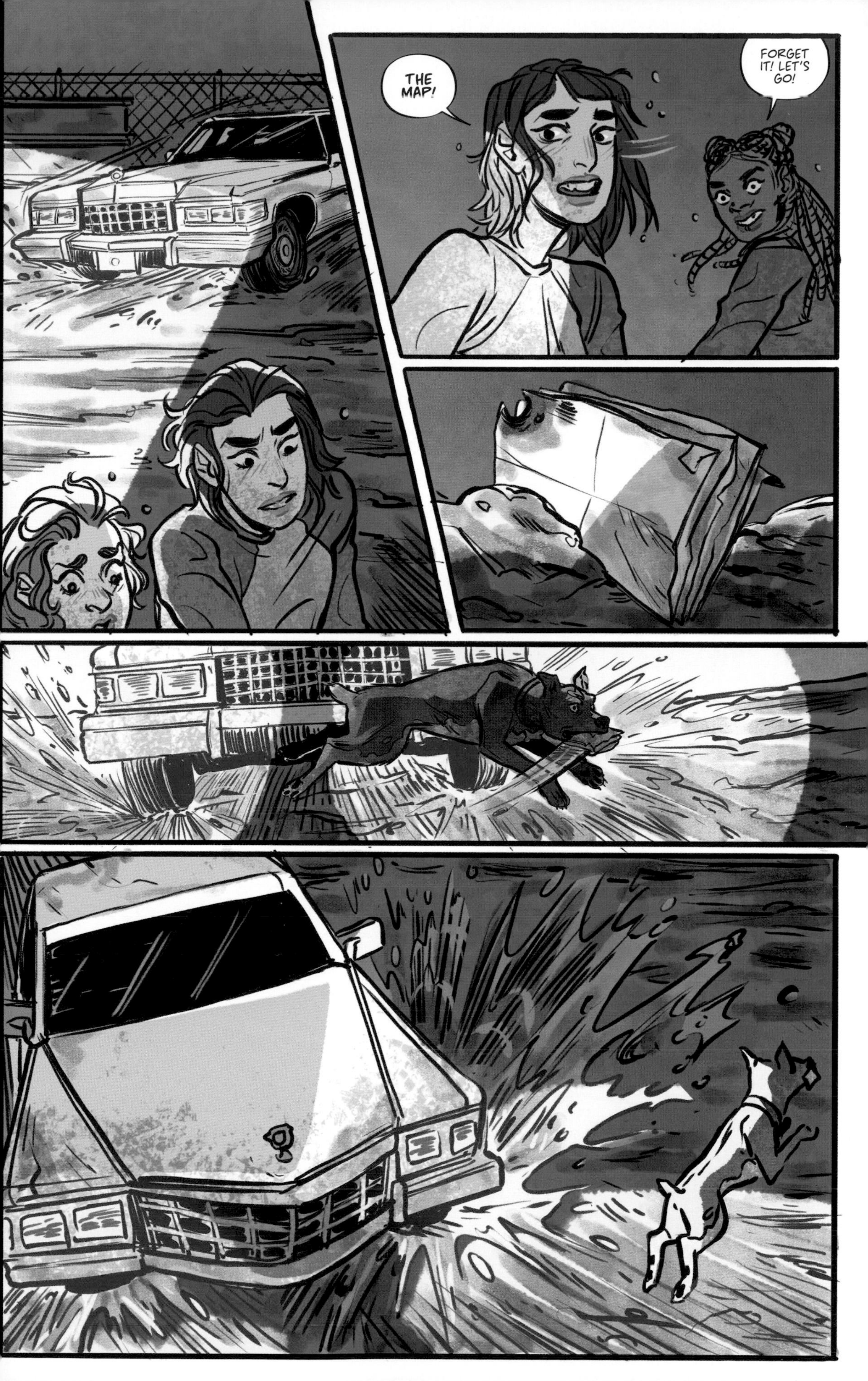
THE MAP!
FORGET IT! LET'S GO!

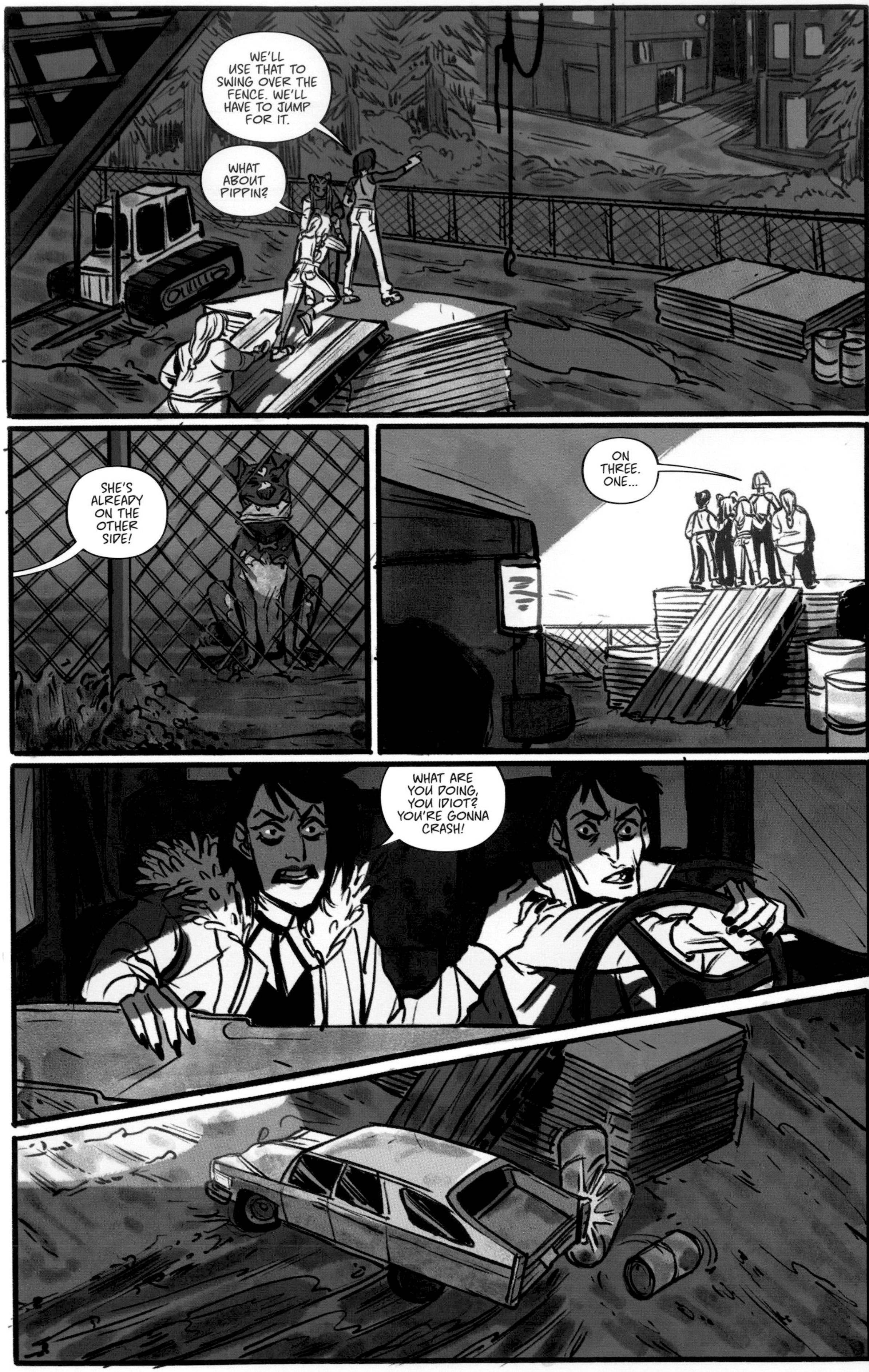
WE'LL USE THAT TO SWING OVER THE FENCE. WE'LL HAVE TO JUMP FOR IT.
WHAT ABOUT PIPPIN?
SHE'S ALREADY ON THE OTHER SIDE!
ON THREE. ONE...
WHAT ARE YOU DOING, YOU IDIOT? YOU'RE GONNA CRASH!

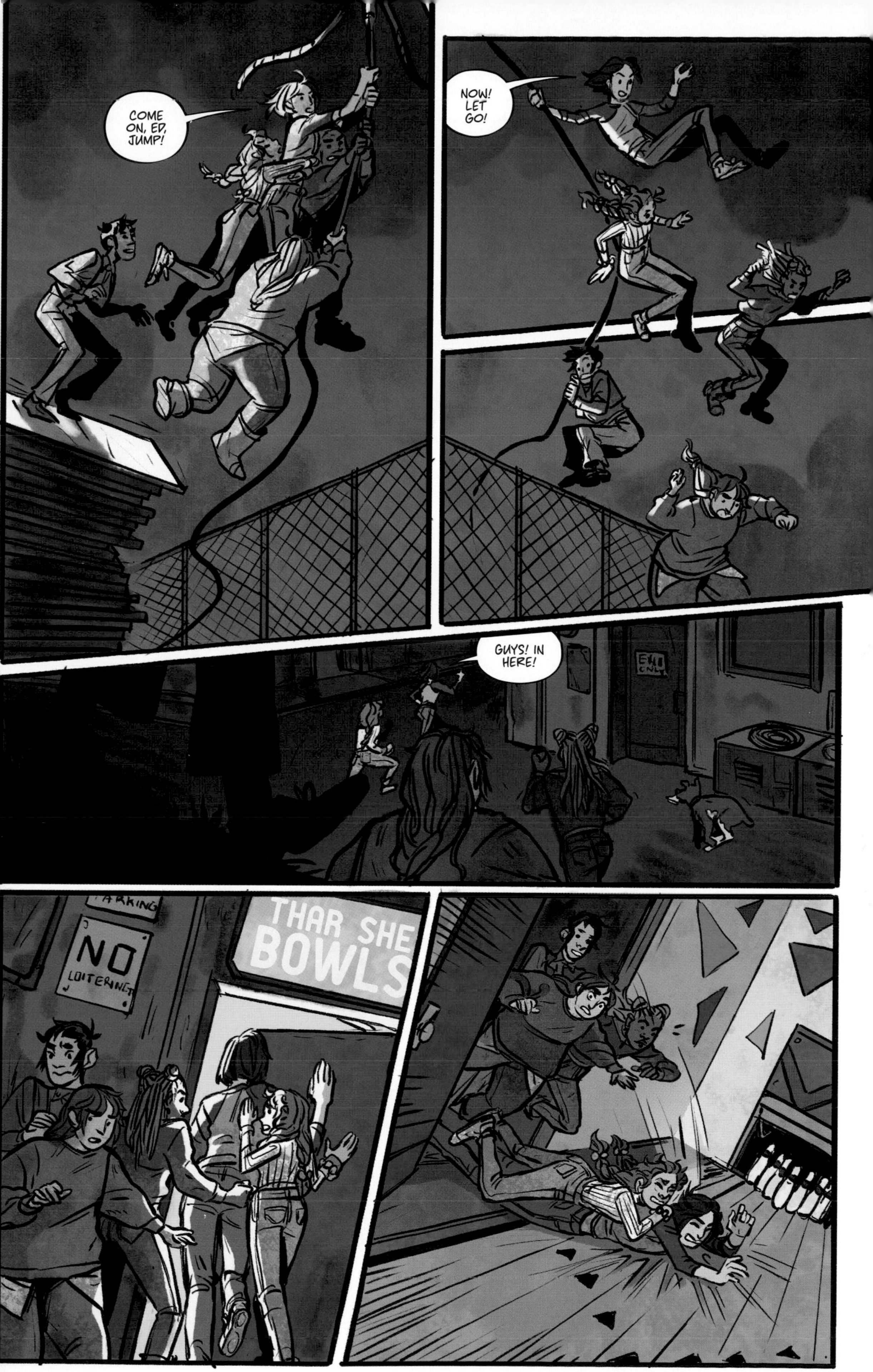
COME ON, ED, JUMP!
NOW! LET GO!
GUYS! IN HERE!
NO LOITERING
THAR SHE BOWLS

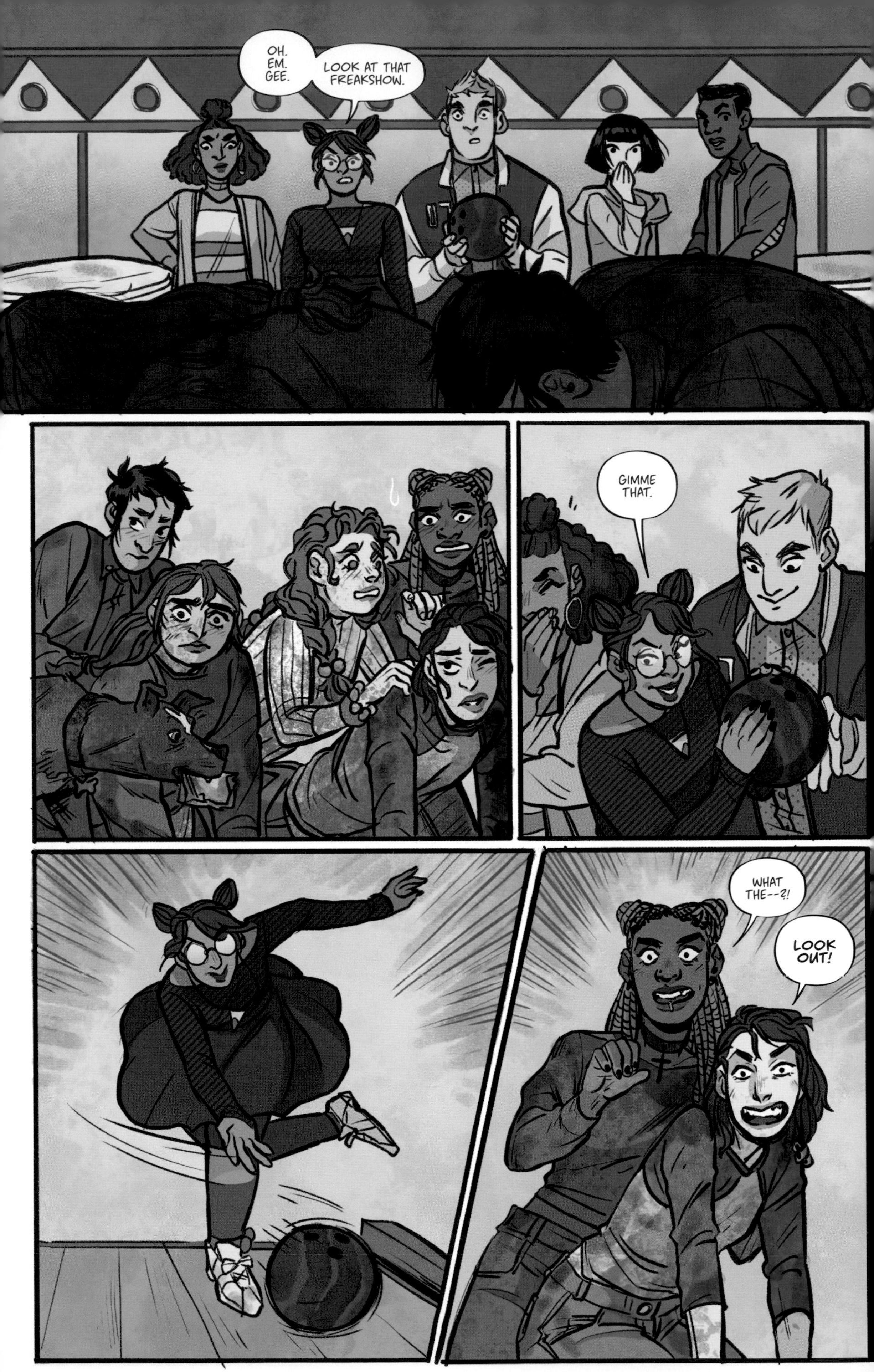
OH. EM. GEE.
LOOK AT THAT FREAKSHOW.
GIMME THAT.
WHAT THE--?!
LOOK OUT!

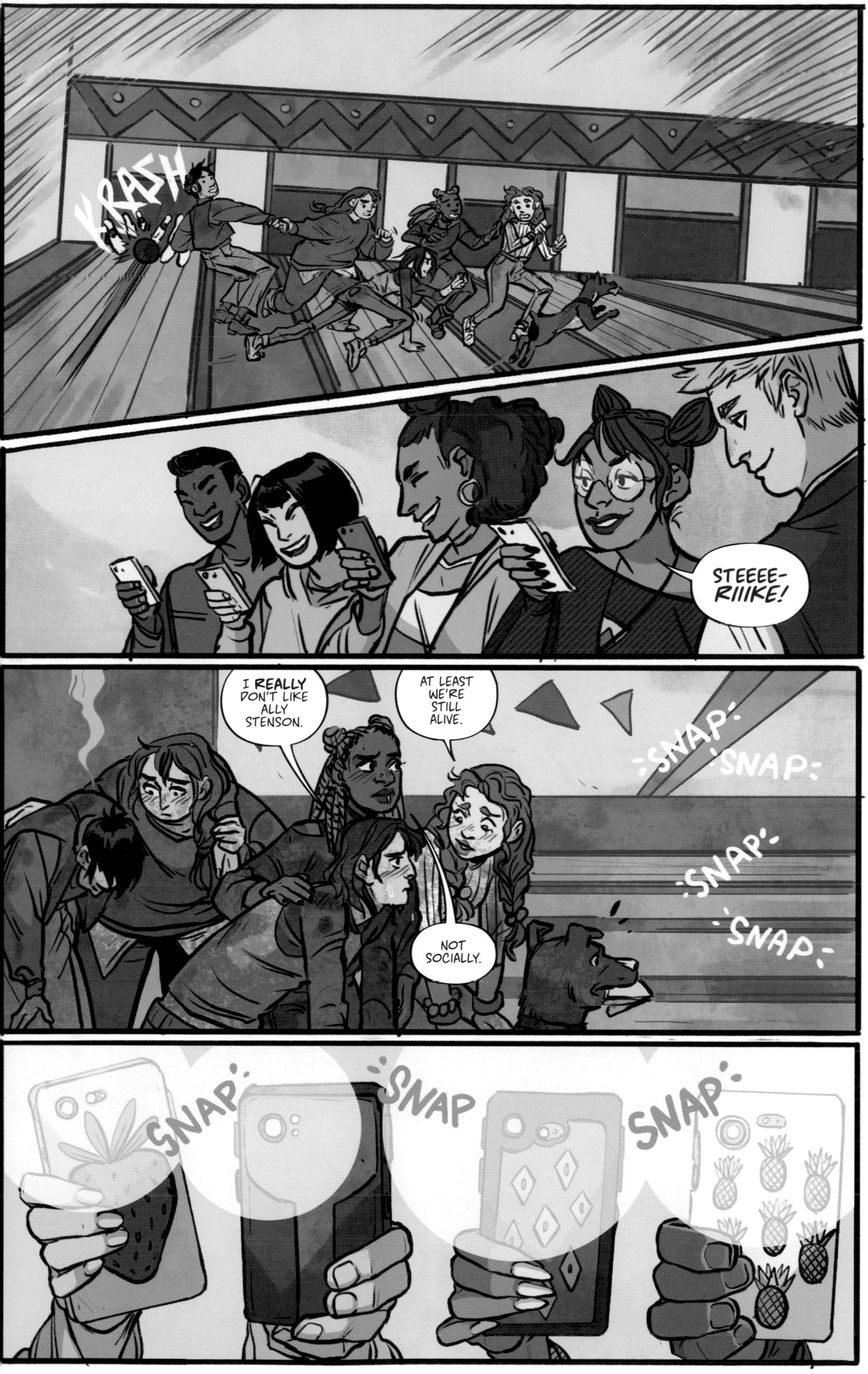
KRASH
STEEEE-RIIIKE!
I REALLY DON'T LIKE ALLY STENSON.
AT LEAST WE'RE STILL ALIVE.
NOT SOCIALLY.
SNAP SNAP
SNAP SNAP
SNAP SNAP SNAP

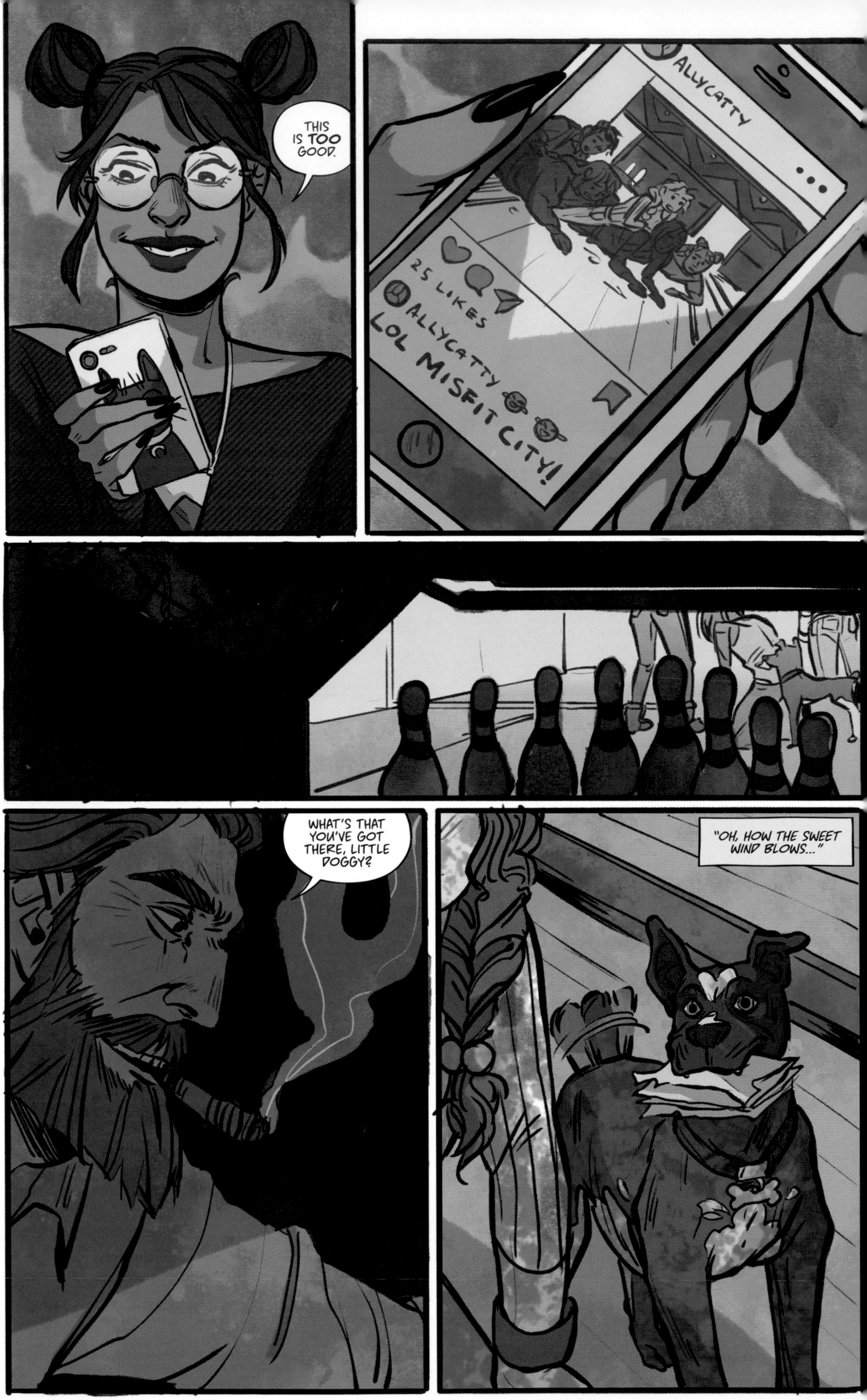
THIS IS TOO GOOD.
ALLYCATTY
25 LIKES
ALLYCATTY
LOL MISFIT CITY!
WHAT'S THAT YOU'VE GOT THERE, LITTLE DOGGY?
"OH, HOW THE SWEET WIND BLOWS..."

CHAPTER III

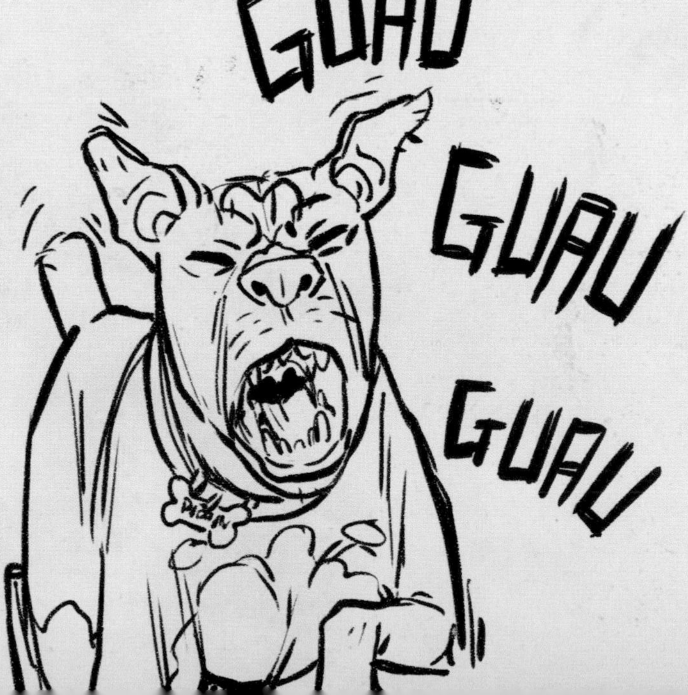
GUAU
GUAU
GUAU

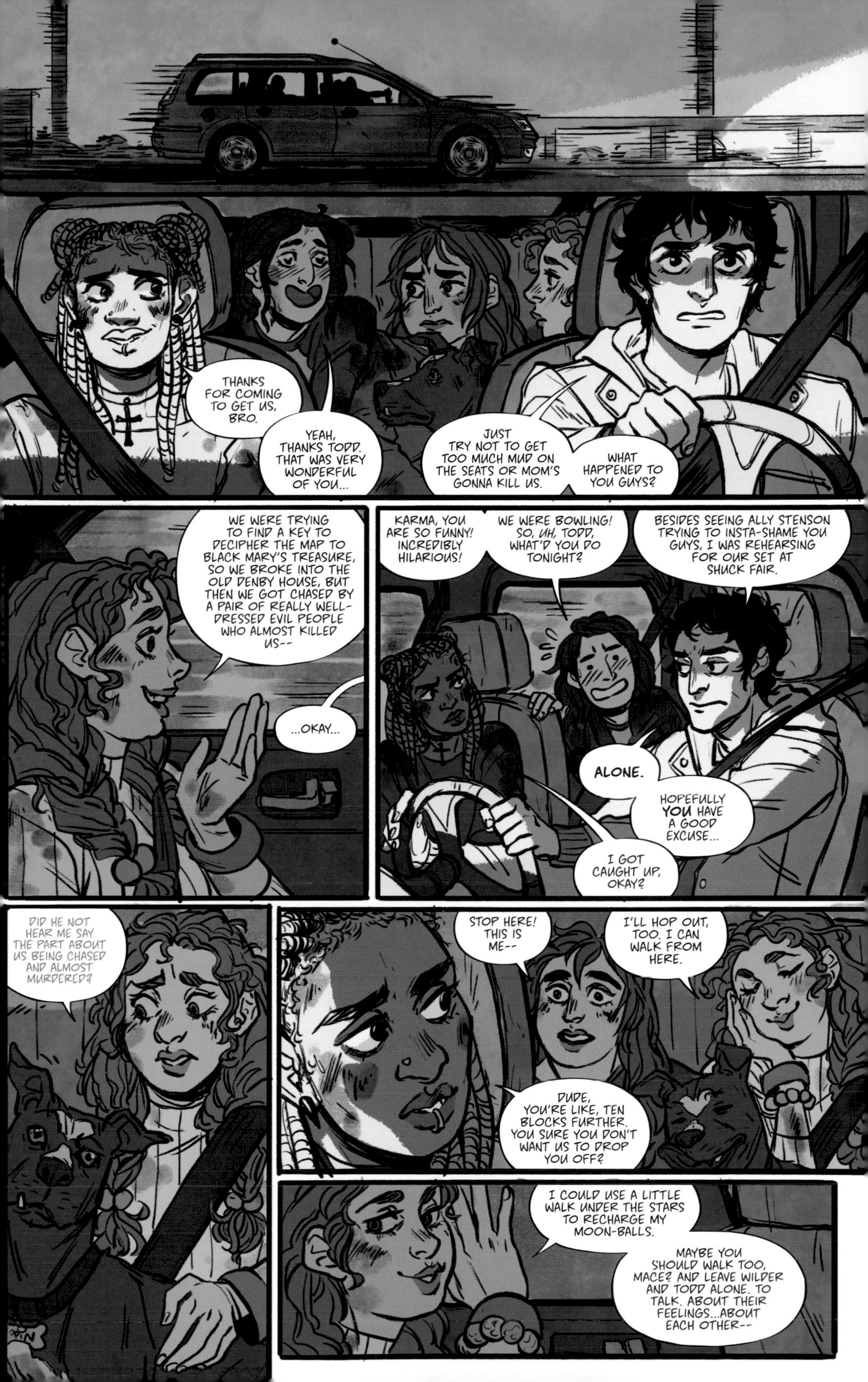
THANKS FOR COMING TO GET US, BRO.
YEAH, THANKS TODD. THAT WAS VERY WONDERFUL OF YOU...
JUST TRY NOT TO GET TOO MUCH MUD ON THE SEATS OR MOM'S GONNA KILL US.
WHAT HAPPENED TO YOU GUYS?
WE WERE TRYING TO FIND A KEY TO DECIPHER THE MAP TO BLACK MARY'S TREASURE, SO WE BROKE INTO THE OLD DENBY HOUSE, BUT THEN WE GOT CHASED BY A PAIR OF REALLY WELL-DRESSED EVIL PEOPLE WHO ALMOST KILLED US--
...OKAY...
KARMA, YOU ARE SO FUNNY! INCREDIBLY HILARIOUS!
WE WERE BOWLING! SO, UH, TODD, WHAT'D YOU DO TONIGHT?
BESIDES SEEING ALLY STENSON TRYING TO INSTA-SHAME YOU GUYS, I WAS REHEARSING FOR OUR SET AT SHUCK FAIR.
ALONE.
HOPEFULLY YOU HAVE A GOOD EXCUSE...
I GOT CAUGHT UP, OKAY?
DID HE NOT HEAR ME SAY THE PART ABOUT US BEING CHASED AND ALMOST MURDERED?
STOP HERE! THIS IS ME--
I'LL HOP OUT, TOO. I CAN WALK FROM HERE.
DUDE, YOU'RE LIKE, TEN BLOCKS FURTHER. YOU SURE YOU DON'T WANT US TO DROP YOU OFF?
I COULD USE A LITTLE WALK UNDER THE STARS TO RECHARGE MY MOON-BALLS.
MAYBE YOU SHOULD WALK TOO, MACE? AND LEAVE WILDER AND TODD ALONE. TO TALK. ABOUT THEIR FEELINGS...ABOUT EACH OTHER--

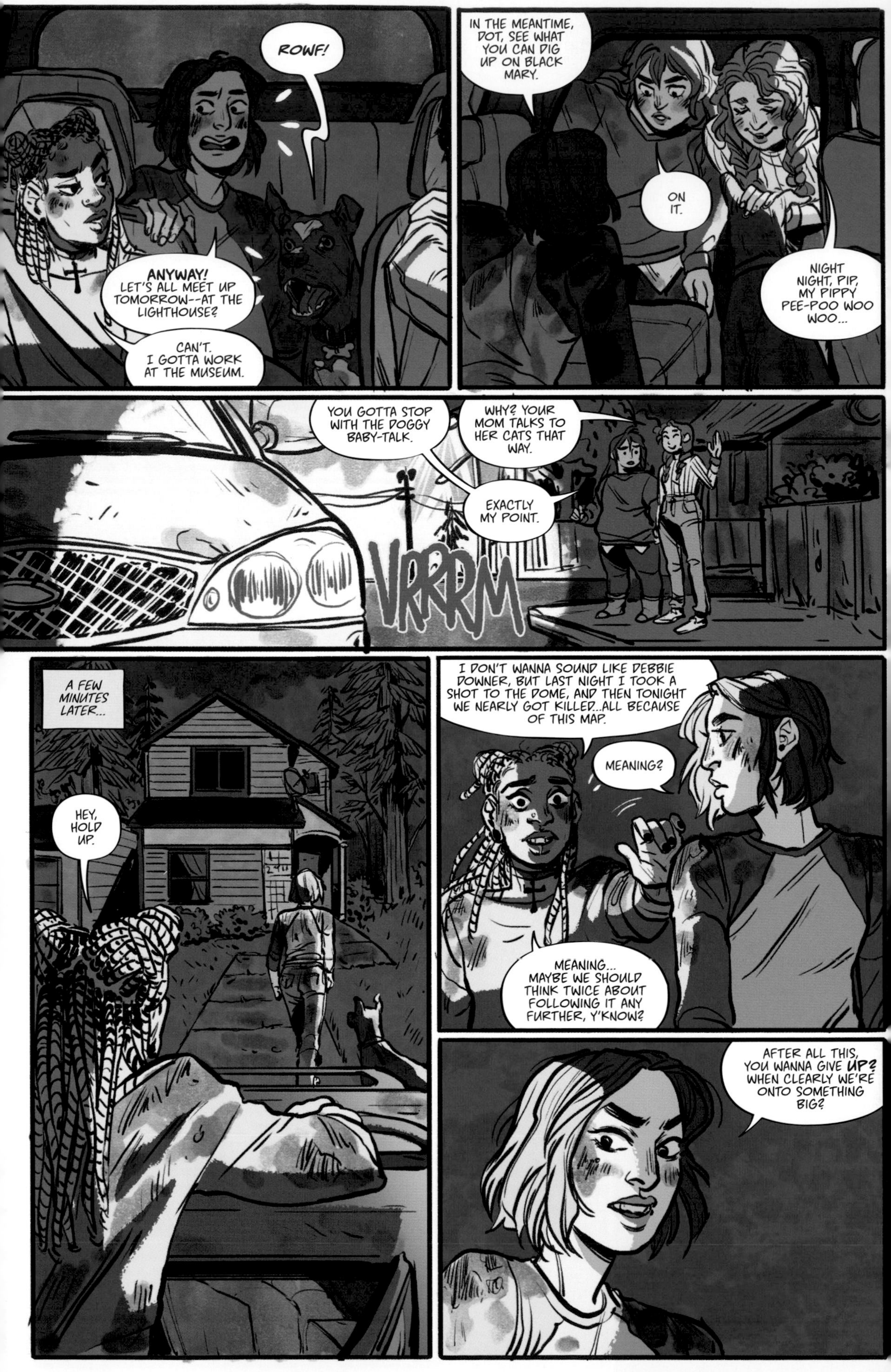
ROWF!
ANYWAY! LET'S ALL MEET UP TOMORROW--AT THE LIGHTHOUSE?
CAN'T. I GOTTA WORK AT THE MUSEUM.
IN THE MEANTIME, DOT, SEE WHAT YOU CAN DIG UP ON BLACK MARY.
ON IT.
NIGHT NIGHT, PIP, MY PIPPY PEE-POO WOO WOO...
YOU GOTTA STOP WITH THE DOGGY BABY-TALK.
WHY? YOUR MOM TALKS TO HER CATS THAT WAY.
EXACTLY MY POINT.
VRRRM
A FEW MINUTES LATER...
HEY, HOLD UP.
I DON'T WANNA SOUND LIKE DEBBIE DOWNER, BUT LAST NIGHT I TOOK A SHOT TO THE DOME, AND THEN TONIGHT WE NEARLY GOT KILLED...ALL BECAUSE OF THIS MAP.
MEANING?
MEANING... MAYBE WE SHOULD THINK TWICE ABOUT FOLLOWING IT ANY FURTHER, Y'KNOW?
AFTER ALL THIS, YOU WANNA GIVE UP? WHEN CLEARLY WE'RE ONTO SOMETHING BIG?

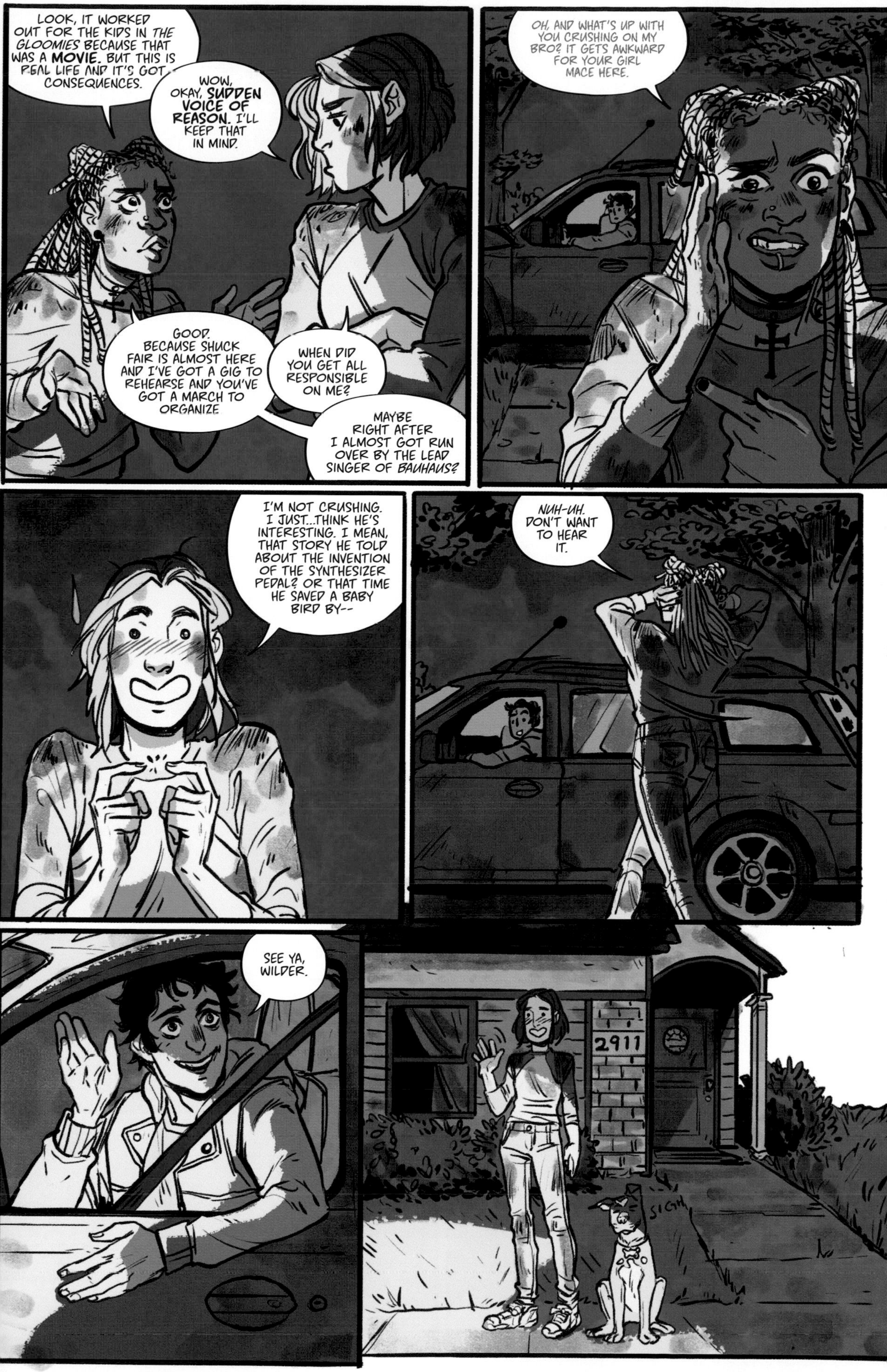
LOOK, IT WORKED OUT FOR THE KIDS IN THE GLOOMIES BECAUSE THAT WAS A MOVIE. BUT THIS IS REAL LIFE AND IT'S GOT CONSEQUENCES.
WOW, OKAY, SUDDEN VOICE OF REASON. I'LL KEEP THAT IN MIND.
GOOD. BECAUSE SHUCK FAIR IS ALMOST HERE AND I'VE GOT A GIG TO REHEARSE AND YOU'VE GOT A MARCH TO ORGANIZE.
WHEN DID YOU GET ALL RESPONSIBLE ON ME?
MAYBE RIGHT AFTER I ALMOST GOT RUN OVER BY THE LEAD SINGER OF BAUHAUS?
OH, AND WHAT'S UP WITH YOU CRUSHING ON MY BRO? IT GETS AWKWARD FOR YOUR GIRL MACE HERE.
I'M NOT CRUSHING. I JUST...THINK HE'S INTERESTING. I MEAN, THAT STORY HE TOLD ABOUT THE INVENTION OF THE SYNTHESIZER PEDAL? OR THAT TIME HE SAVED A BABY BIRD BY--
NUH-UH. DON'T WANT TO HEAR IT.
SEE YA, WILDER.
2911
SIGH

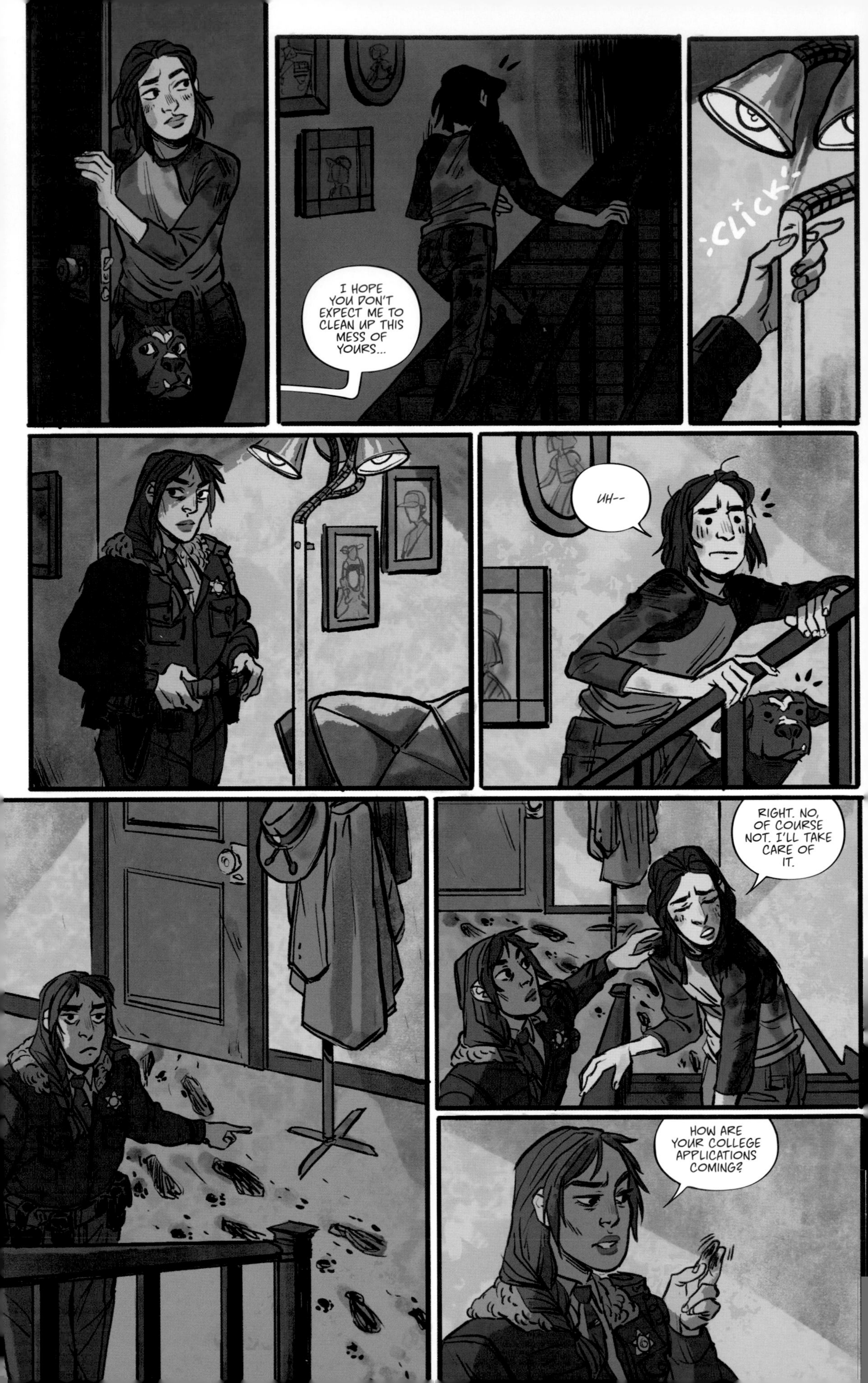
I HOPE YOU DON'T EXPECT ME TO CLEAN UP THIS MESS OF YOURS...
CLICK
UH--
RIGHT. NO, OF COURSE NOT. I'LL TAKE CARE OF IT.
HOW ARE YOUR COLLEGE APPLICATIONS COMING?

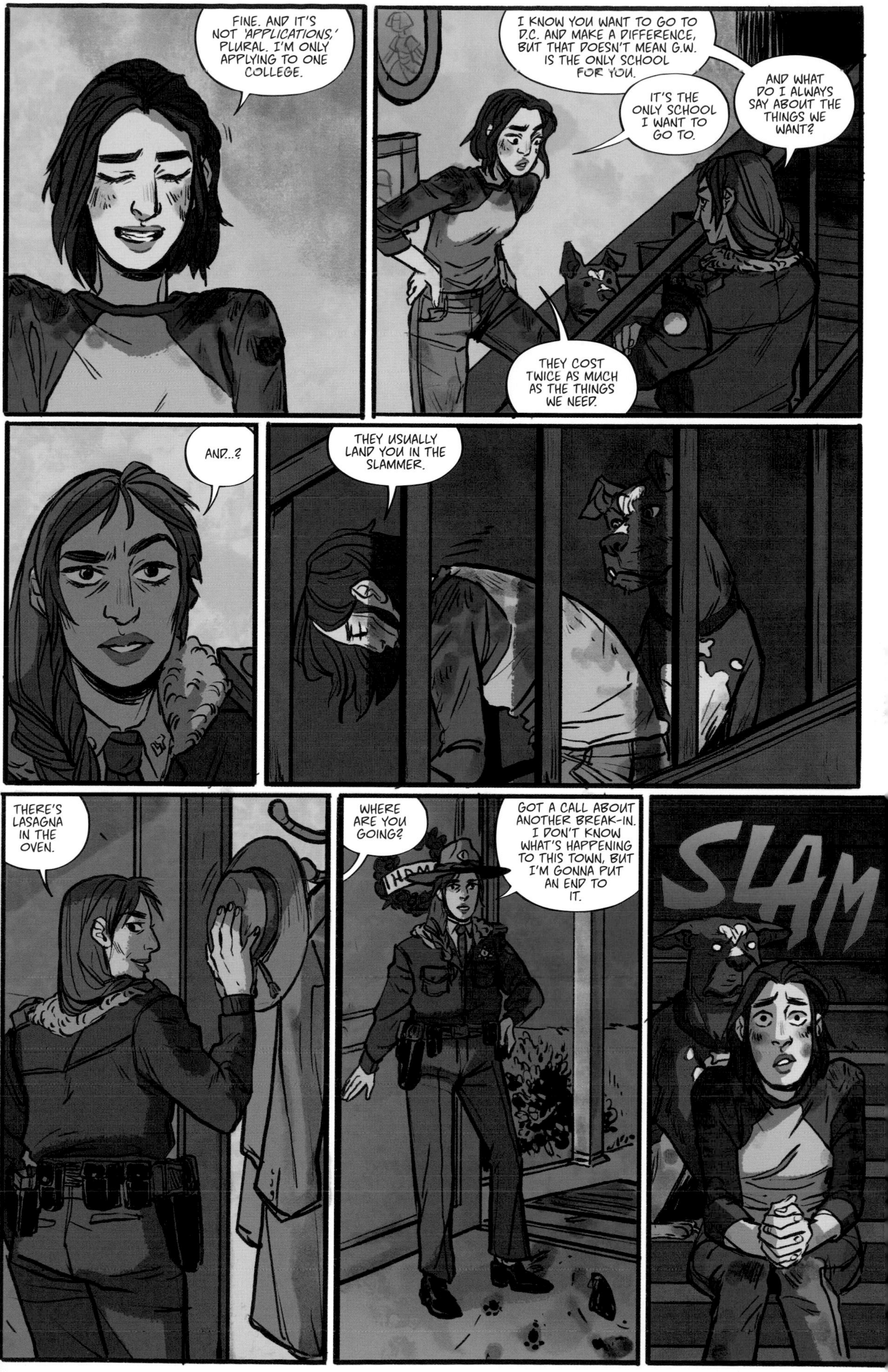
FINE. AND IT'S NOT 'APPLICATIONS,' PLURAL. I'M ONLY APPLYING TO ONE COLLEGE.
I KNOW YOU WANT TO GO TO D.C. AND MAKE A DIFFERENCE, BUT THAT DOESN'T MEAN G.W. IS THE ONLY SCHOOL FOR YOU.
IT'S THE ONLY SCHOOL I WANT TO GO TO.
AND WHAT DO I ALWAYS SAY ABOUT THE THINGS WE WANT?
THEY COST TWICE AS MUCH AS THE THINGS WE NEED.
AND...?
THEY USUALLY LAND YOU IN THE SLAMMER.
THERE'S LASAGNA IN THE OVEN.
WHERE ARE YOU GOING?
GOT A CALL ABOUT ANOTHER BREAK-IN. I DON'T KNOW WHAT'S HAPPENING TO THIS TOWN, BUT I'M GONNA PUT AN END TO IT.
SLAM

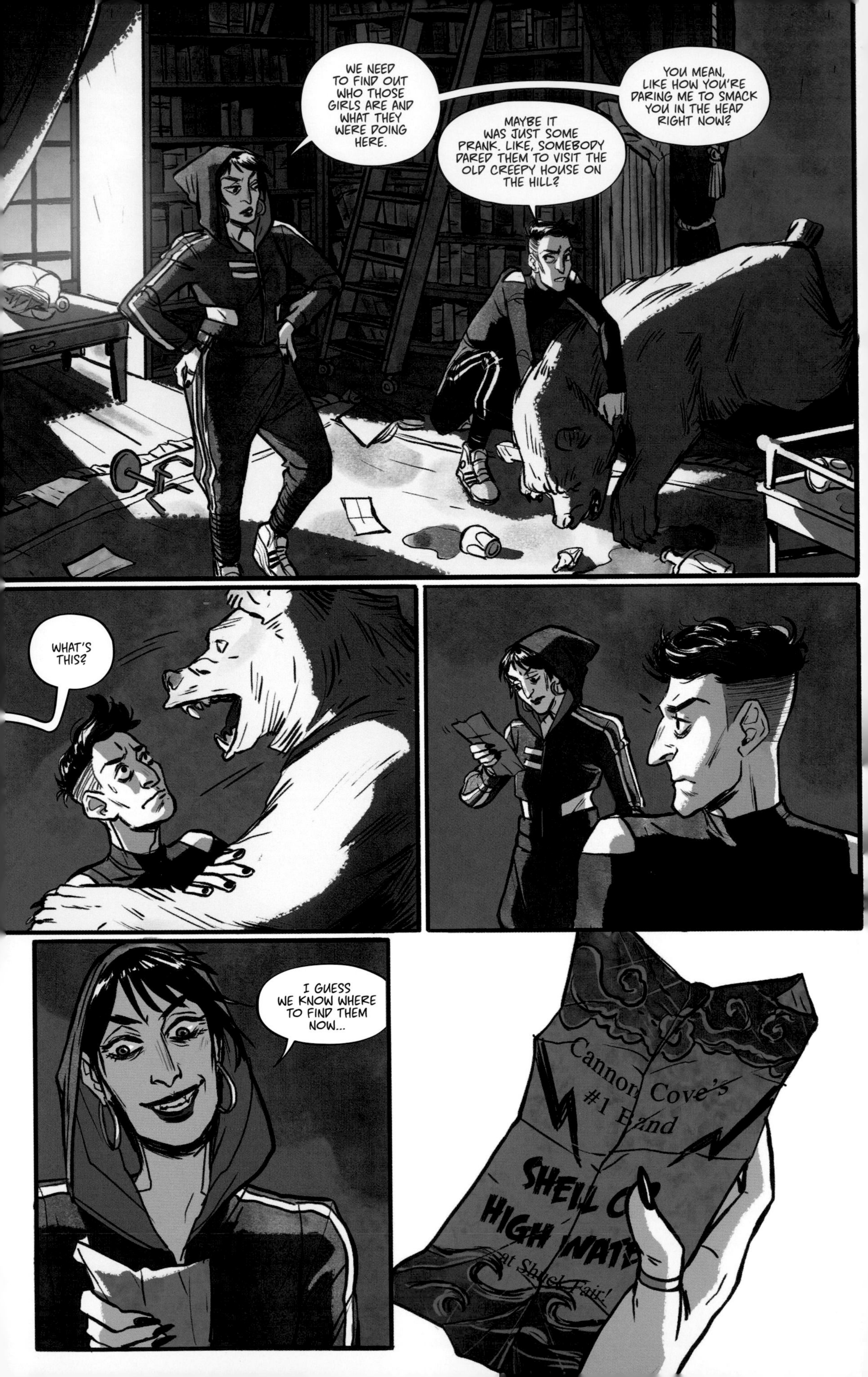
WE NEED TO FIND OUT WHO THOSE GIRLS ARE AND WHAT THEY WERE DOING HERE.
MAYBE IT WAS JUST SOME PRANK. LIKE, SOMEBODY DARED THEM TO VISIT THE OLD CREEPY HOUSE ON THE HILL?
YOU MEAN, LIKE HOW YOU'RE DARING ME TO SMACK YOU IN THE HEAD RIGHT NOW?
WHAT'S THIS?
I GUESS WE KNOW WHERE TO FIND THEM NOW...
Cannon Cove's
#1
at Shuck Fair!

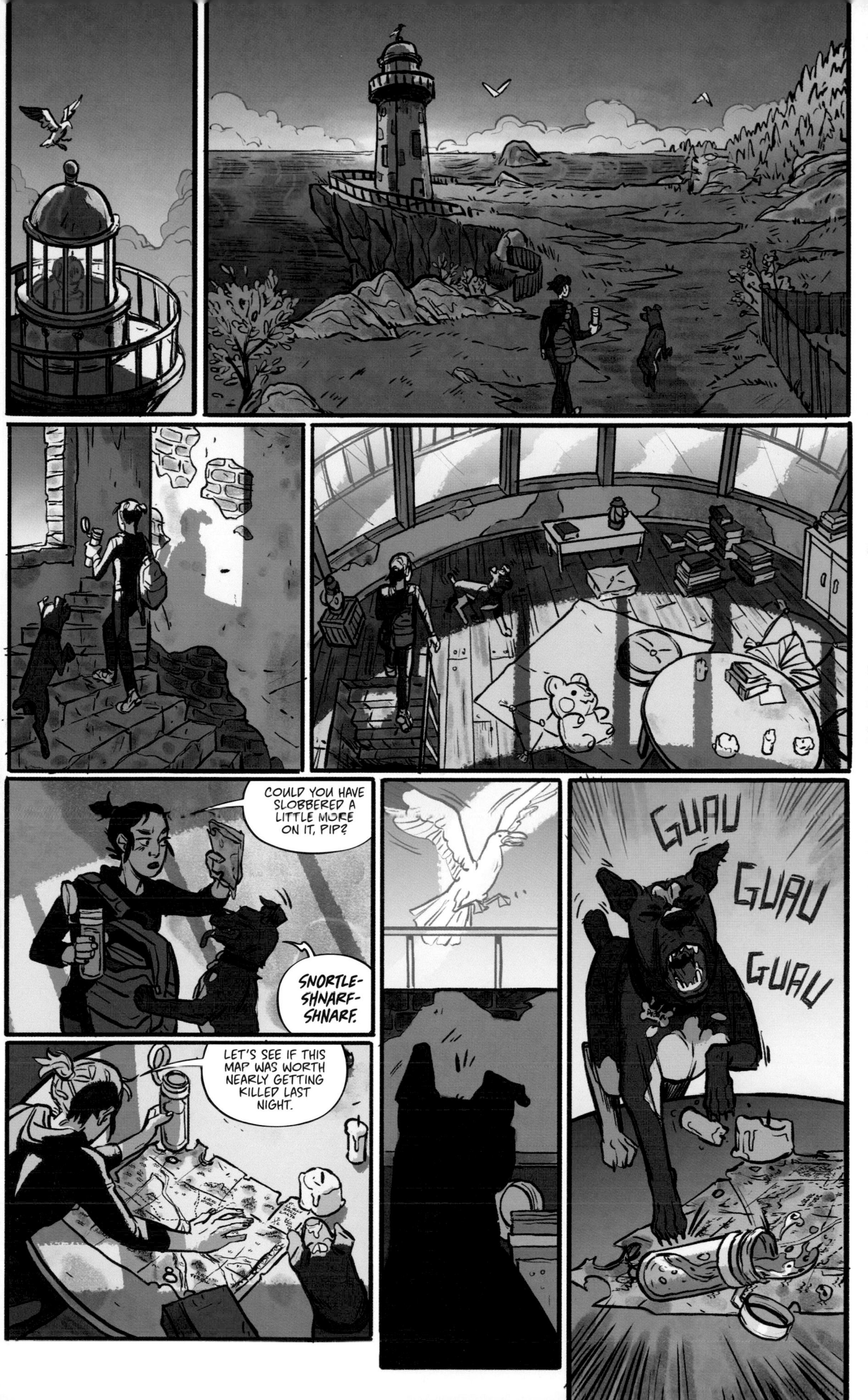
COULD YOU HAVE SLOBBERED A LITTLE MORE ON IT, PIP?
SNORTLE-SHNARF-SHNARF.
LET'S SEE IF THIS MAP WAS WORTH NEARLY GETTING KILLED LAST NIGHT.
GUAU
GUAU
GUAU

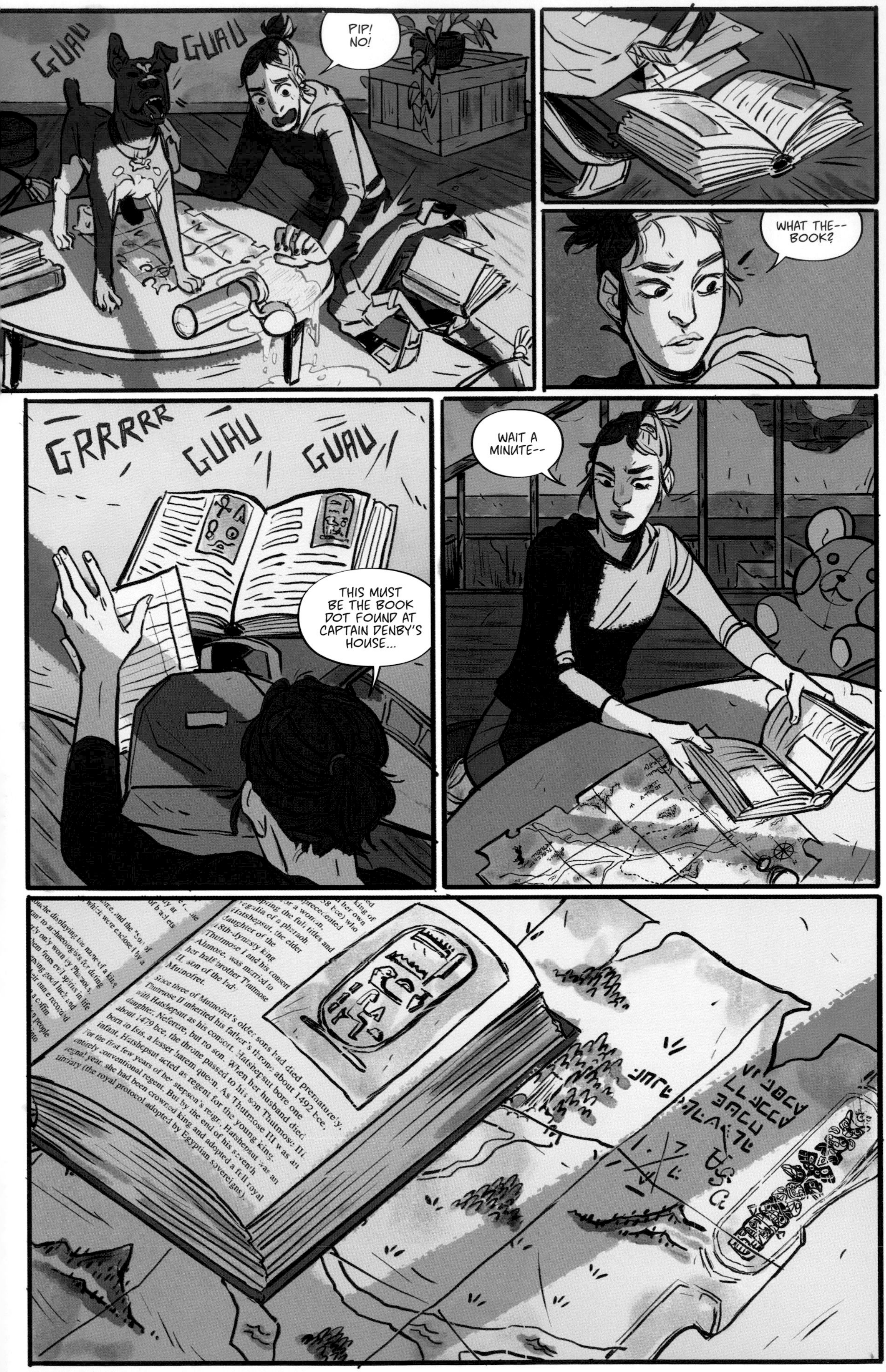
GUAU
GUAU
PIP! NO!
WHAT THE-- BOOK?
GRRRRR
GUAU
GUAU
THIS MUST BE THE BOOK DOT FOUND AT CAPTAIN DENBY'S HOUSE...
WAIT A MINUTE--

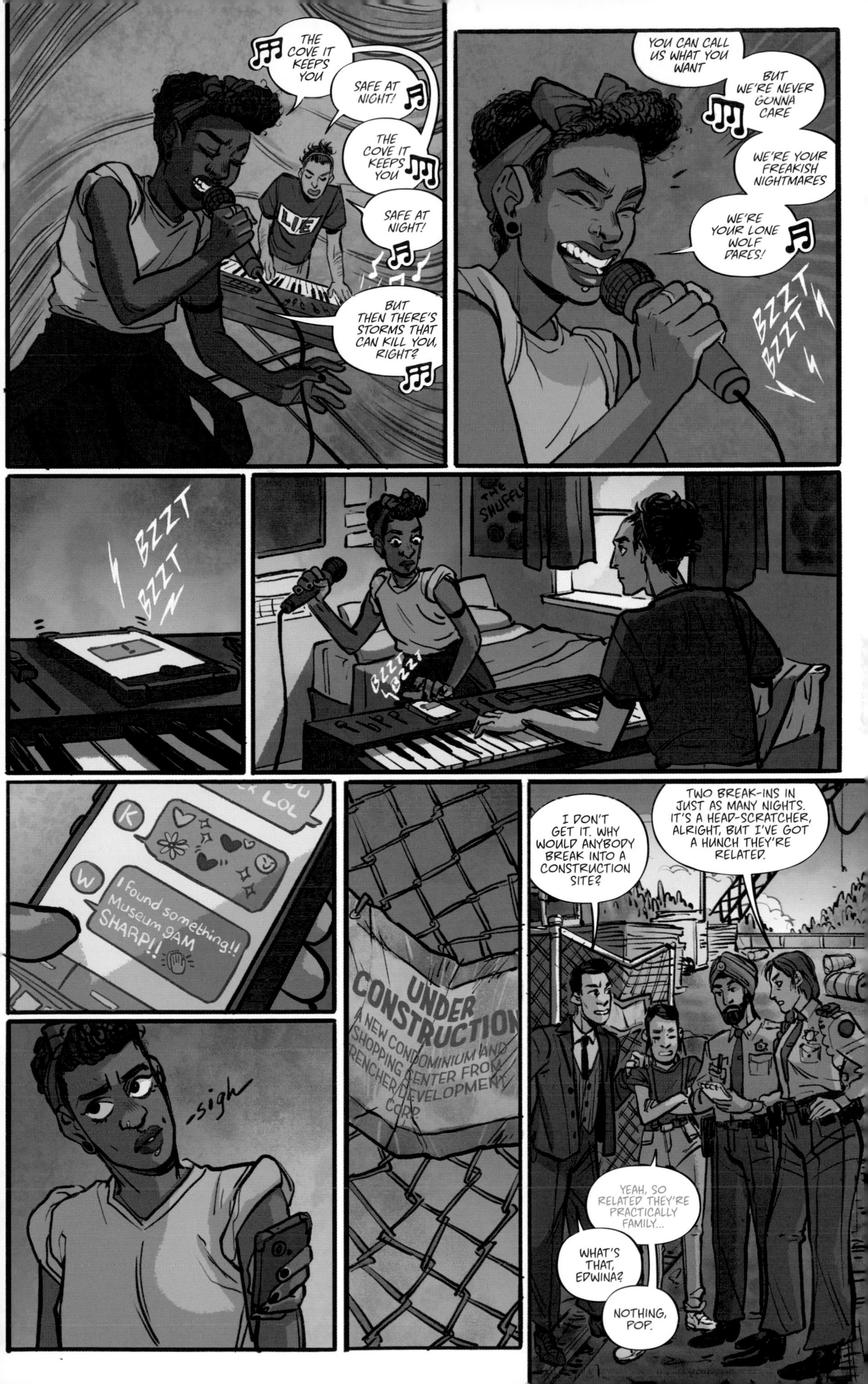
THE COVE IT KEEPS YOU
SAFE AT NIGHT!
THE COVE IT KEEPS YOU
SAFE AT NIGHT!
BUT THEN THERE'S STORMS THAT CAN KILL YOU, RIGHT?
LIE
YOU CAN CALL US WHAT YOU WANT
BUT WE'RE NEVER GONNA CARE
WE'RE YOUR FREAKISH NIGHTMARES
WE'RE YOUR LONE WOLF DARES!
BZZT BZZT
BZZT BZZT
THE SHUFFL
BZZT BZZT
I found something!! Museum 9AM SHARP!!
-sigh
UNDER CONSTRUCTION
A NEW CONDOMINIUM AND SHOPPING CENTER FROM FRENCHER DEVELOPMENT CORP.
I DON'T GET IT. WHY WOULD ANYBODY BREAK INTO A CONSTRUCTION SITE?
TWO BREAK-INS IN JUST AS MANY NIGHTS. IT'S A HEAD-SCRATCHER, ALRIGHT, BUT I'VE GOT A HUNCH THEY'RE RELATED.
YEAH, SO RELATED THEY'RE PRACTICALLY FAMILY...
WHAT'S THAT, EDWINA?
NOTHING, POP.

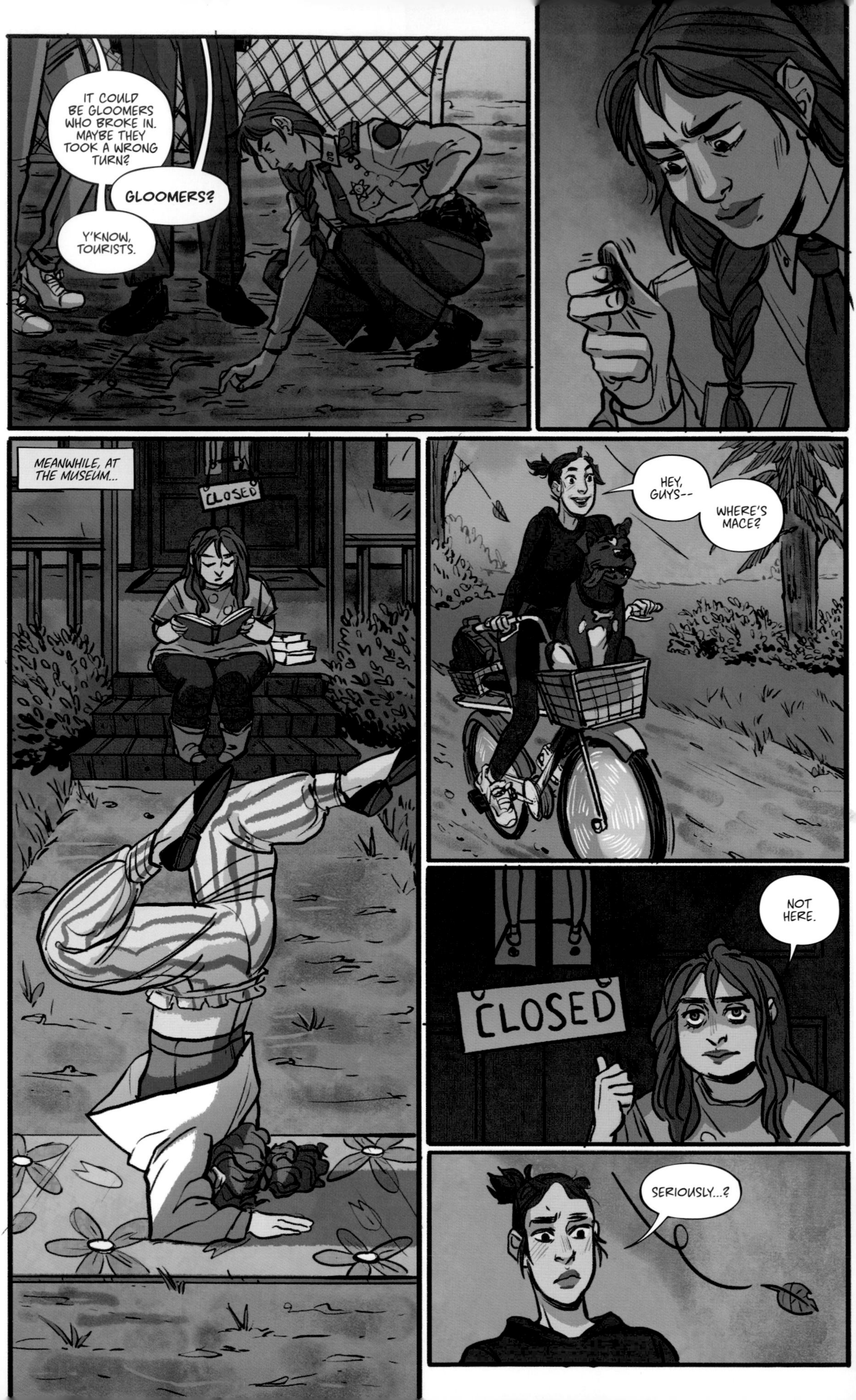
IT COULD BE GLOOMERS WHO BROKE IN. MAYBE THEY TOOK A WRONG TURN?
GLOOMERS?
Y'KNOW, TOURISTS.
MEANWHILE, AT THE MUSEUM...
CLOSED
HEY, GUYS--
WHERE'S MACE?
CLOSED
NOT HERE.
SERIOUSLY...?

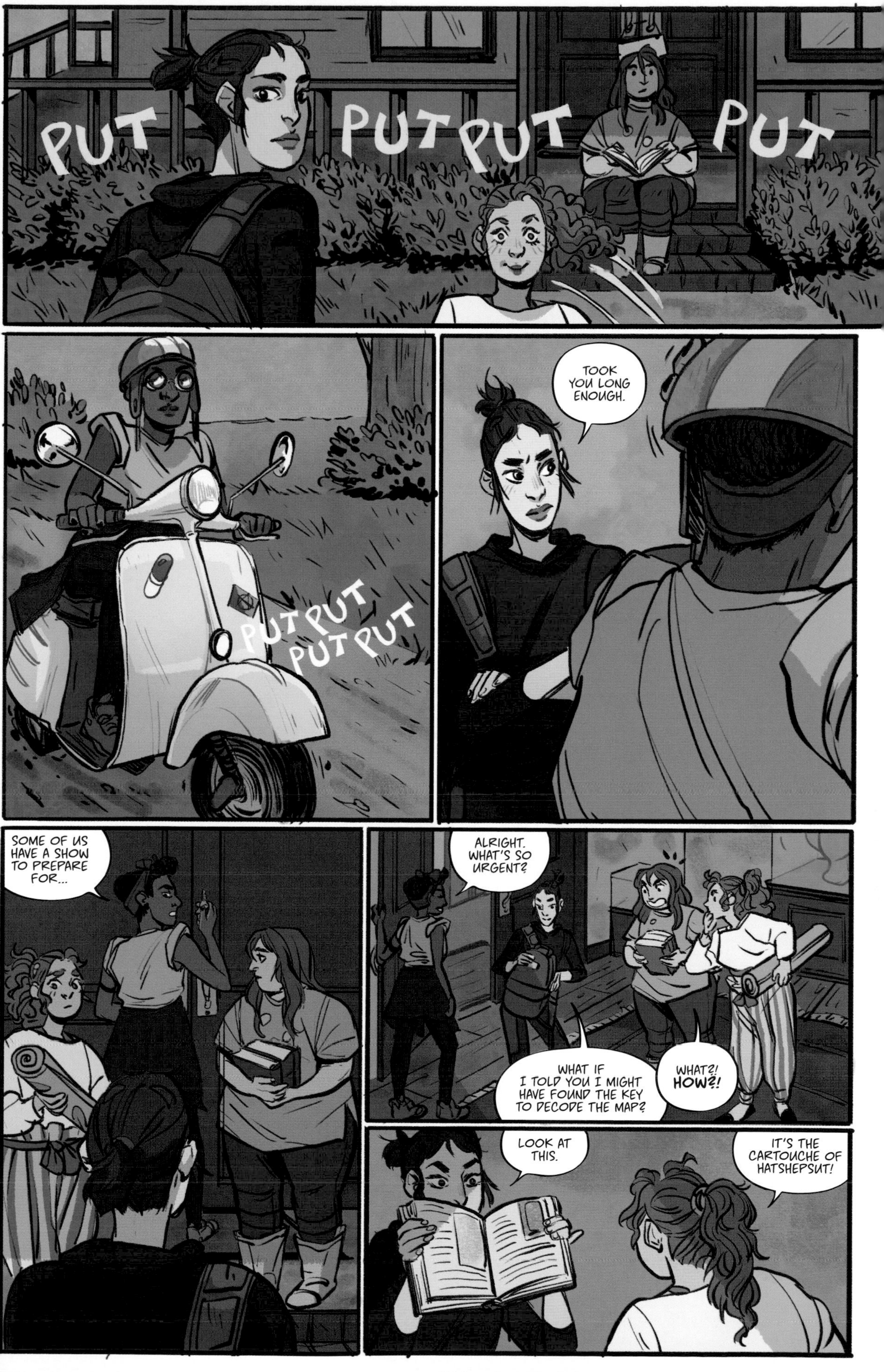
PUT PUT PUT PUT
PUT PUT PUT PUT
TOOK YOU LONG ENOUGH.
SOME OF US HAVE A SHOW TO PREPARE FOR...
ALRIGHT. WHAT'S SO URGENT?
WHAT IF I TOLD YOU I MIGHT HAVE FOUND THE KEY TO DECODE THE MAP?
WHAT?! HOW?!
LOOK AT THIS.
IT'S THE CARTOUCHE OF HATSHEPSUT!

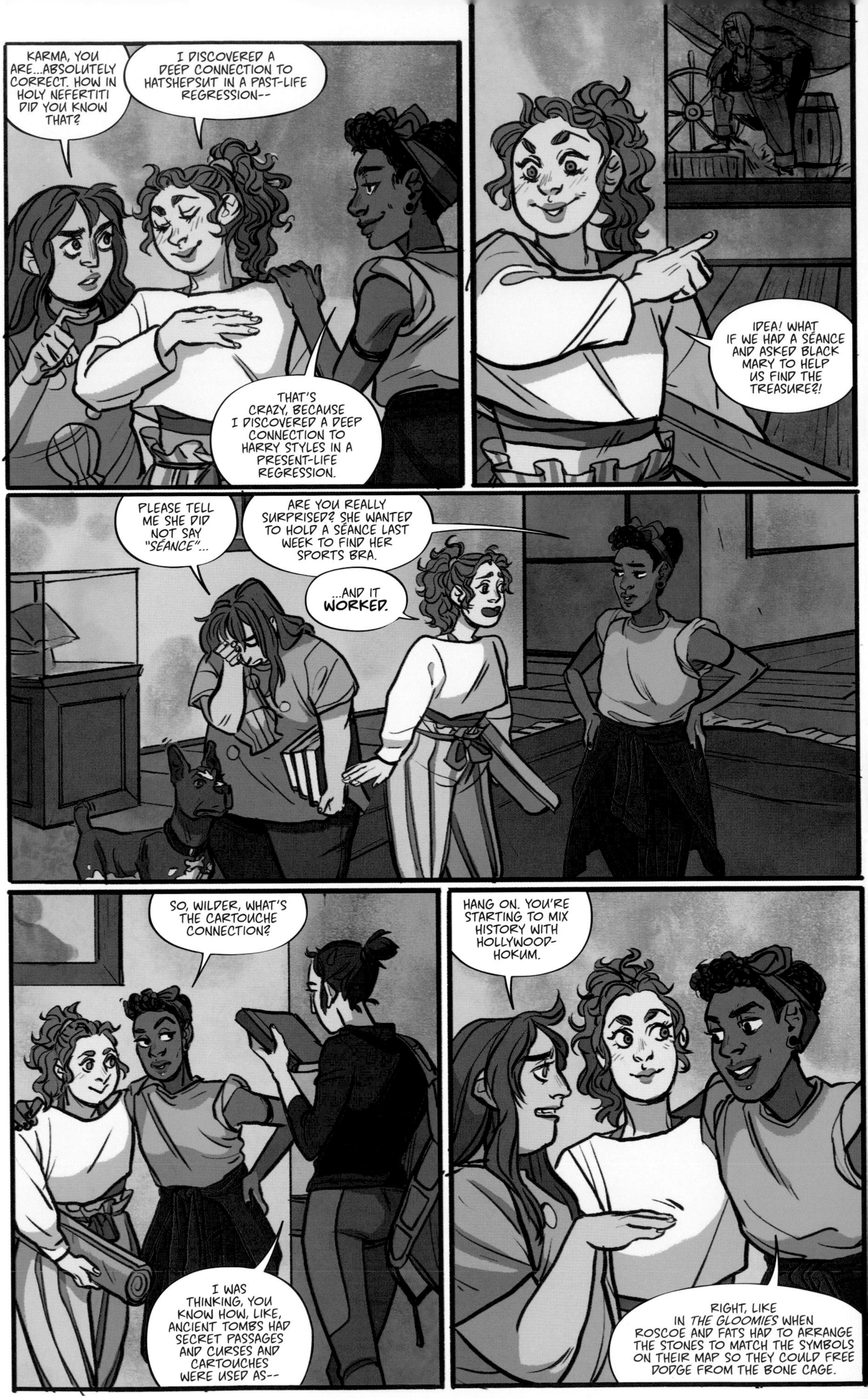

KARMA, YOU ARE...ABSOLUTELY CORRECT. HOW IN HOLY NEFERTITI DID YOU KNOW THAT?
I DISCOVERED A DEEP CONNECTION TO HATSHEPSUT IN A PAST-LIFE REGRESSION--
THAT'S CRAZY, BECAUSE I DISCOVERED A DEEP CONNECTION TO HARRY STYLES IN A PRESENT-LIFE REGRESSION.
IDEA! WHAT IF WE HAD A SÉANCE AND ASKED BLACK MARY TO HELP US FIND THE TREASURE?!
PLEASE TELL ME SHE DID NOT SAY *"SÉANCE"*...
ARE YOU REALLY SURPRISED? SHE WANTED TO HOLD A SÉANCE LAST WEEK TO FIND HER SPORTS BRA.
...AND IT **WORKED.**
SO, WILDER, WHAT'S THE CARTOUCHE CONNECTION?
I WAS THINKING, YOU KNOW HOW, LIKE, ANCIENT TOMBS HAD SECRET PASSAGES AND CURSES AND CARTOUCHES WERE USED AS--
HANG ON. YOU'RE STARTING TO MIX HISTORY WITH HOLLYWOOD-HOKUM.
RIGHT, LIKE IN *THE GLOOMIES* WHEN ROSCOE AND FATS HAD TO ARRANGE THE STONES TO MATCH THE SYMBOLS ON THEIR MAP SO THEY COULD FREE DODGE FROM THE BONE CAGE.

ACTUALLY, I WAS THINKING THAT CARTOUCHES TYPICALLY JUST CONTAINED THE BURIED PERSON'S NAME.

BESIDES, WE HAVEN'T FOUND ANY CARTOUCHES.

UNTIL NOW.

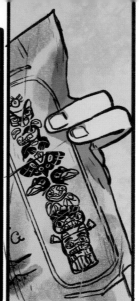

NOW THAT'S PRETTY COOL.

THAT ONE LOOKS LIKE PIPPIN!

THIS LINES UP WITH MY RESEARCH ON BLACK MARY!

THESE DESIGNS ARE SIMILAR TO THOSE FOUND AMONG **INDIGENOUS ARTISANS OF THE REGION.** AND GUESS WHO HER CREW CONSISTED OF?

THE TILLAMOOK?

RIGHT. EACH OF THESE ANIMALS HAS A SPECIAL MEANING IN THEIR CULTURE.

OKAY, SO, WHO DO WE KNOW WHO'S TILLAMOOK?

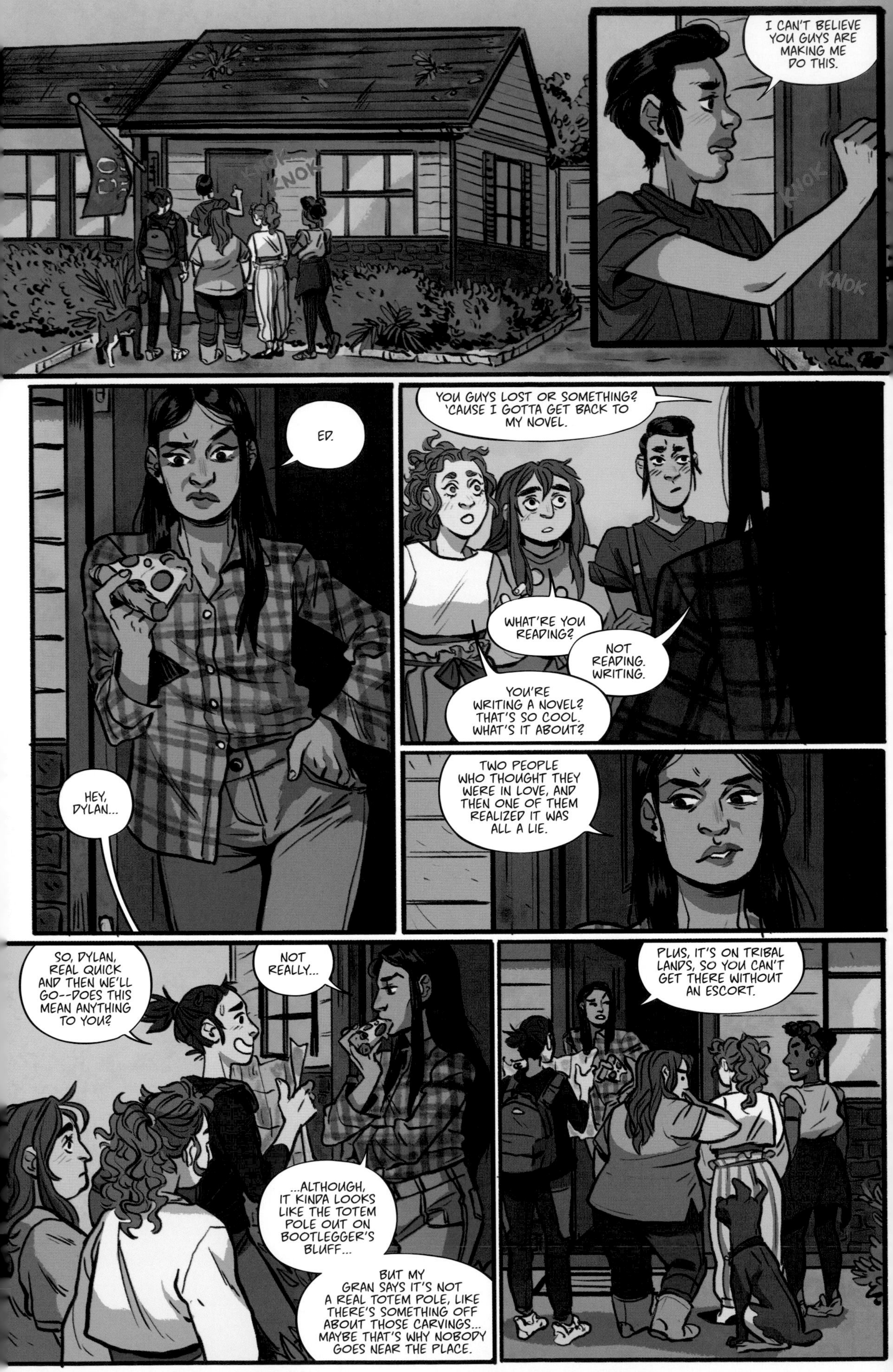
KNOK KNOK
I CAN'T BELIEVE YOU GUYS ARE MAKING ME DO THIS.
KNOK
KNOK
ED.
HEY, DYLAN...
YOU GUYS LOST OR SOMETHING? 'CAUSE I GOTTA GET BACK TO MY NOVEL.
WHAT'RE YOU READING?
NOT READING. WRITING.
YOU'RE WRITING A NOVEL? THAT'S SO COOL. WHAT'S IT ABOUT?
TWO PEOPLE WHO THOUGHT THEY WERE IN LOVE, AND THEN ONE OF THEM REALIZED IT WAS ALL A LIE.
SO, DYLAN, REAL QUICK AND THEN WE'LL GO--DOES THIS MEAN ANYTHING TO YOU?
NOT REALLY...
...ALTHOUGH, IT KINDA LOOKS LIKE THE TOTEM POLE OUT ON BOOTLEGGER'S BLUFF...
BUT MY GRAN SAYS IT'S NOT A REAL TOTEM POLE, LIKE THERE'S SOMETHING OFF ABOUT THOSE CARVINGS... MAYBE THAT'S WHY NOBODY GOES NEAR THE PLACE.
PLUS, IT'S ON TRIBAL LANDS, SO YOU CAN'T GET THERE WITHOUT AN ESCORT.

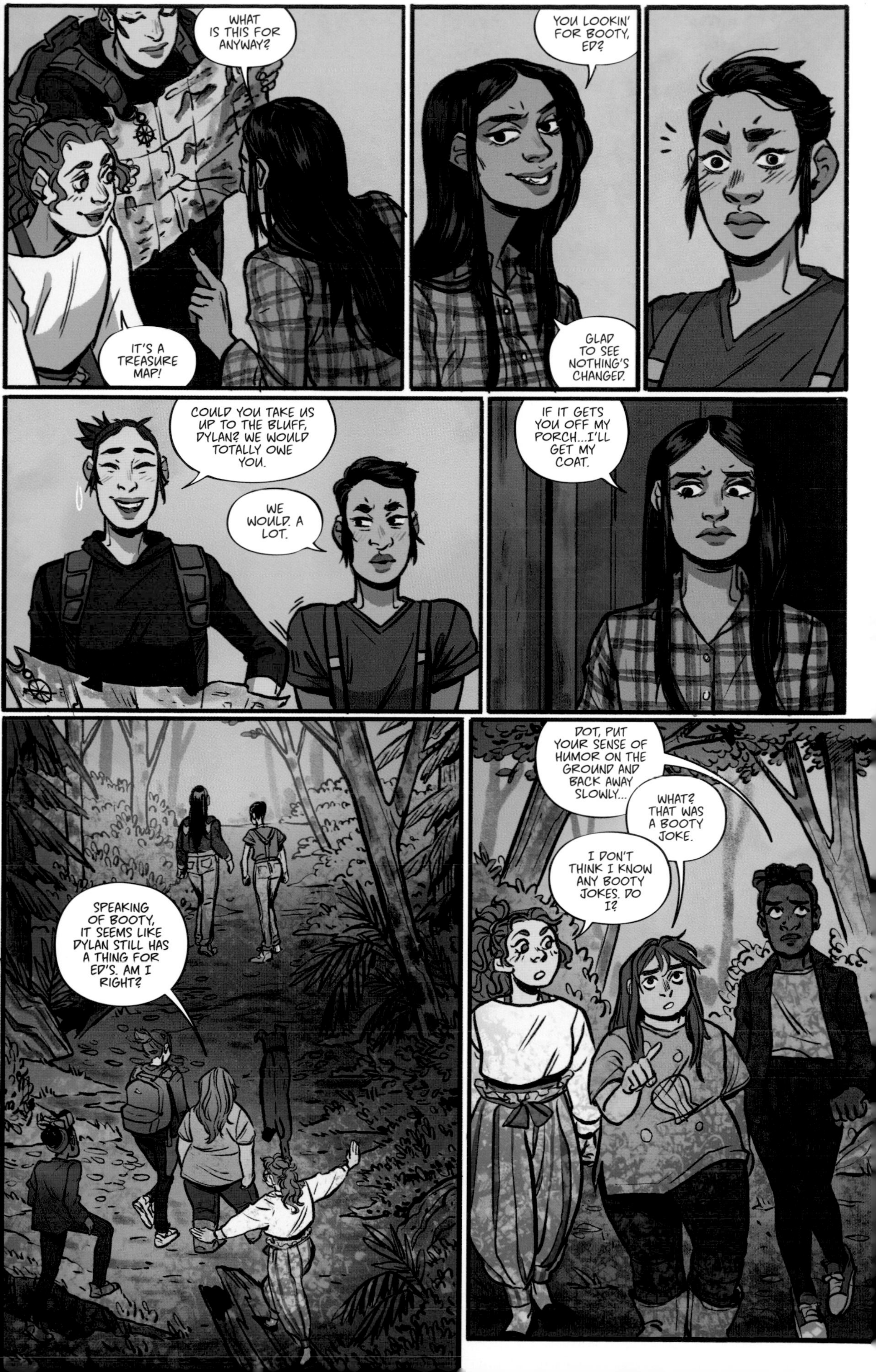
WHAT IS THIS FOR ANYWAY?
IT'S A TREASURE MAP!
YOU LOOKIN' FOR BOOTY, ED?
GLAD TO SEE NOTHING'S CHANGED.
COULD YOU TAKE US UP TO THE BLUFF, DYLAN? WE WOULD TOTALLY OWE YOU.
WE WOULD. A LOT.
IF IT GETS YOU OFF MY PORCH...I'LL GET MY COAT.
SPEAKING OF BOOTY, IT SEEMS LIKE DYLAN STILL HAS A THING FOR ED'S. AM I RIGHT?
DOT, PUT YOUR SENSE OF HUMOR ON THE GROUND AND BACK AWAY SLOWLY...
WHAT? THAT WAS A BOOTY JOKE.
I DON'T THINK I KNOW ANY BOOTY JOKES. DO I?

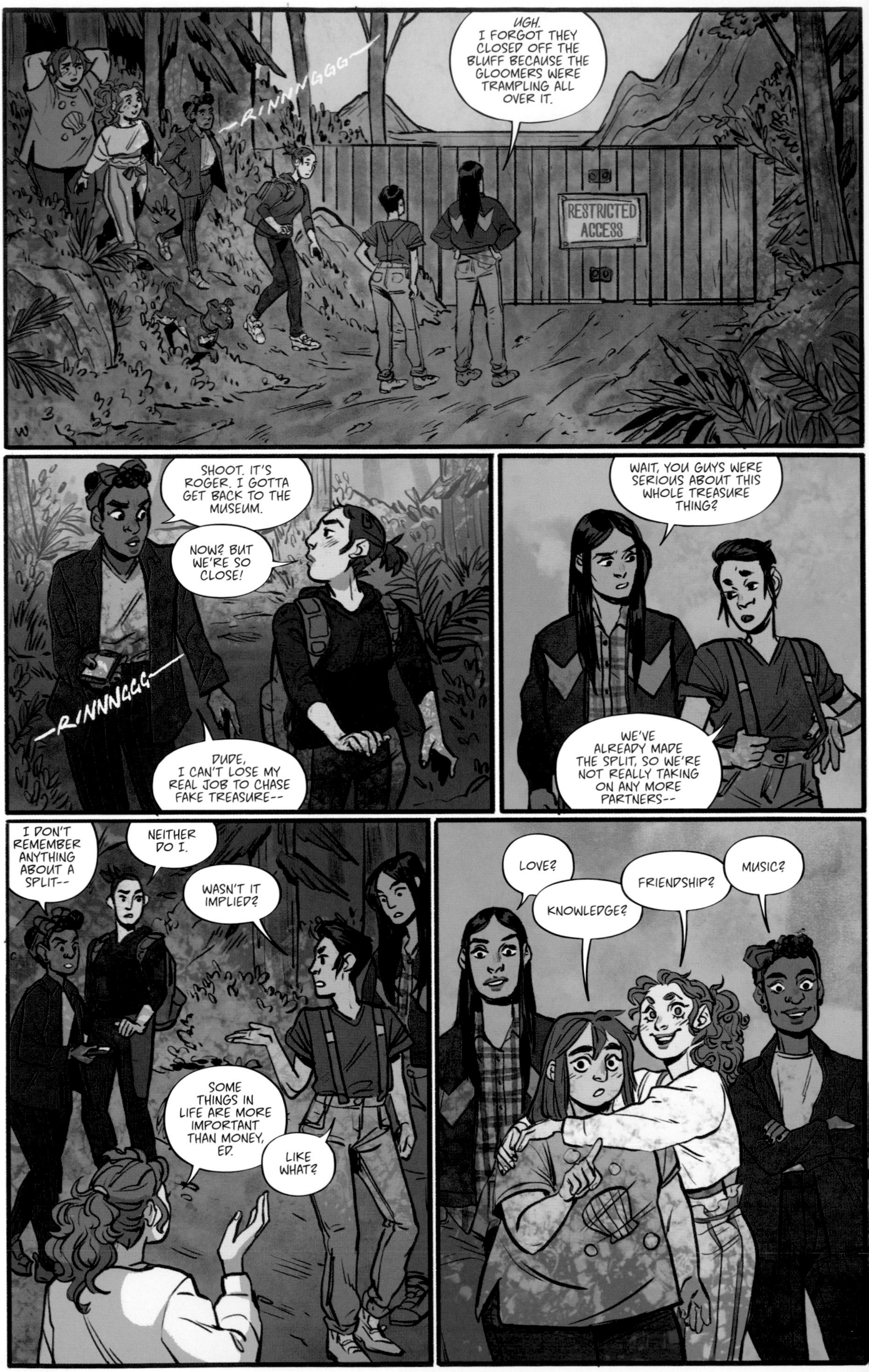
—RINNNGGG—
UGH. I FORGOT THEY CLOSED OFF THE BLUFF BECAUSE THE GLOOMERS WERE TRAMPLING ALL OVER IT.
RESTRICTED ACCESS
SHOOT. IT'S ROGER. I GOTTA GET BACK TO THE MUSEUM.
NOW? BUT WE'RE SO CLOSE!
—RINNNGGG—
DUDE, I CAN'T LOSE MY REAL JOB TO CHASE FAKE TREASURE--
WAIT, YOU GUYS WERE SERIOUS ABOUT THIS WHOLE TREASURE THING?
WE'VE ALREADY MADE THE SPLIT, SO WE'RE NOT REALLY TAKING ON ANY MORE PARTNERS--
I DON'T REMEMBER ANYTHING ABOUT A SPLIT--
NEITHER DO I.
WASN'T IT IMPLIED?
SOME THINGS IN LIFE ARE MORE IMPORTANT THAN MONEY, ED.
LIKE WHAT?
LOVE?
KNOWLEDGE?
FRIENDSHIP?
MUSIC?

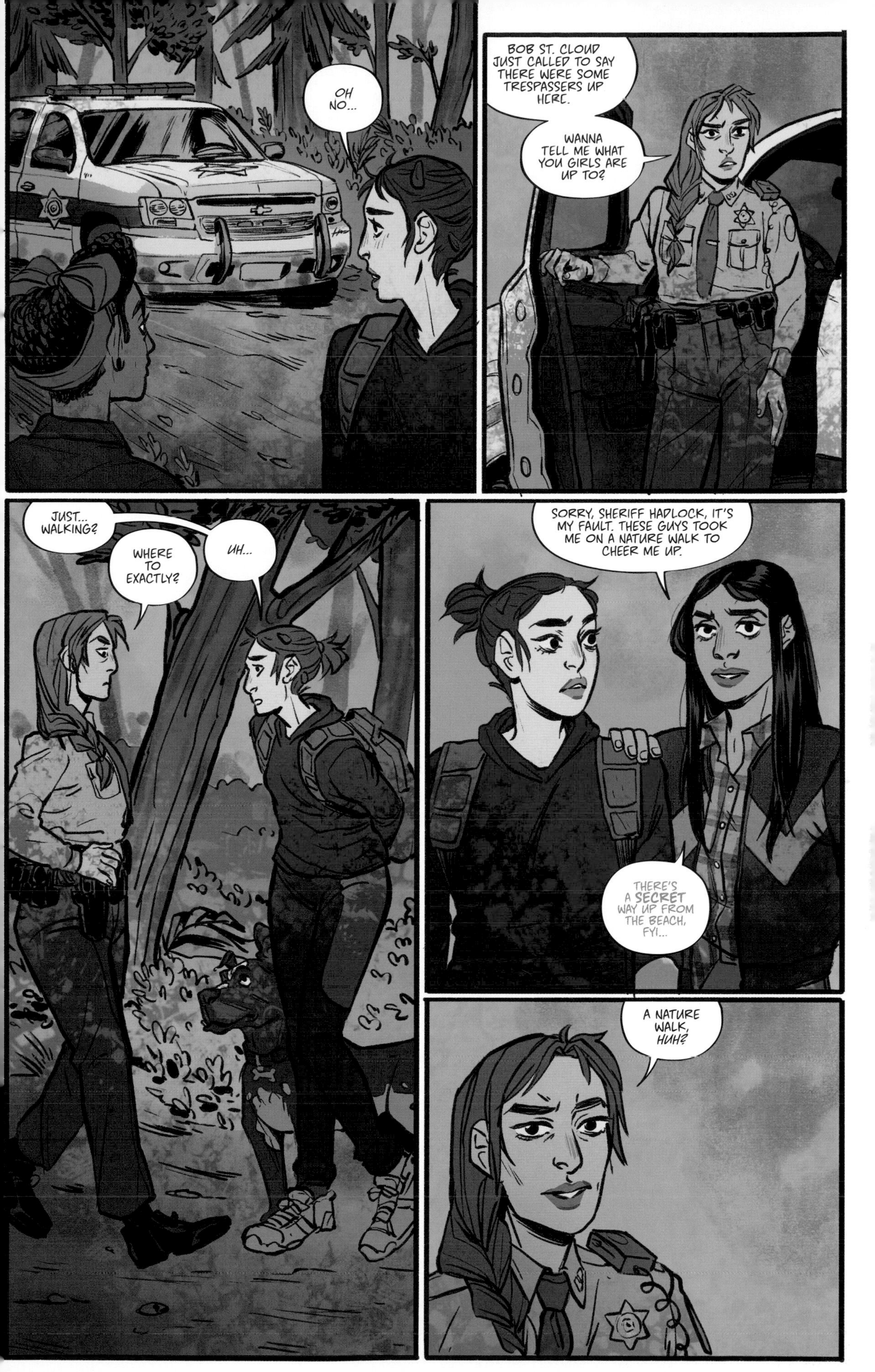
OH NO...
BOB ST. CLOUD JUST CALLED TO SAY THERE WERE SOME TRESPASSERS UP HERE.
WANNA TELL ME WHAT YOU GIRLS ARE UP TO?
JUST... WALKING?
UH...
WHERE TO EXACTLY?
SORRY, SHERIFF HADLOCK, IT'S MY FAULT. THESE GUYS TOOK ME ON A NATURE WALK TO CHEER ME UP.
THERE'S A SECRET WAY UP FROM THE BEACH, FYI...
A NATURE WALK, HUH?

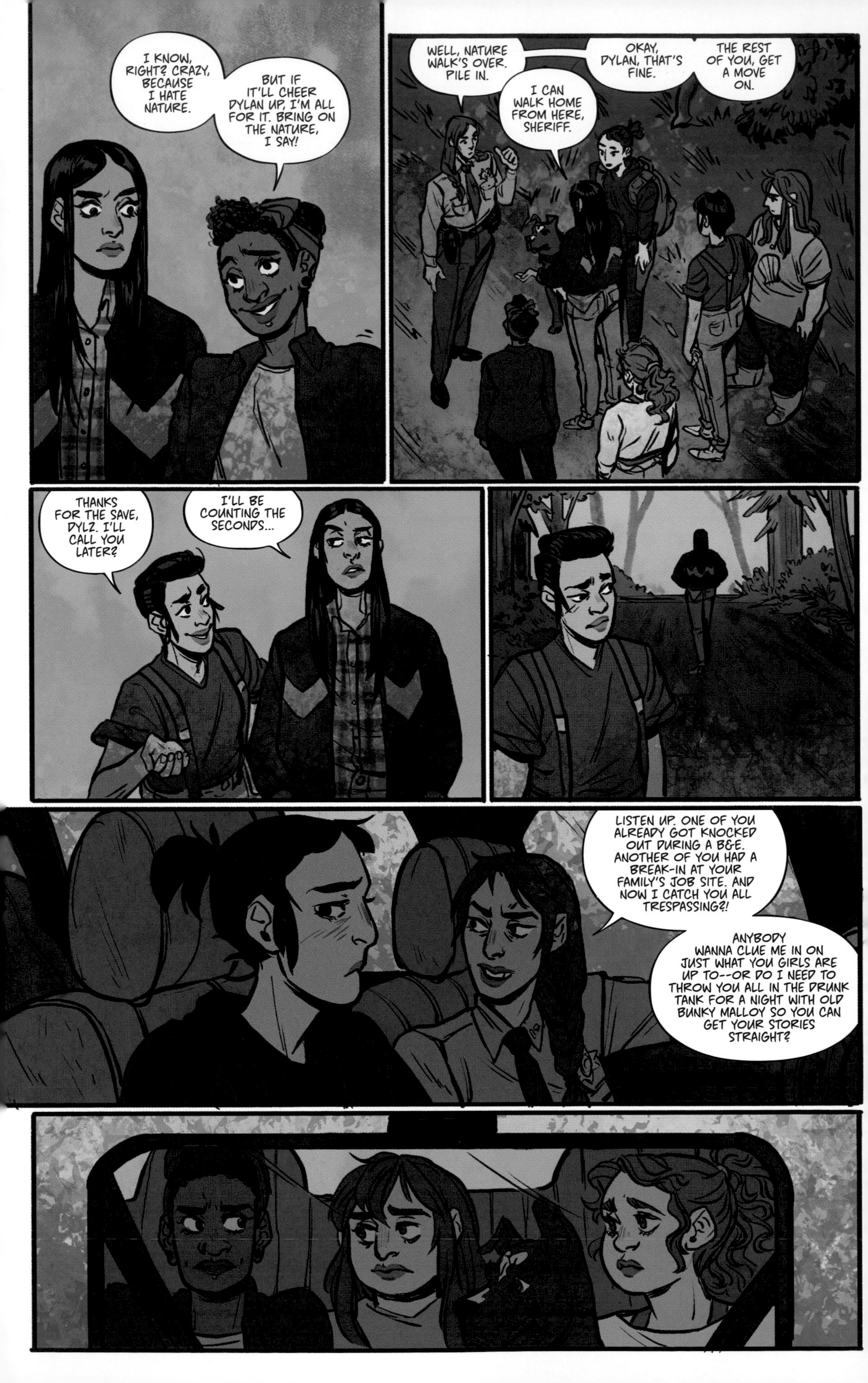
I KNOW, RIGHT? CRAZY, BECAUSE I HATE NATURE.
BUT IF IT'LL CHEER DYLAN UP, I'M ALL FOR IT. BRING ON THE NATURE, I SAY!
WELL, NATURE WALK'S OVER. PILE IN.
I CAN WALK HOME FROM HERE, SHERIFF.
OKAY, DYLAN, THAT'S FINE.
THE REST OF YOU, GET A MOVE ON.
THANKS FOR THE SAVE, DYLZ. I'LL CALL YOU LATER?
I'LL BE COUNTING THE SECONDS...
LISTEN UP. ONE OF YOU ALREADY GOT KNOCKED OUT DURING A B&E. ANOTHER OF YOU HAD A BREAK-IN AT YOUR FAMILY'S JOB SITE. AND NOW I CATCH YOU ALL TRESPASSING?!
ANYBODY WANNA CLUE ME IN ON JUST WHAT YOU GIRLS ARE UP TO--OR DO I NEED TO THROW YOU ALL IN THE DRUNK TANK FOR A NIGHT WITH OLD BUNKY MALLOY SO YOU CAN GET YOUR STORIES STRAIGHT?

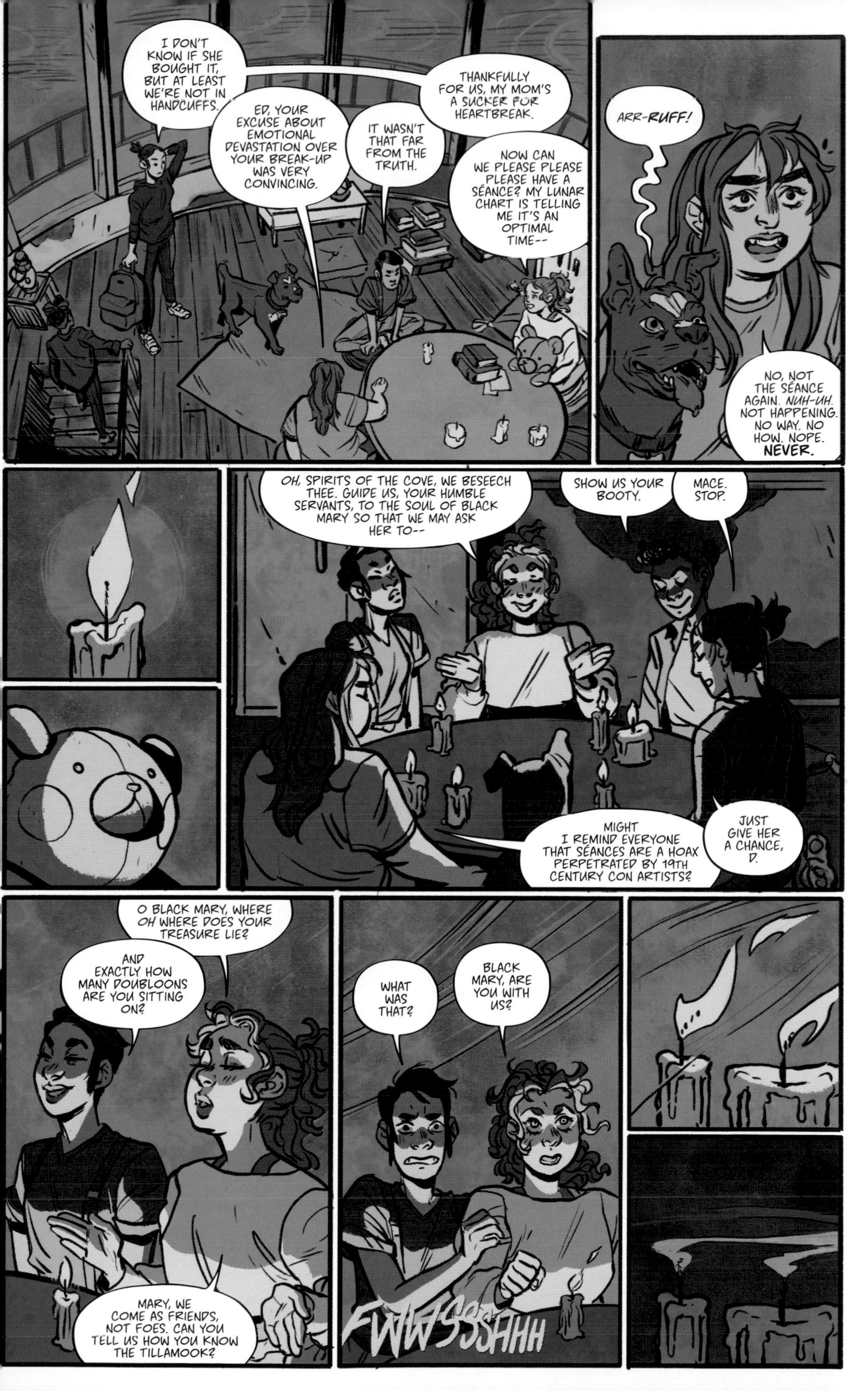
I DON'T KNOW IF SHE BOUGHT IT, BUT AT LEAST WE'RE NOT IN HANDCUFFS.
ED, YOUR EXCUSE ABOUT EMOTIONAL DEVASTATION OVER YOUR BREAK-UP WAS VERY CONVINCING.
IT WASN'T THAT FAR FROM THE TRUTH.
THANKFULLY FOR US, MY MOM'S A SUCKER FOR HEARTBREAK.
NOW CAN WE PLEASE PLEASE PLEASE HAVE A SÉANCE? MY LUNAR CHART IS TELLING ME IT'S AN OPTIMAL TIME--
ARR-RUFF!
NO, NOT THE SÉANCE AGAIN. NUH-UH. NOT HAPPENING. NO WAY. NO HOW. NOPE. NEVER.
OH, SPIRITS OF THE COVE, WE BESEECH THEE. GUIDE US, YOUR HUMBLE SERVANTS, TO THE SOUL OF BLACK MARY SO THAT WE MAY ASK HER TO--
SHOW US YOUR BOOTY.
MACE. STOP.
MIGHT I REMIND EVERYONE THAT SÉANCES ARE A HOAX PERPETRATED BY 19TH CENTURY CON ARTISTS?
JUST GIVE HER A CHANCE, D.
O BLACK MARY, WHERE OH WHERE DOES YOUR TREASURE LIE?
AND EXACTLY HOW MANY DOUBLOONS ARE YOU SITTING ON?
MARY, WE COME AS FRIENDS, NOT FOES. CAN YOU TELL US HOW YOU KNOW THE TILLAMOOK?
FWWSSSHHH
WHAT WAS THAT?
BLACK MARY, ARE YOU WITH US?

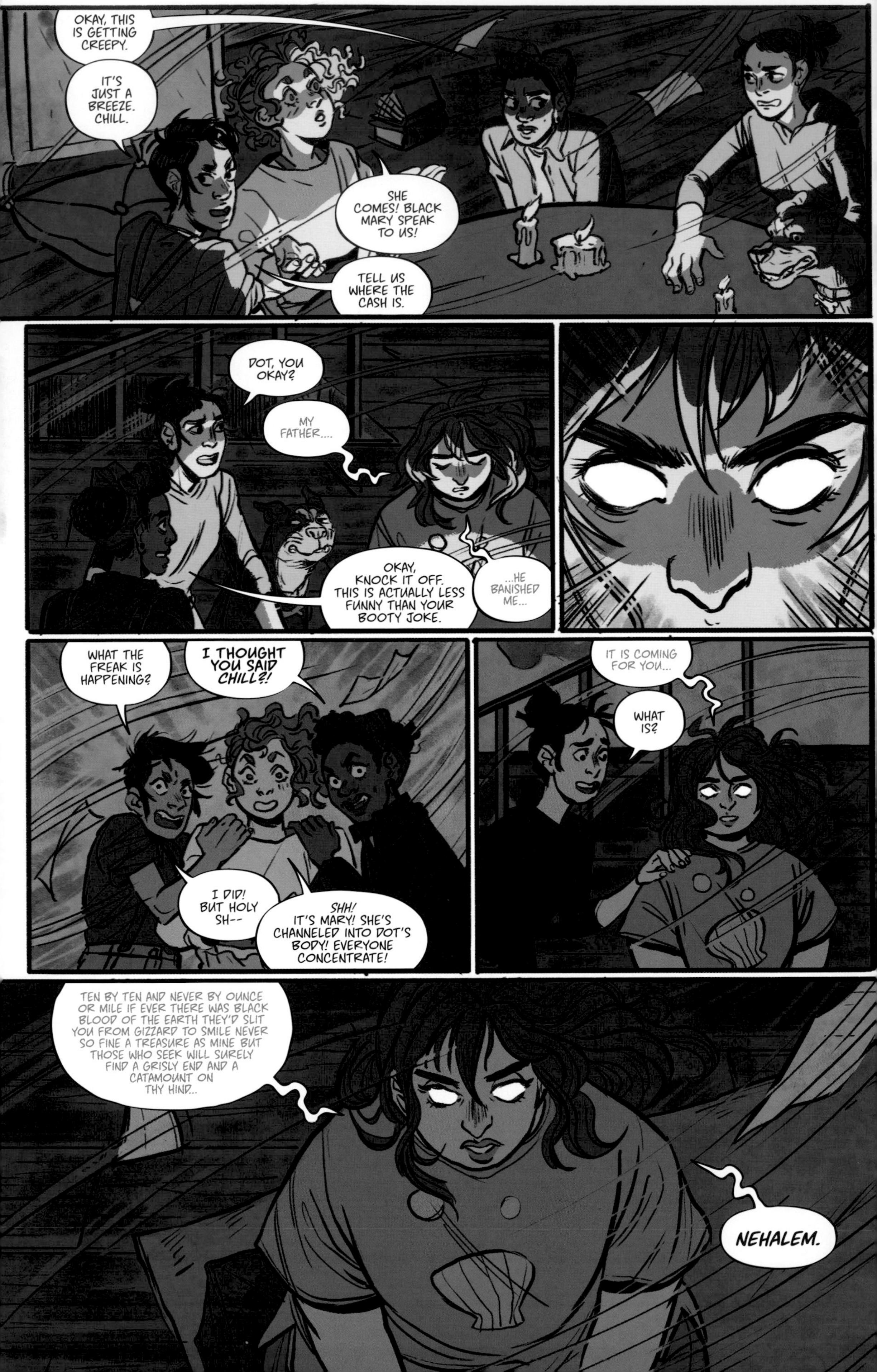
OKAY, THIS IS GETTING CREEPY.
IT'S JUST A BREEZE. CHILL.
SHE COMES! BLACK MARY SPEAK TO US!
TELL US WHERE THE CASH IS.
DOT, YOU OKAY?
MY FATHER....
OKAY, KNOCK IT OFF. THIS IS ACTUALLY LESS FUNNY THAN YOUR BOOTY JOKE.
...HE BANISHED ME...
WHAT THE FREAK IS HAPPENING?
I THOUGHT YOU SAID CHILL?!
I DID! BUT HOLY SH--
SHH! IT'S MARY! SHE'S CHANNELED INTO DOT'S BODY! EVERYONE CONCENTRATE!
IT IS COMING FOR YOU...
WHAT IS?
TEN BY TEN AND NEVER BY OUNCE OR MILE IF EVER THERE WAS BLACK BLOOD OF THE EARTH THEY'D SLIT YOU FROM GIZZARD TO SMILE NEVER SO FINE A TREASURE AS MINE BUT THOSE WHO SEEK WILL SURELY FIND A GRISLY END AND A CATAMOUNT ON THY HIND...
NEHALEM.

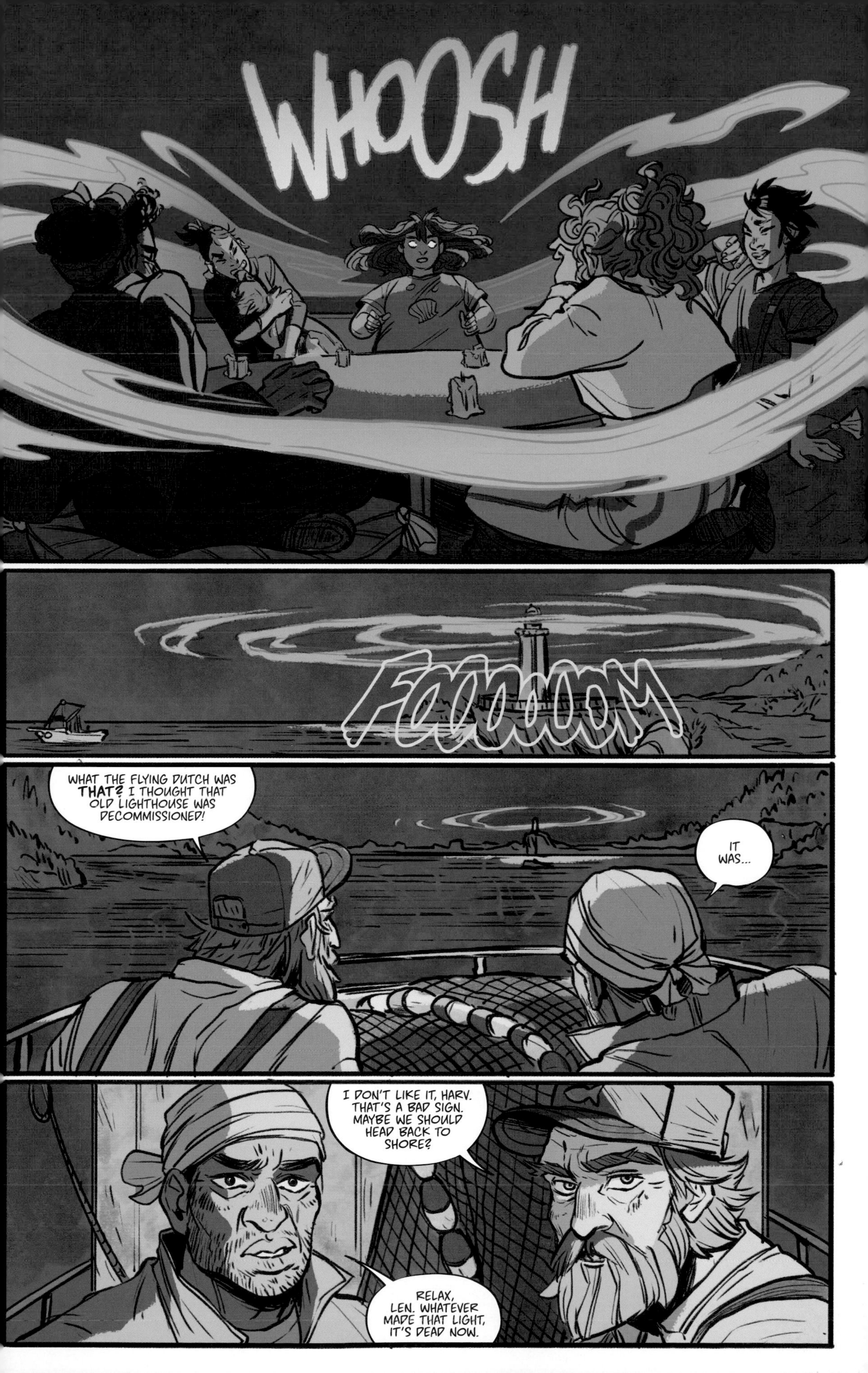
WHOOSH
FOOOOOOM
WHAT THE FLYING DUTCH WAS THAT? I THOUGHT THAT OLD LIGHTHOUSE WAS DECOMMISSIONED!
IT WAS...
I DON'T LIKE IT, HARV. THAT'S A BAD SIGN. MAYBE WE SHOULD HEAD BACK TO SHORE?
RELAX, LEN. WHATEVER MADE THAT LIGHT, IT'S DEAD NOW.

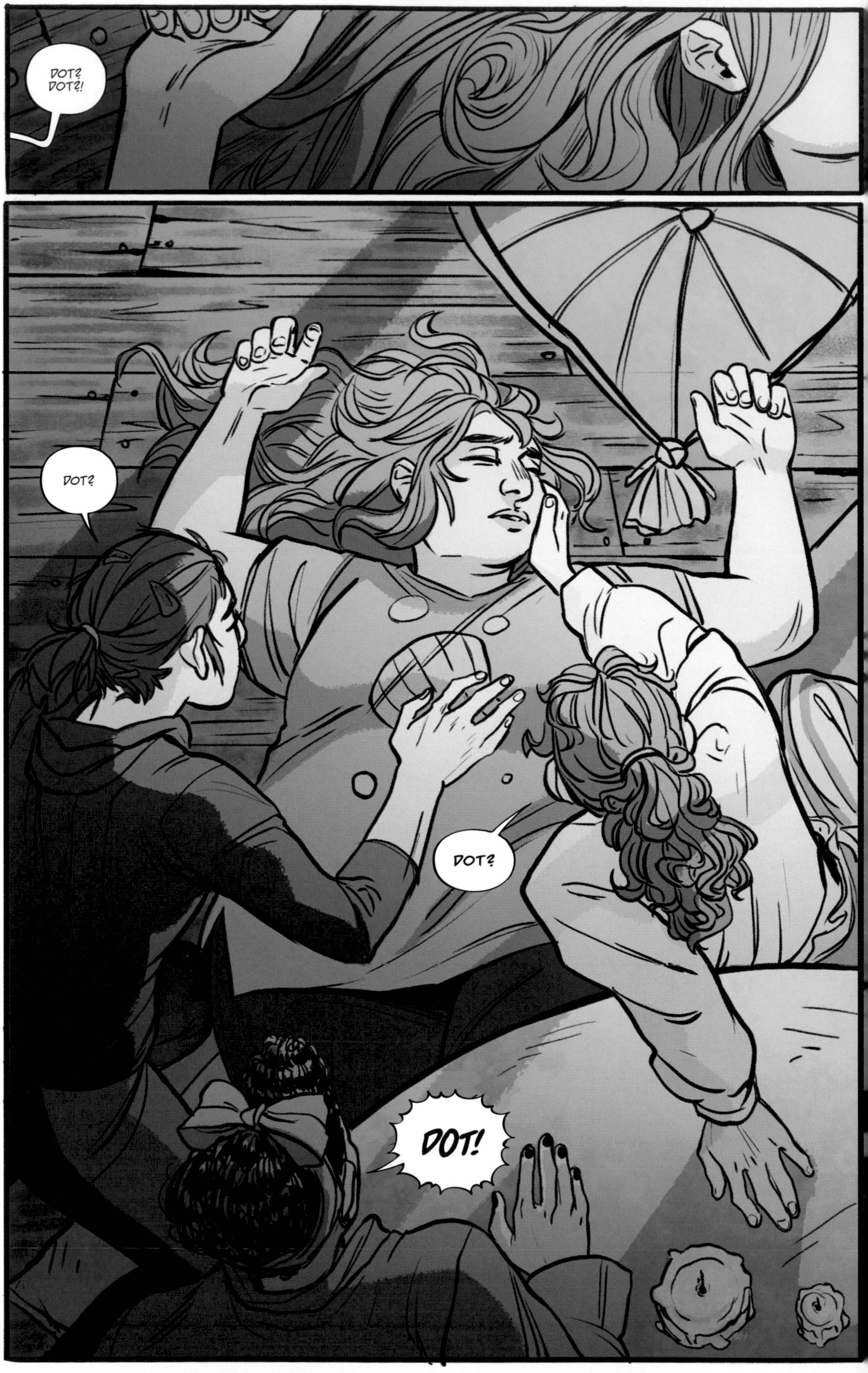
DOT? DOT?!
DOT?
DOT?
DOT!

CHAPTER
IV

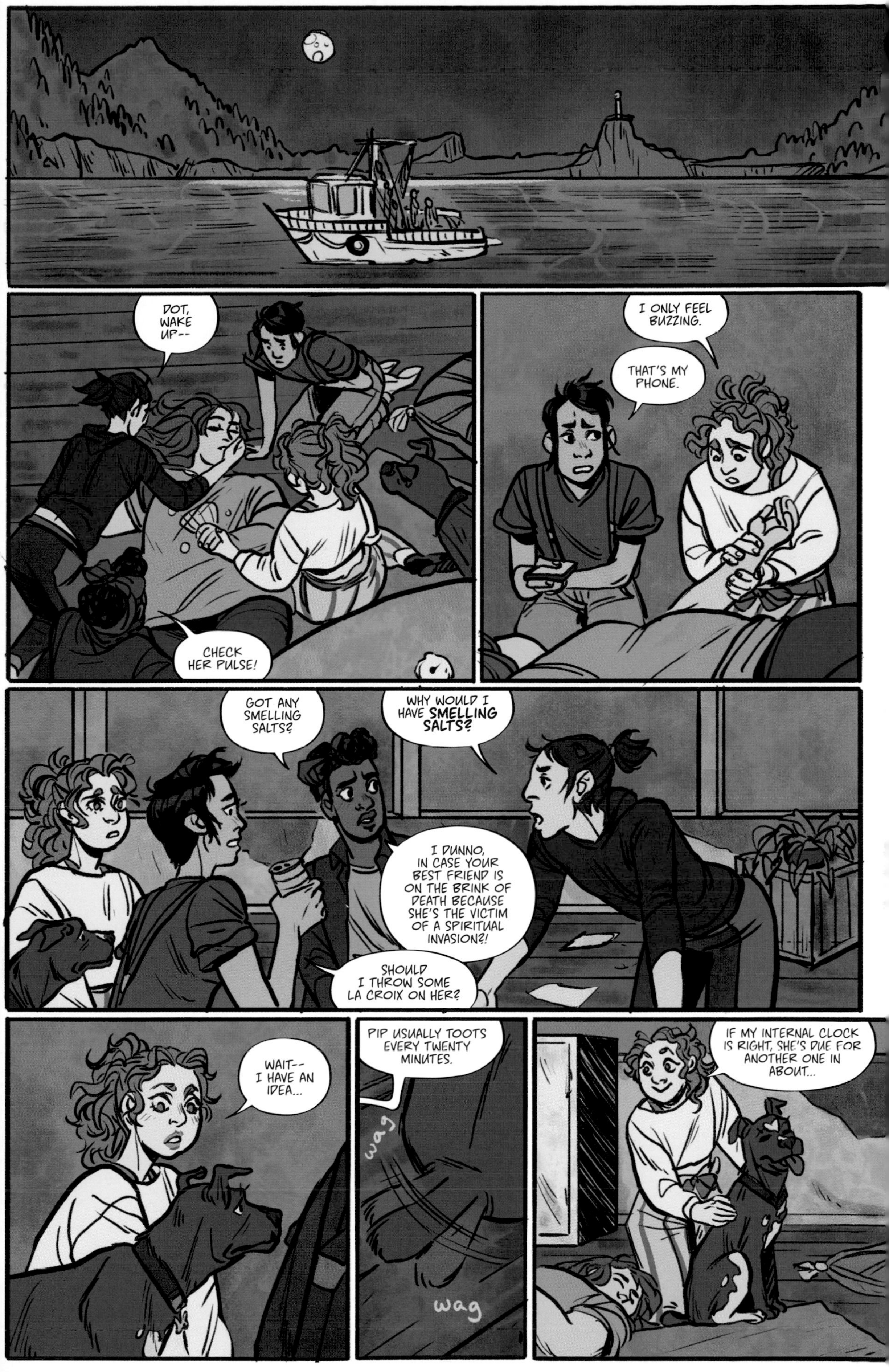
DOT, WAKE UP--
CHECK HER PULSE!
I ONLY FEEL BUZZING.
THAT'S MY PHONE.
GOT ANY SMELLING SALTS?
WHY WOULD I HAVE **SMELLING SALTS?**
I DUNNO, IN CASE YOUR BEST FRIEND IS ON THE BRINK OF DEATH BECAUSE SHE'S THE VICTIM OF A SPIRITUAL INVASION?!
SHOULD I THROW SOME LA CROIX ON HER?
WAIT-- I HAVE AN IDEA...
PIP USUALLY TOOTS EVERY TWENTY MINUTES.
wag
wag
IF MY INTERNAL CLOCK IS RIGHT, SHE'S DUE FOR ANOTHER ONE IN ABOUT...

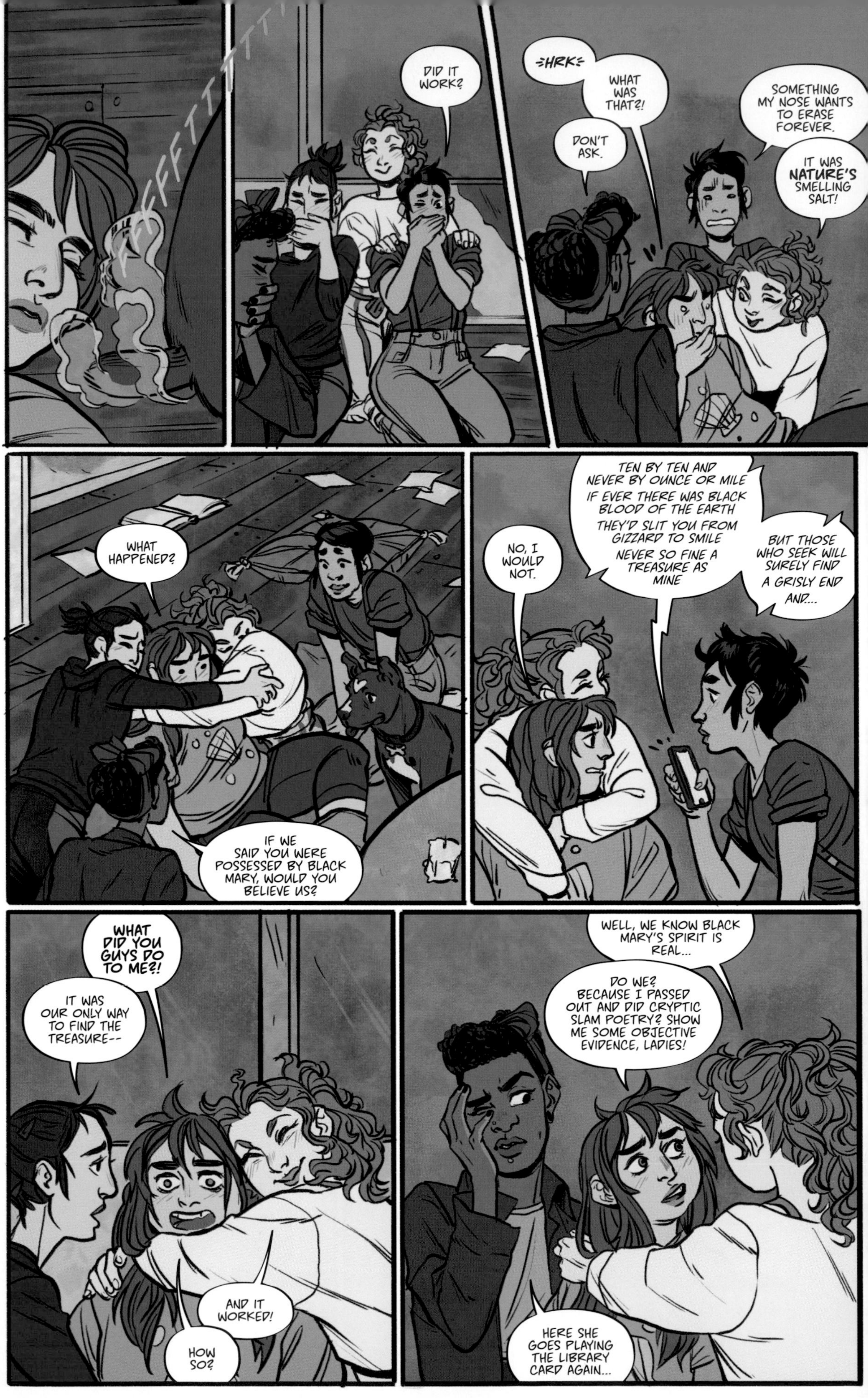
FFFFTTTTT
DID IT WORK?
HRK
WHAT WAS THAT?!
DON'T ASK.
SOMETHING MY NOSE WANTS TO ERASE FOREVER.
IT WAS NATURE'S SMELLING SALT!
WHAT HAPPENED?
IF WE SAID YOU WERE POSSESSED BY BLACK MARY, WOULD YOU BELIEVE US?
NO, I WOULD NOT.
TEN BY TEN AND NEVER BY OUNCE OR MILE IF EVER THERE WAS BLACK BLOOD OF THE EARTH THEY'D SLIT YOU FROM GIZZARD TO SMILE NEVER SO FINE A TREASURE AS MINE
BUT THOSE WHO SEEK WILL SURELY FIND A GRISLY END AND...
WHAT DID YOU GUYS DO TO ME?!
IT WAS OUR ONLY WAY TO FIND THE TREASURE--
AND IT WORKED!
HOW SO?
WELL, WE KNOW BLACK MARY'S SPIRIT IS REAL...
DO WE? BECAUSE I PASSED OUT AND DID CRYPTIC SLAM POETRY? SHOW ME SOME OBJECTIVE EVIDENCE, LADIES!
HERE SHE GOES PLAYING THE LIBRARY CARD AGAIN...

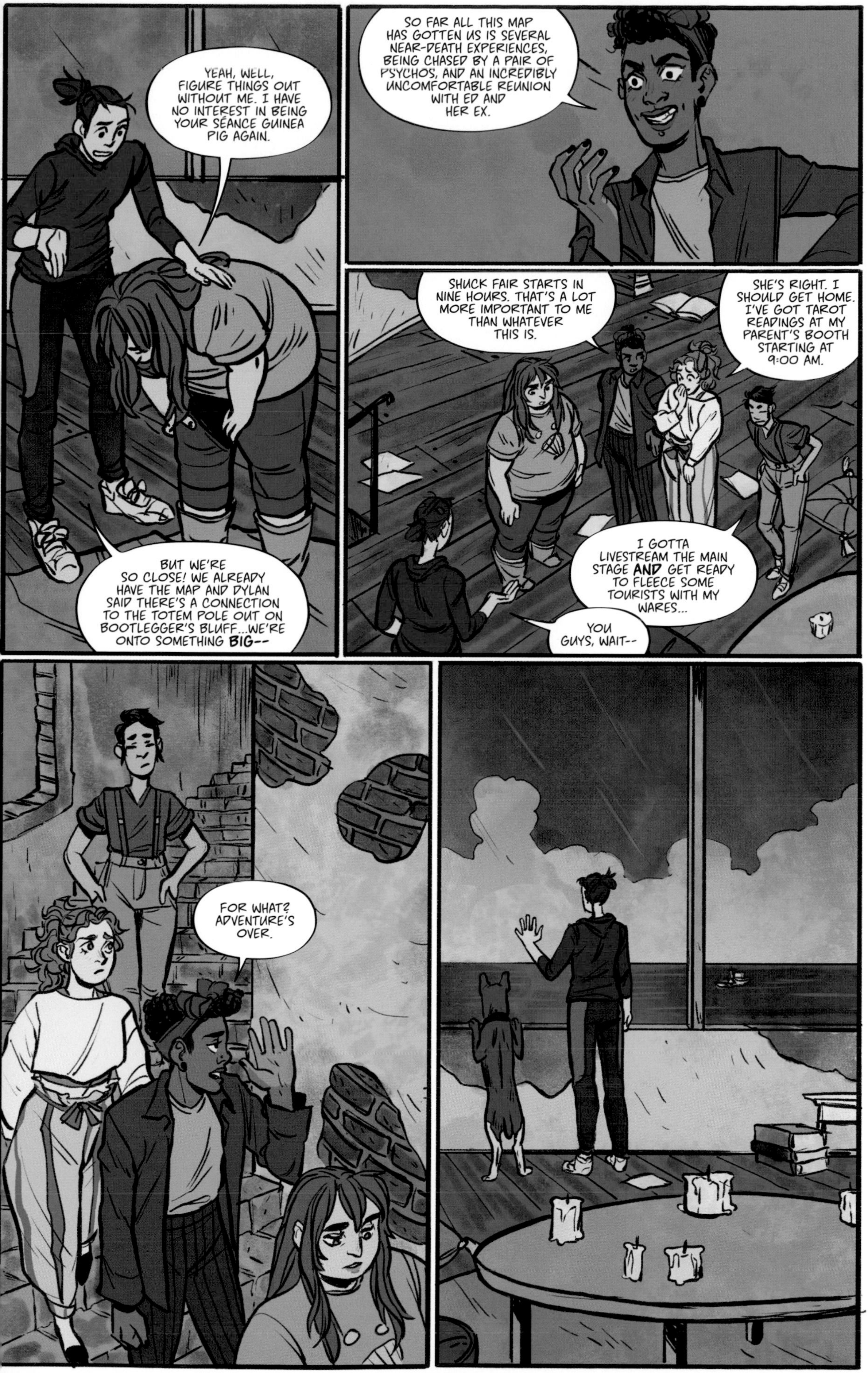
YEAH, WELL, FIGURE THINGS OUT WITHOUT ME. I HAVE NO INTEREST IN BEING YOUR SÉANCE GUINEA PIG AGAIN.
SO FAR ALL THIS MAP HAS GOTTEN US IS SEVERAL NEAR-DEATH EXPERIENCES, BEING CHASED BY A PAIR OF PSYCHOS, AND AN INCREDIBLY UNCOMFORTABLE REUNION WITH ED AND HER EX.
BUT WE'RE SO CLOSE! WE ALREADY HAVE THE MAP AND DYLAN SAID THERE'S A CONNECTION TO THE TOTEM POLE OUT ON BOOTLEGGER'S BLUFF...WE'RE ONTO SOMETHING BIG--
SHUCK FAIR STARTS IN NINE HOURS. THAT'S A LOT MORE IMPORTANT TO ME THAN WHATEVER THIS IS.
SHE'S RIGHT. I SHOULD GET HOME. I'VE GOT TAROT READINGS AT MY PARENT'S BOOTH STARTING AT 9:00 AM.
I GOTTA LIVESTREAM THE MAIN STAGE AND GET READY TO FLEECE SOME TOURISTS WITH MY WARES...
YOU GUYS, WAIT--
FOR WHAT? ADVENTURE'S OVER.

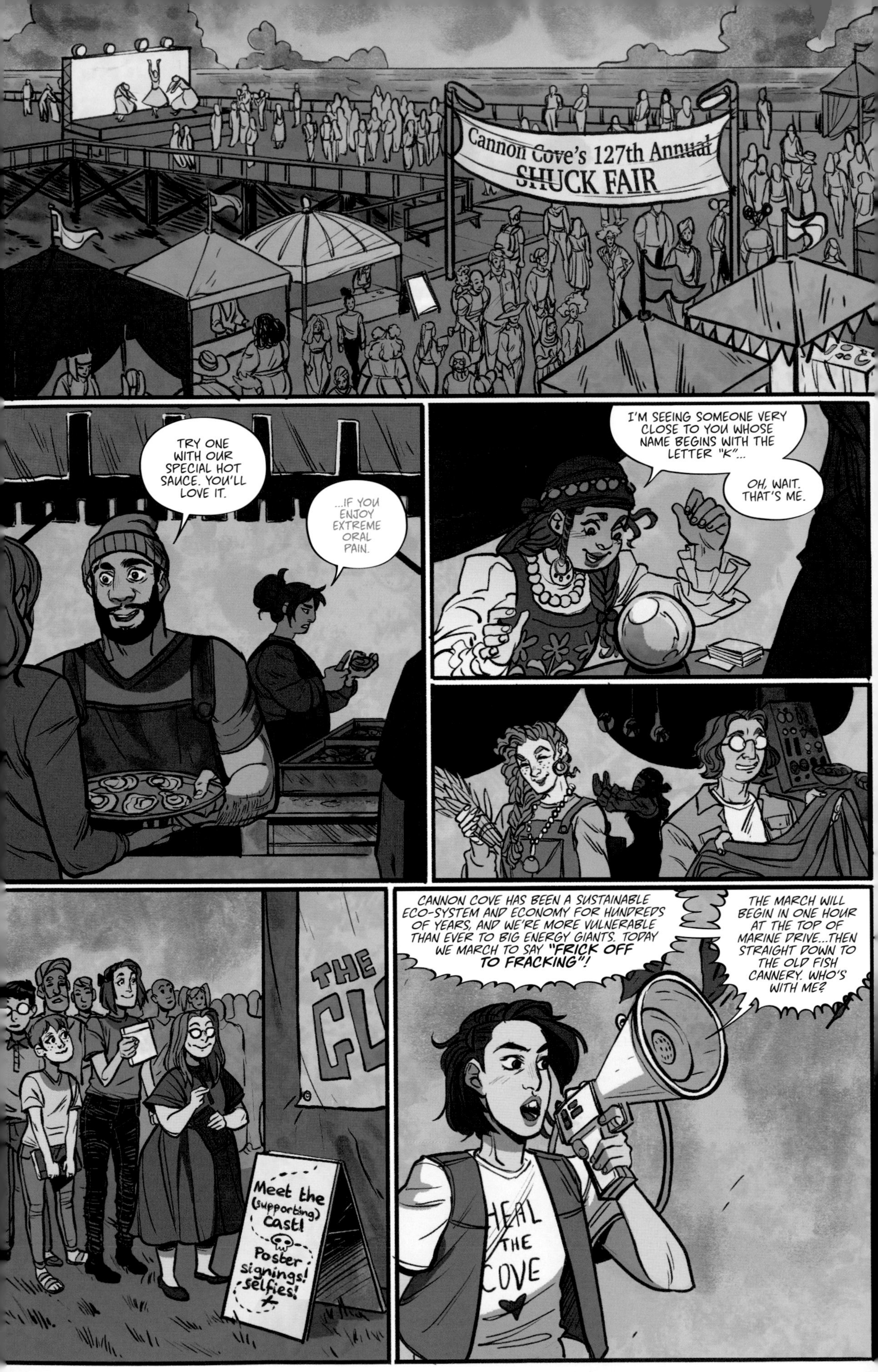
Cannon Cove's 127th Annual
SHUCK FAIR
TRY ONE WITH OUR SPECIAL HOT SAUCE. YOU'LL LOVE IT.
...IF YOU ENJOY EXTREME ORAL PAIN.
I'M SEEING SOMEONE VERY CLOSE TO YOU WHOSE NAME BEGINS WITH THE LETTER "K"...
OH, WAIT. THAT'S ME.
THE
Meet the (supporting) cast!
Poster signings! selfies!
CANNON COVE HAS BEEN A SUSTAINABLE ECO-SYSTEM AND ECONOMY FOR HUNDREDS OF YEARS, AND WE'RE MORE VULNERABLE THAN EVER TO BIG ENERGY GIANTS. TODAY WE MARCH TO SAY "FRICK OFF TO FRACKING"!
THE MARCH WILL BEGIN IN ONE HOUR AT THE TOP OF MARINE DRIVE...THEN STRAIGHT DOWN TO THE OLD FISH CANNERY. WHO'S WITH ME?
HEAL THE COVE

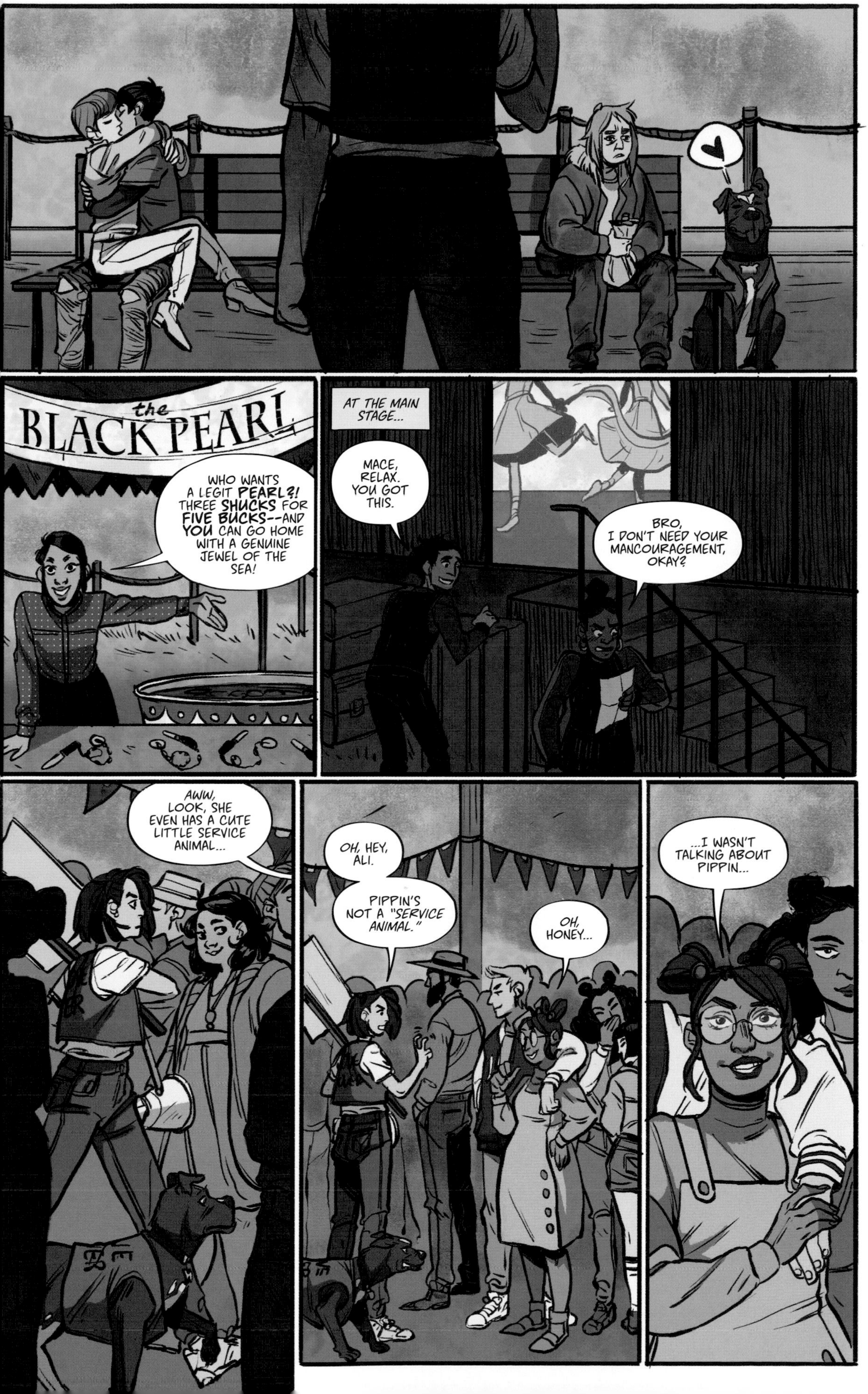
the BLACK PEARL
WHO WANTS A LEGIT PEARL?! THREE SHUCKS FOR FIVE BUCKS--AND YOU CAN GO HOME WITH A GENUINE JEWEL OF THE SEA!
AT THE MAIN STAGE...
MACE, RELAX. YOU GOT THIS.
BRO, I DON'T NEED YOUR MANCOURAGEMENT, OKAY?
AWW, LOOK, SHE EVEN HAS A CUTE LITTLE SERVICE ANIMAL...
OH, HEY, ALI.
PIPPIN'S NOT A "SERVICE ANIMAL."
OH, HONEY...
...I WASN'T TALKING ABOUT PIPPIN...

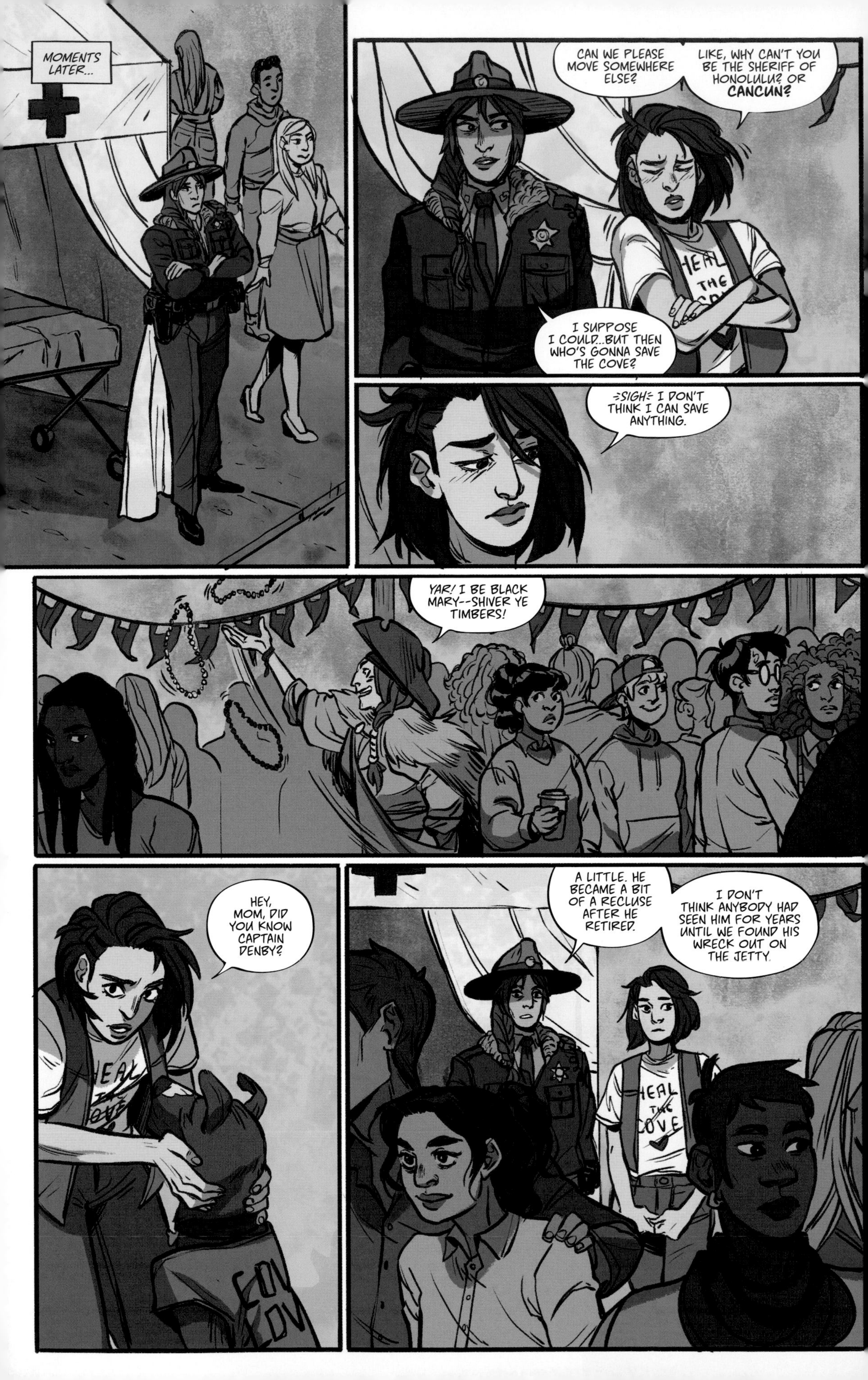
MOMENTS LATER...
CAN WE PLEASE MOVE SOMEWHERE ELSE?
LIKE, WHY CAN'T YOU BE THE SHERIFF OF HONOLULU? OR **CANCUN?**
I SUPPOSE I COULD...BUT THEN WHO'S GONNA SAVE THE COVE?
=SIGH= I DON'T THINK I CAN SAVE ANYTHING.
YAR! I BE BLACK MARY--SHIVER YE TIMBERS!
HEY, MOM, DID YOU KNOW CAPTAIN DENBY?
A LITTLE. HE BECAME A BIT OF A RECLUSE AFTER HE RETIRED.
I DON'T THINK ANYBODY HAD SEEN HIM FOR YEARS UNTIL WE FOUND HIS WRECK OUT ON THE JETTY.

YOU WERE THE ONE WHO FOUND THE BODY?

NOPE. NO ONE DID. PROBABLY GOT PULLED OUT WITH THE TIDE. I IMAGINE THAT'S JUST WHAT A PROUD OLD SEAWOLF LIKE DENBY WOULD'VE WANTED--

Y'KNOW, IF YOU'RE CURIOUS ABOUT CAPTAIN DENBY, THE MAN TO TALK TO IS HORACE SHIPP. THEY USED TO SAIL TOGETHER.

COVE LOVER

ELSEWHERE...

I HATE PUBLIC REVELRY.

THEN WHY ARE WE HERE?

Cannon C____ ___th Annual
SHUC____AIR

BECAUSE WE FOUND **THIS**, YOU IDIOT...AND THOSE GIRLS ARE BOUND TO BE AT THIS LOSER-FEST.

OOH, IS THAT GARTH HEMMING?

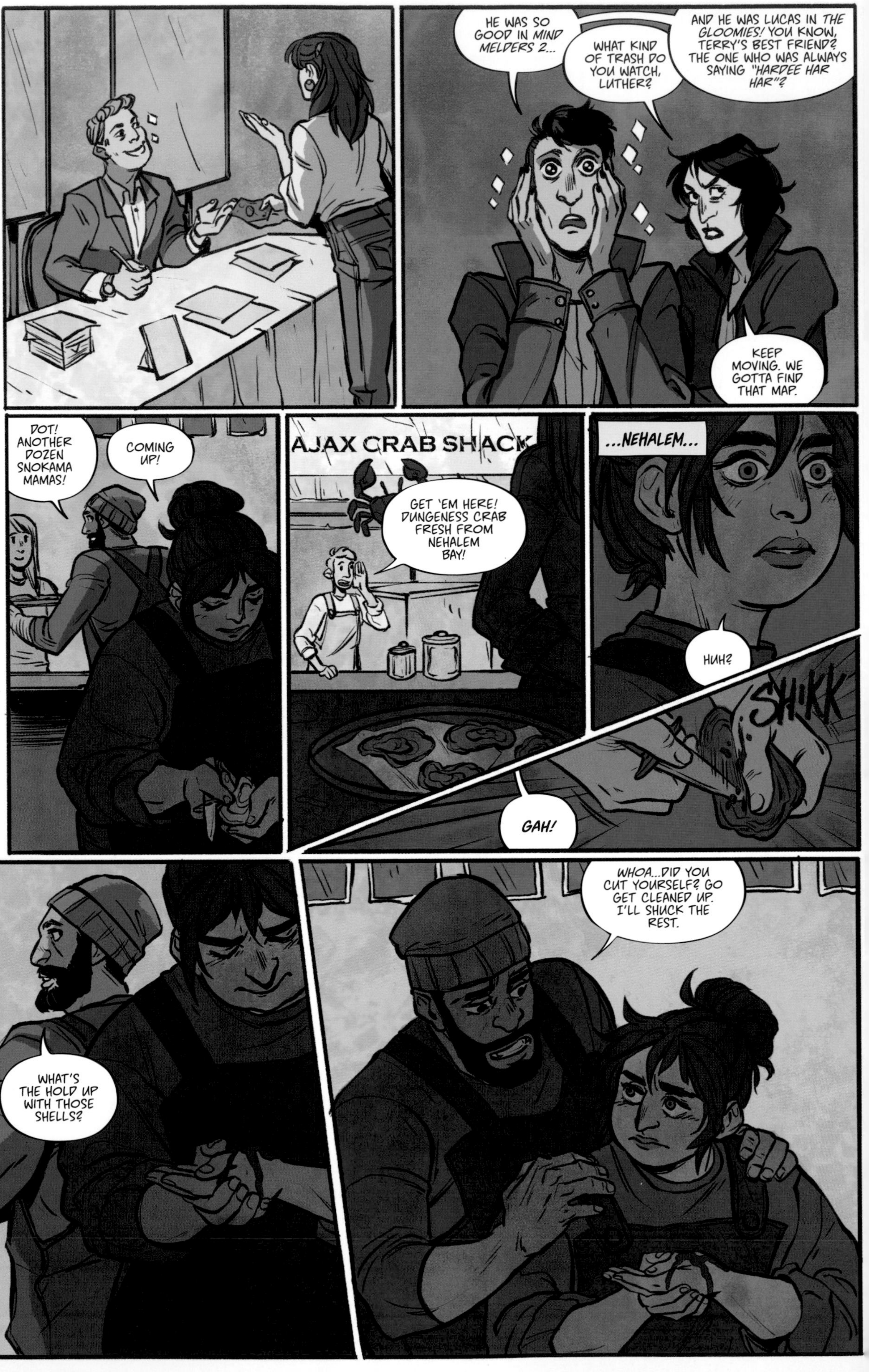
HE WAS SO GOOD IN MIND MELDERS 2...
WHAT KIND OF TRASH DO YOU WATCH, LUTHER?
AND HE WAS LUCAS IN THE GLOOMIES! YOU KNOW, TERRY'S BEST FRIEND? THE ONE WHO WAS ALWAYS SAYING "HARDEE HAR HAR"?
KEEP MOVING. WE GOTTA FIND THAT MAP.
DOT! ANOTHER DOZEN SNOKAMA MAMAS!
COMING UP!
AJAX CRAB SHACK
GET 'EM HERE! DUNGENESS CRAB FRESH FROM NEHALEM BAY!
...NEHALEM...
HUH?
SHIKK
GAH!
WHAT'S THE HOLD UP WITH THOSE SHELLS?
WHOA...DID YOU CUT YOURSELF? GO GET CLEANED UP. I'LL SHUCK THE REST.

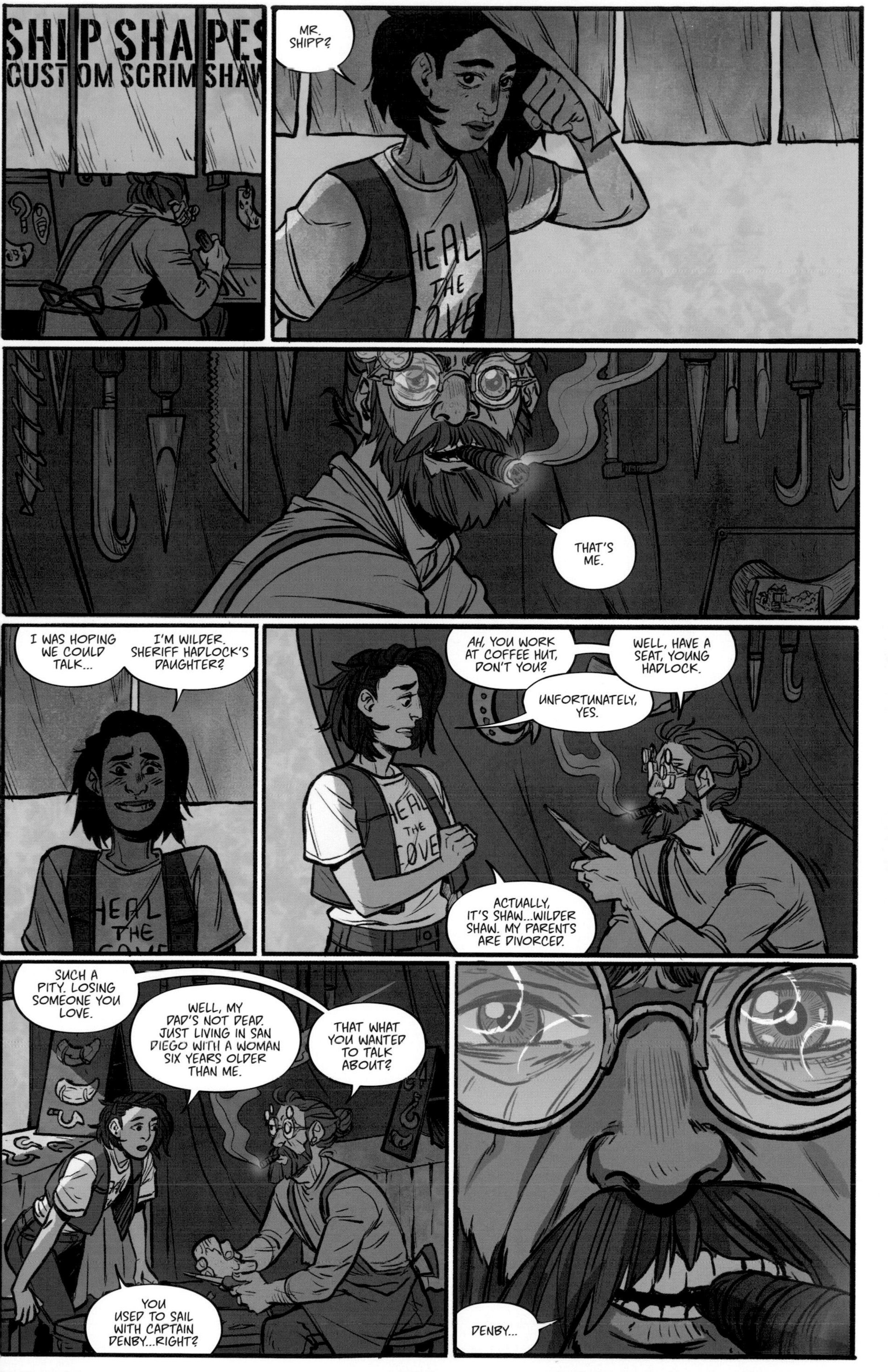
SHIP SHAPES
CUSTOM SCRIMSHAW
MR. SHIPP?
HEAL THE COVE
THAT'S ME.
I WAS HOPING WE COULD TALK...
I'M WILDER. SHERIFF HADLOCK'S DAUGHTER?
AH, YOU WORK AT COFFEE HUT, DON'T YOU?
WELL, HAVE A SEAT, YOUNG HADLOCK.
UNFORTUNATELY, YES.
ACTUALLY, IT'S SHAW...WILDER SHAW. MY PARENTS ARE DIVORCED.
SUCH A PITY. LOSING SOMEONE YOU LOVE.
WELL, MY DAD'S NOT DEAD. JUST LIVING IN SAN DIEGO WITH A WOMAN SIX YEARS OLDER THAN ME.
THAT WHAT YOU WANTED TO TALK ABOUT?
YOU USED TO SAIL WITH CAPTAIN DENBY...RIGHT?
DENBY...

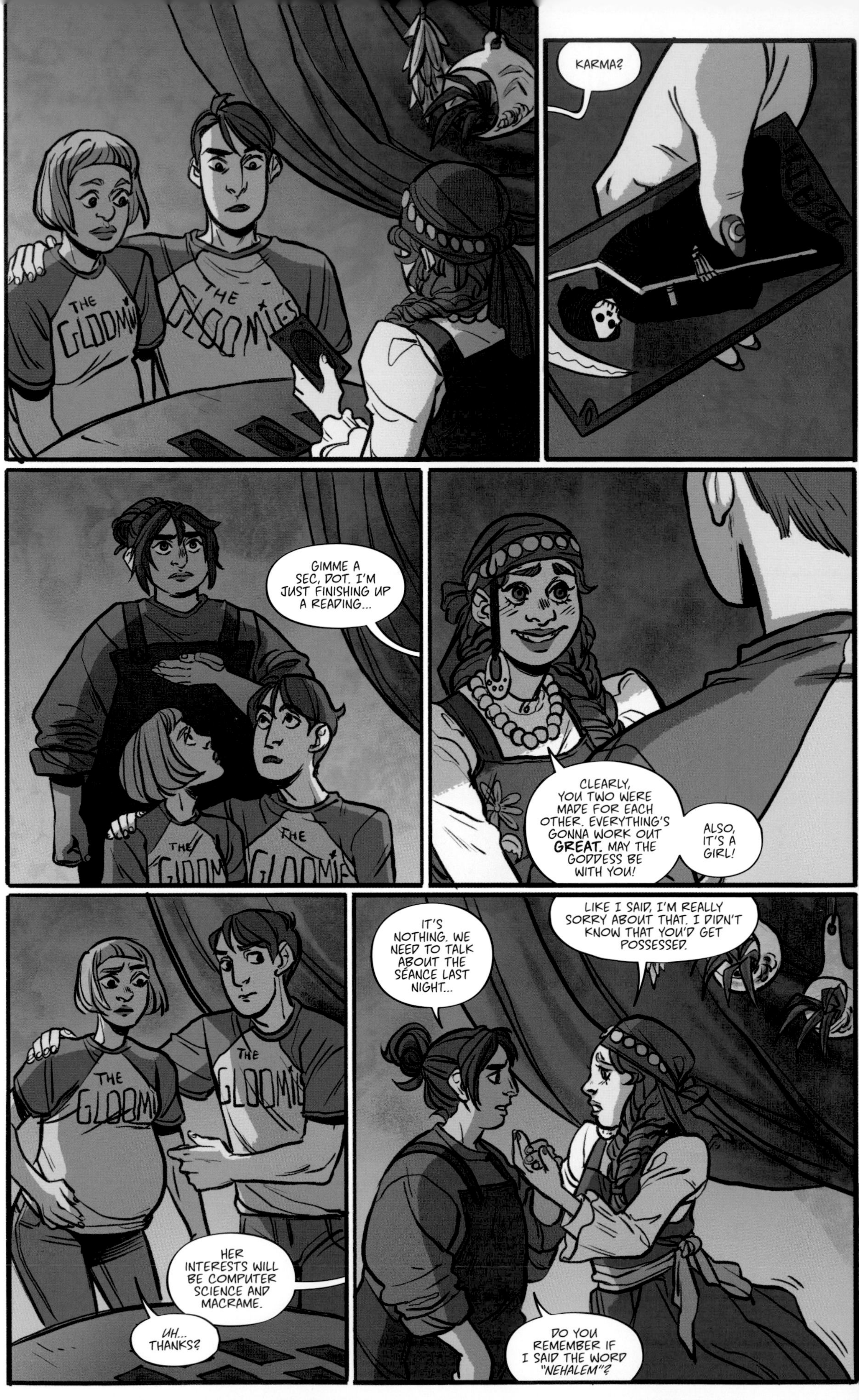
KARMA?
GIMME A SEC, DOT. I'M JUST FINISHING UP A READING...
CLEARLY, YOU TWO WERE MADE FOR EACH OTHER. EVERYTHING'S GONNA WORK OUT **GREAT.** MAY THE GODDESS BE WITH YOU!
ALSO, IT'S A GIRL!
HER INTERESTS WILL BE COMPUTER SCIENCE AND MACRAME.
UH... THANKS?
IT'S NOTHING. WE NEED TO TALK ABOUT THE SÉANCE LAST NIGHT...
LIKE I SAID, I'M REALLY SORRY ABOUT THAT. I DIDN'T KNOW THAT YOU'D GET POSSESSED.
DO YOU REMEMBER IF I SAID THE WORD *"NEHALEM"*?

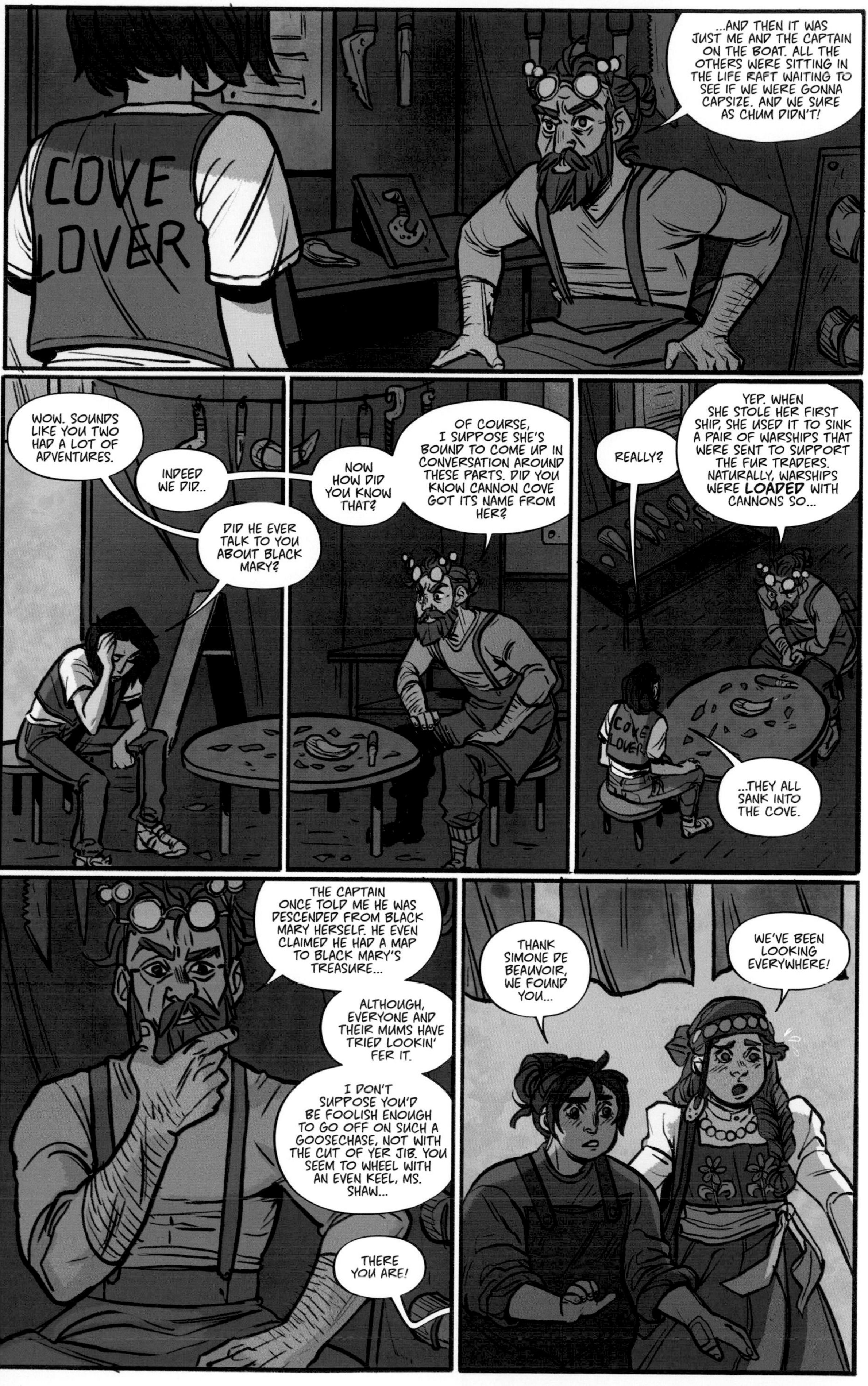
...AND THEN IT WAS JUST ME AND THE CAPTAIN ON THE BOAT. ALL THE OTHERS WERE SITTING IN THE LIFE RAFT WAITING TO SEE IF WE WERE GONNA CAPSIZE. AND WE SURE AS CHUM DIDN'T!
COVE LOVER
WOW. SOUNDS LIKE YOU TWO HAD A LOT OF ADVENTURES.
INDEED WE DID...
DID HE EVER TALK TO YOU ABOUT BLACK MARY?
NOW HOW DID YOU KNOW THAT?
OF COURSE, I SUPPOSE SHE'S BOUND TO COME UP IN CONVERSATION AROUND THESE PARTS. DID YOU KNOW CANNON COVE GOT ITS NAME FROM HER?
REALLY?
YEP. WHEN SHE STOLE HER FIRST SHIP, SHE USED IT TO SINK A PAIR OF WARSHIPS THAT WERE SENT TO SUPPORT THE FUR TRADERS. NATURALLY, WARSHIPS WERE **LOADED** WITH CANNONS SO...
COVE LOVER
...THEY ALL SANK INTO THE COVE.
THE CAPTAIN ONCE TOLD ME HE WAS DESCENDED FROM BLACK MARY HERSELF. HE EVEN CLAIMED HE HAD A MAP TO BLACK MARY'S TREASURE...
ALTHOUGH, EVERYONE AND THEIR MUMS HAVE TRIED LOOKIN' FER IT.
I DON'T SUPPOSE YOU'D BE FOOLISH ENOUGH TO GO OFF ON SUCH A GOOSECHASE, NOT WITH THE CUT OF YER JIB. YOU SEEM TO WHEEL WITH AN EVEN KEEL, MS. SHAW...
THERE YOU ARE!
THANK SIMONE DE BEAUVOIR, WE FOUND YOU...
WE'VE BEEN LOOKING EVERYWHERE!

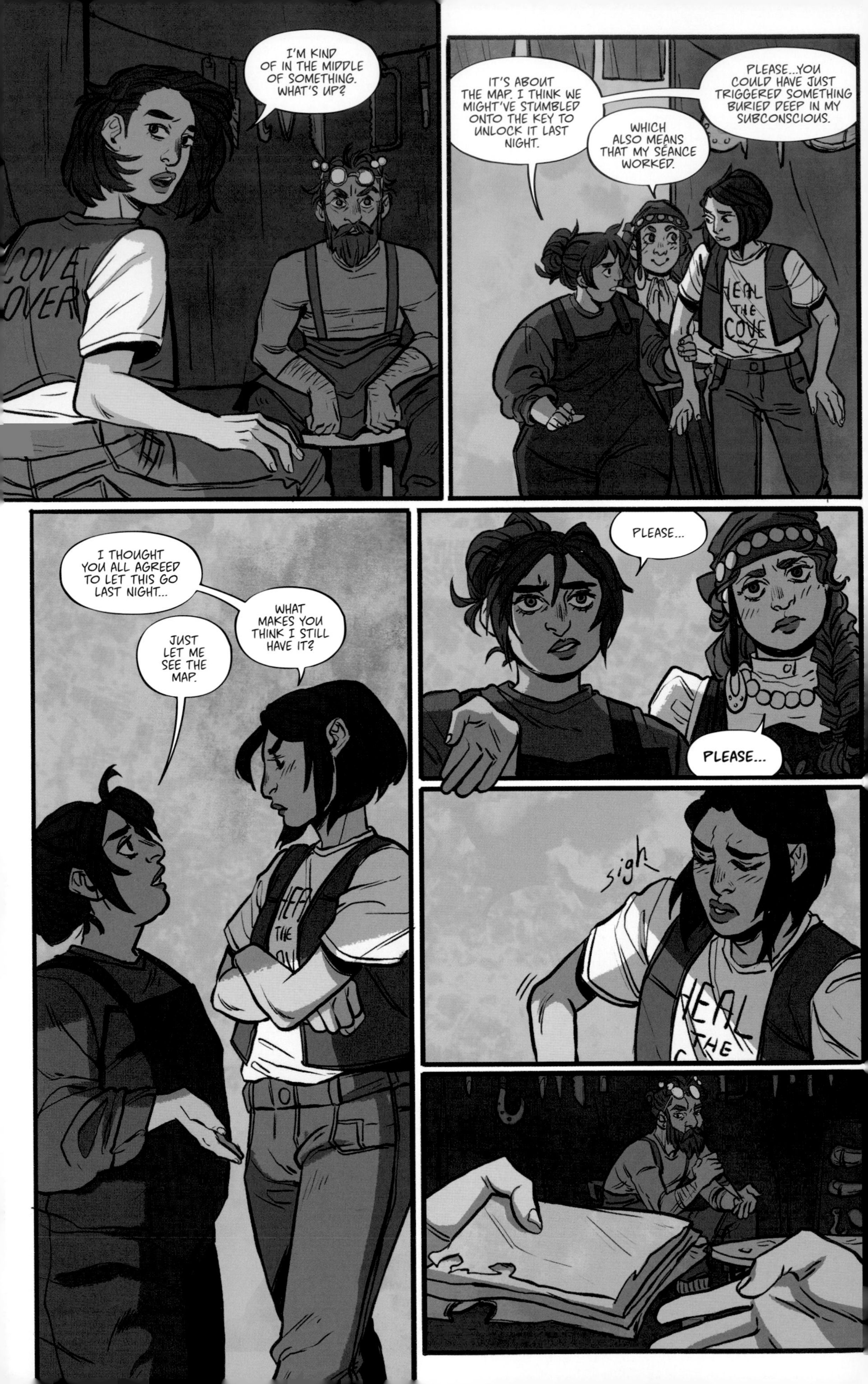
I'M KIND OF IN THE MIDDLE OF SOMETHING. WHAT'S UP?
COVE LOVER
IT'S ABOUT THE MAP. I THINK WE MIGHT'VE STUMBLED ONTO THE KEY TO UNLOCK IT LAST NIGHT.
WHICH ALSO MEANS THAT MY SÉANCE WORKED.
PLEASE...YOU COULD HAVE JUST TRIGGERED SOMETHING BURIED DEEP IN MY SUBCONSCIOUS.
HEAL THE COVE
I THOUGHT YOU ALL AGREED TO LET THIS GO LAST NIGHT...
JUST LET ME SEE THE MAP.
WHAT MAKES YOU THINK I STILL HAVE IT?
PLEASE...
PLEASE...
sigh

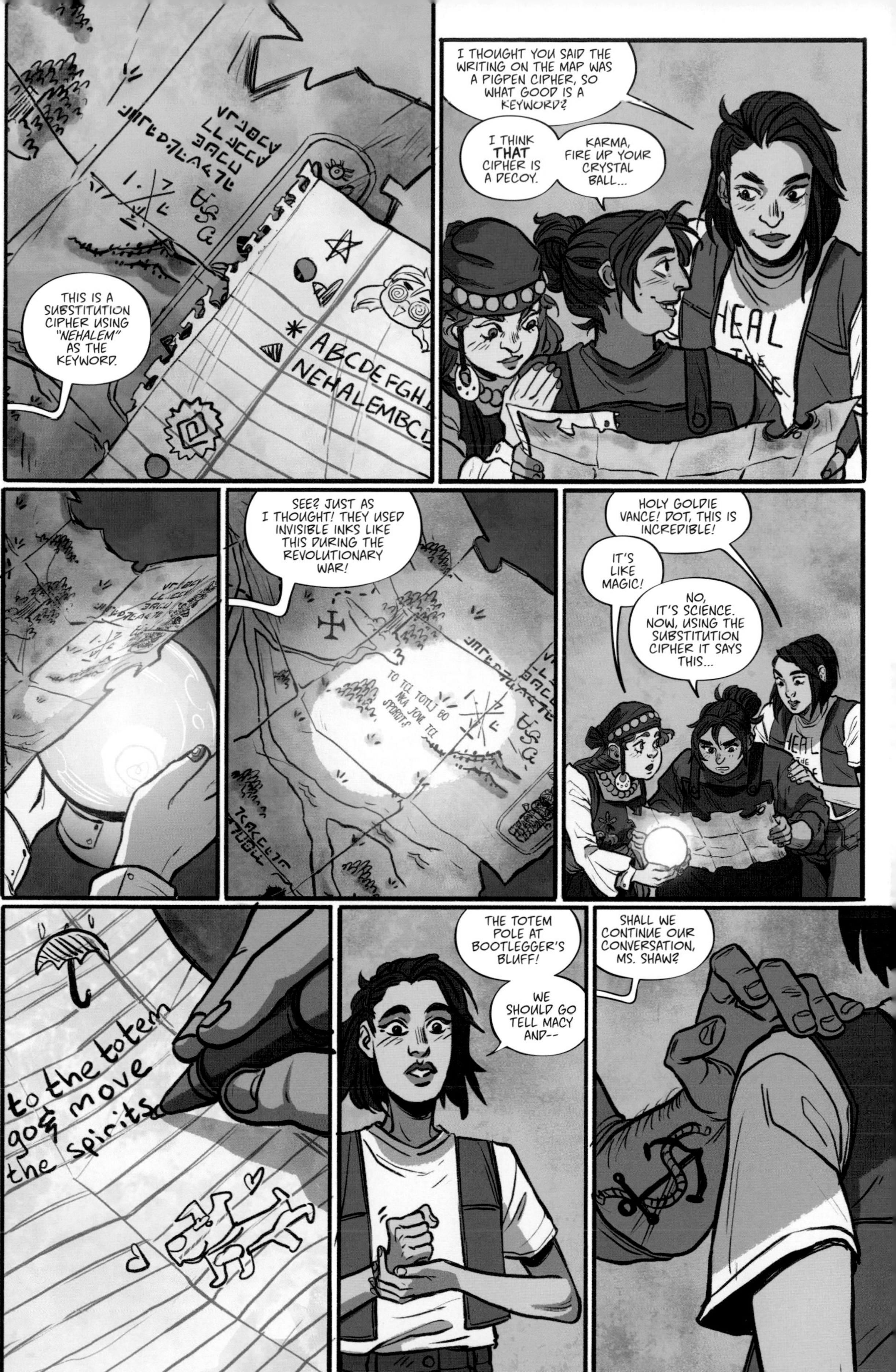
ABCDEFGHI
NEHALEMBCD
THIS IS A SUBSTITUTION CIPHER USING "NEHALEM" AS THE KEYWORD.
I THOUGHT YOU SAID THE WRITING ON THE MAP WAS A PIGPEN CIPHER, SO WHAT GOOD IS A KEYWORD?
I THINK **THAT** CIPHER IS A DECOY.
KARMA, FIRE UP YOUR CRYSTAL BALL...
HEAL
SEE? JUST AS I THOUGHT! THEY USED INVISIBLE INKS LIKE THIS DURING THE REVOLUTIONARY WAR!
HOLY GOLDIE VANCE! DOT, THIS IS INCREDIBLE!
IT'S LIKE MAGIC!
NO, IT'S SCIENCE. NOW, USING THE SUBSTITUTION CIPHER IT SAYS THIS...
HEAL
to the totem go & move the spirits
THE TOTEM POLE AT BOOTLEGGER'S BLUFF!
WE SHOULD GO TELL MACY AND--
SHALL WE CONTINUE OUR CONVERSATION, MS. SHAW?

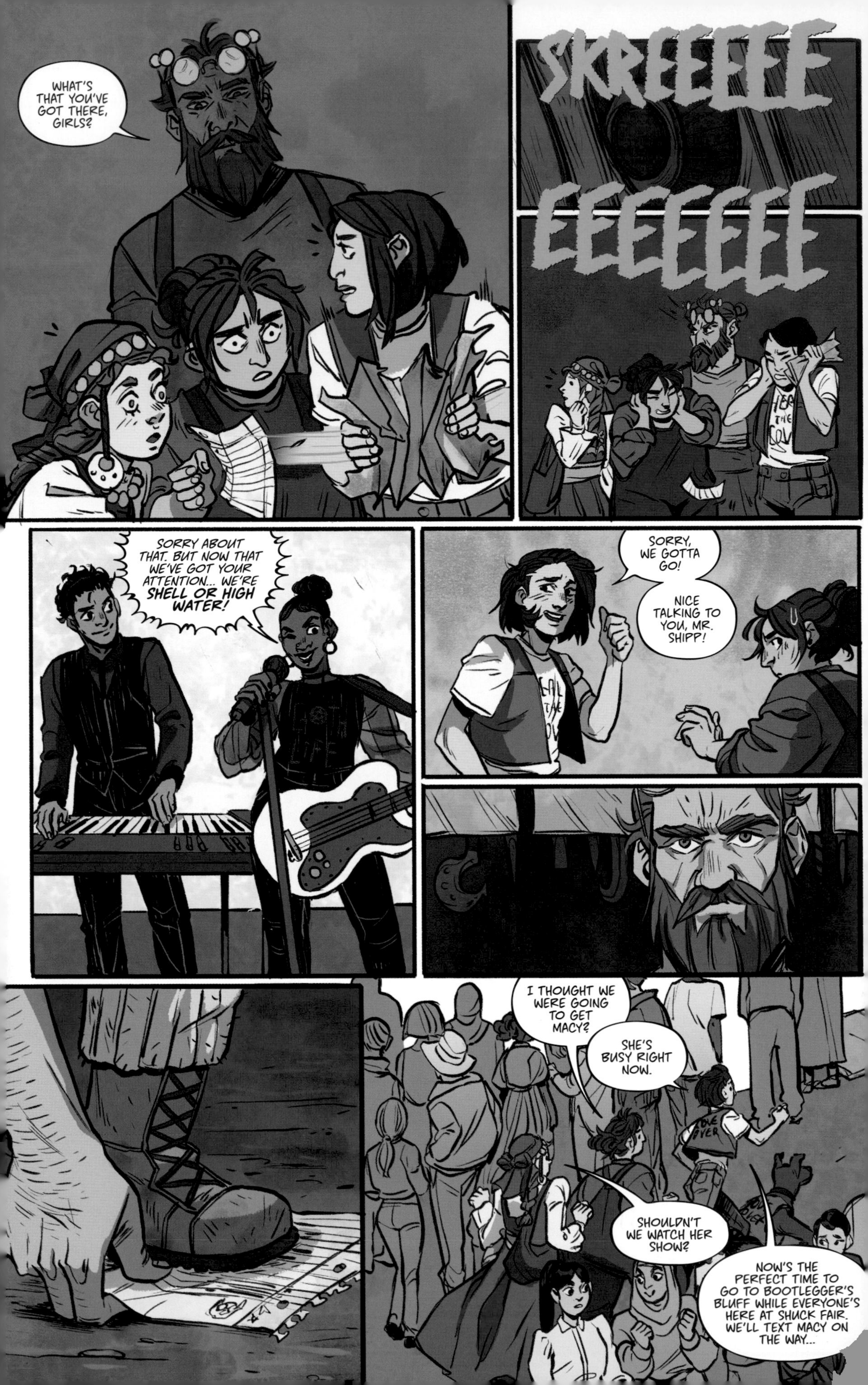
WHAT'S THAT YOU'VE GOT THERE, GIRLS?
SKREEEEEE
EEEEEEE
SORRY ABOUT THAT. BUT NOW THAT WE'VE GOT YOUR ATTENTION... WE'RE **SHELL OR HIGH WATER!**
SORRY, WE GOTTA GO!
NICE TALKING TO YOU, MR. SHIPP!
I THOUGHT WE WERE GOING TO GET MACY?
SHE'S BUSY RIGHT NOW.
SHOULDN'T WE WATCH HER SHOW?
NOW'S THE PERFECT TIME TO GO TO BOOTLEGGER'S BLUFF WHILE EVERYONE'S HERE AT SHUCK FAIR. WE'LL TEXT MACY ON THE WAY...

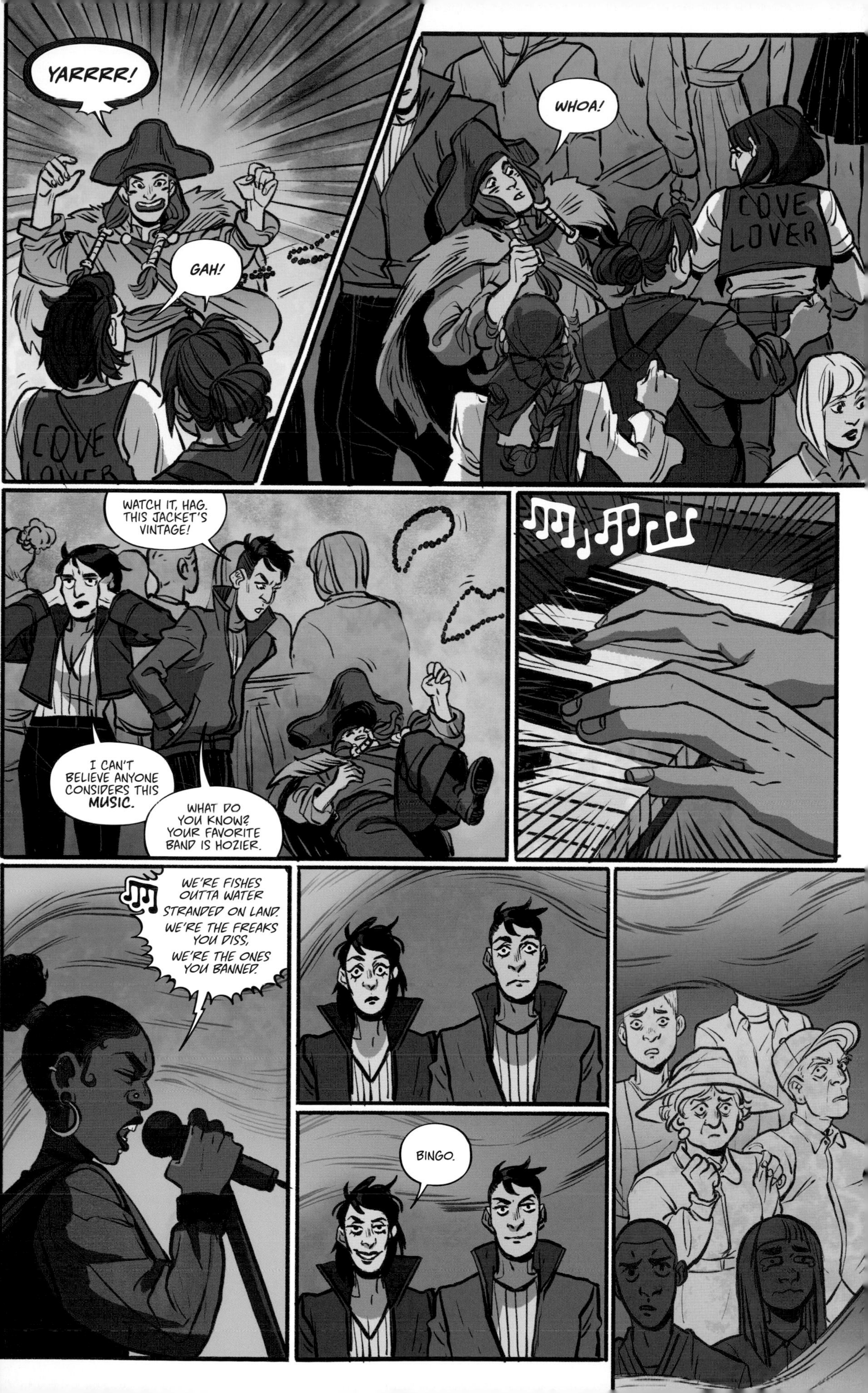

YARRRR!
GAH!
COVE LOVER
WHOA!
COVE LOVER
WATCH IT, HAG. THIS JACKET'S VINTAGE!
I CAN'T BELIEVE ANYONE CONSIDERS THIS MUSIC.
WHAT DO YOU KNOW? YOUR FAVORITE BAND IS HOZIER.
WE'RE FISHES OUTTA WATER STRANDED ON LAND. WE'RE THE FREAKS YOU DISS, WE'RE THE ONES YOU BANNED.
BINGO.

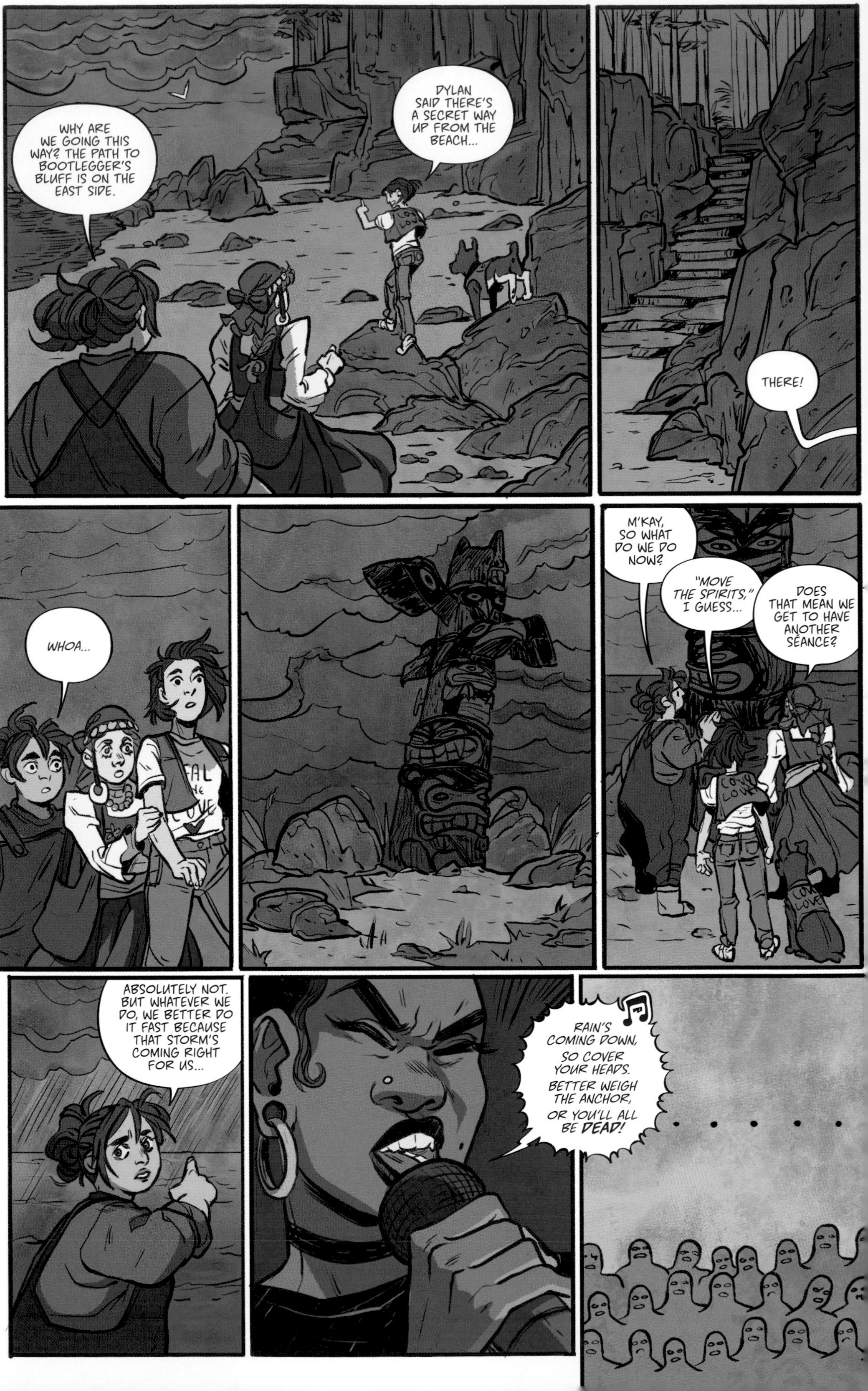
WHY ARE WE GOING THIS WAY? THE PATH TO BOOTLEGGER'S BLUFF IS ON THE EAST SIDE.
DYLAN SAID THERE'S A SECRET WAY UP FROM THE BEACH...
THERE!
WHOA...
M'KAY, SO WHAT DO WE DO NOW?
"MOVE THE SPIRITS," I GUESS...
DOES THAT MEAN WE GET TO HAVE ANOTHER SÉANCE?
ABSOLUTELY NOT. BUT WHATEVER WE DO, WE BETTER DO IT FAST BECAUSE THAT STORM'S COMING RIGHT FOR US...
RAIN'S COMING DOWN, SO COVER YOUR HEADS. BETTER WEIGH THE ANCHOR, OR YOU'LL ALL BE DEAD!
. . . . .

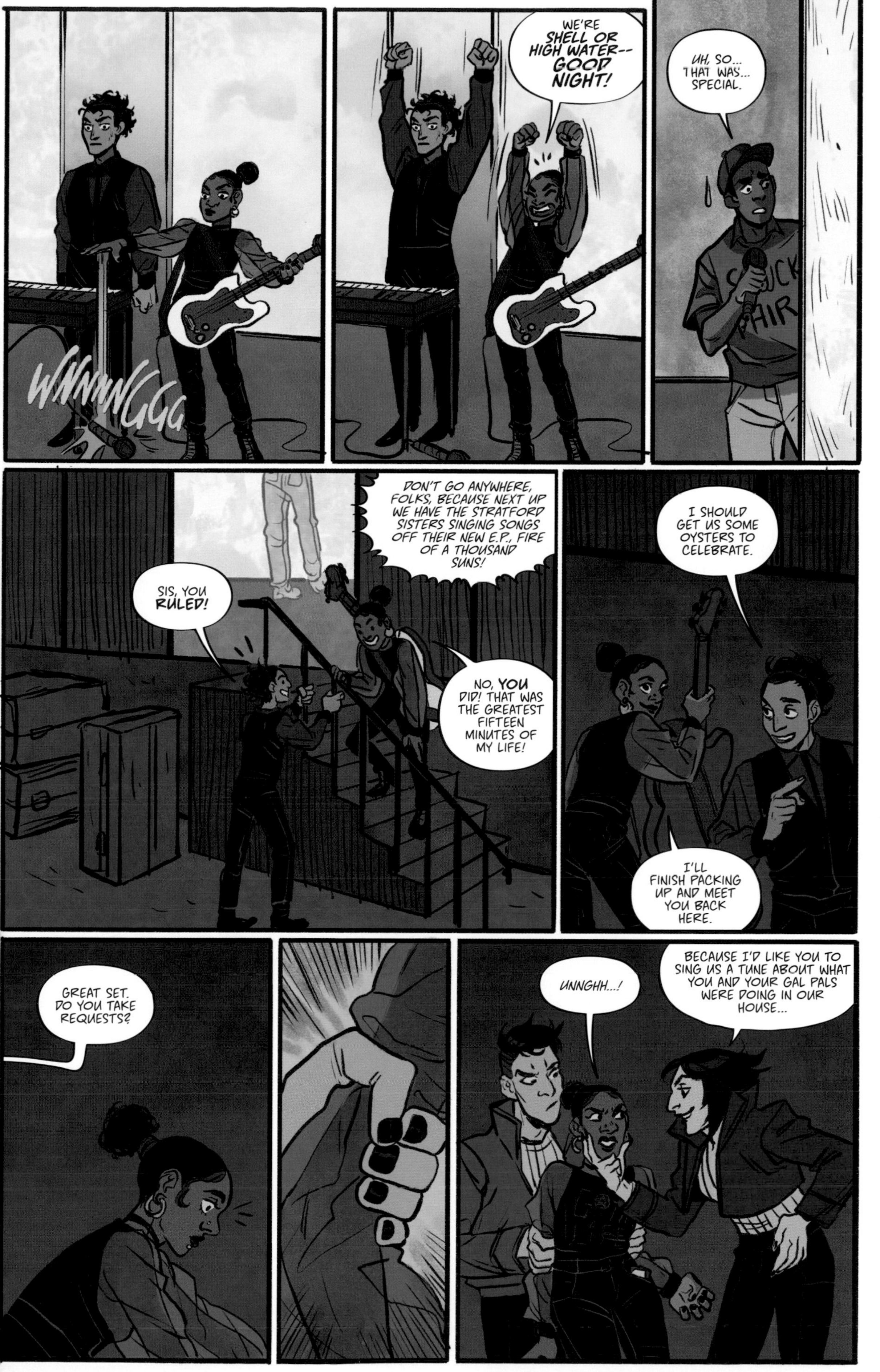
WNNNNGGG
WE'RE SHELL OR HIGH WATER-- GOOD NIGHT!
UH, SO... THAT WAS... SPECIAL.
DON'T GO ANYWHERE, FOLKS, BECAUSE NEXT UP WE HAVE THE STRATFORD SISTERS SINGING SONGS OFF THEIR NEW E.P., FIRE OF A THOUSAND SUNS!
SIS, YOU RULED!
NO, YOU DID! THAT WAS THE GREATEST FIFTEEN MINUTES OF MY LIFE!
I SHOULD GET US SOME OYSTERS TO CELEBRATE.
I'LL FINISH PACKING UP AND MEET YOU BACK HERE.
GREAT SET. DO YOU TAKE REQUESTS?
UNNGHH...!
BECAUSE I'D LIKE YOU TO SING US A TUNE ABOUT WHAT YOU AND YOUR GAL PALS WERE DOING IN OUR HOUSE...

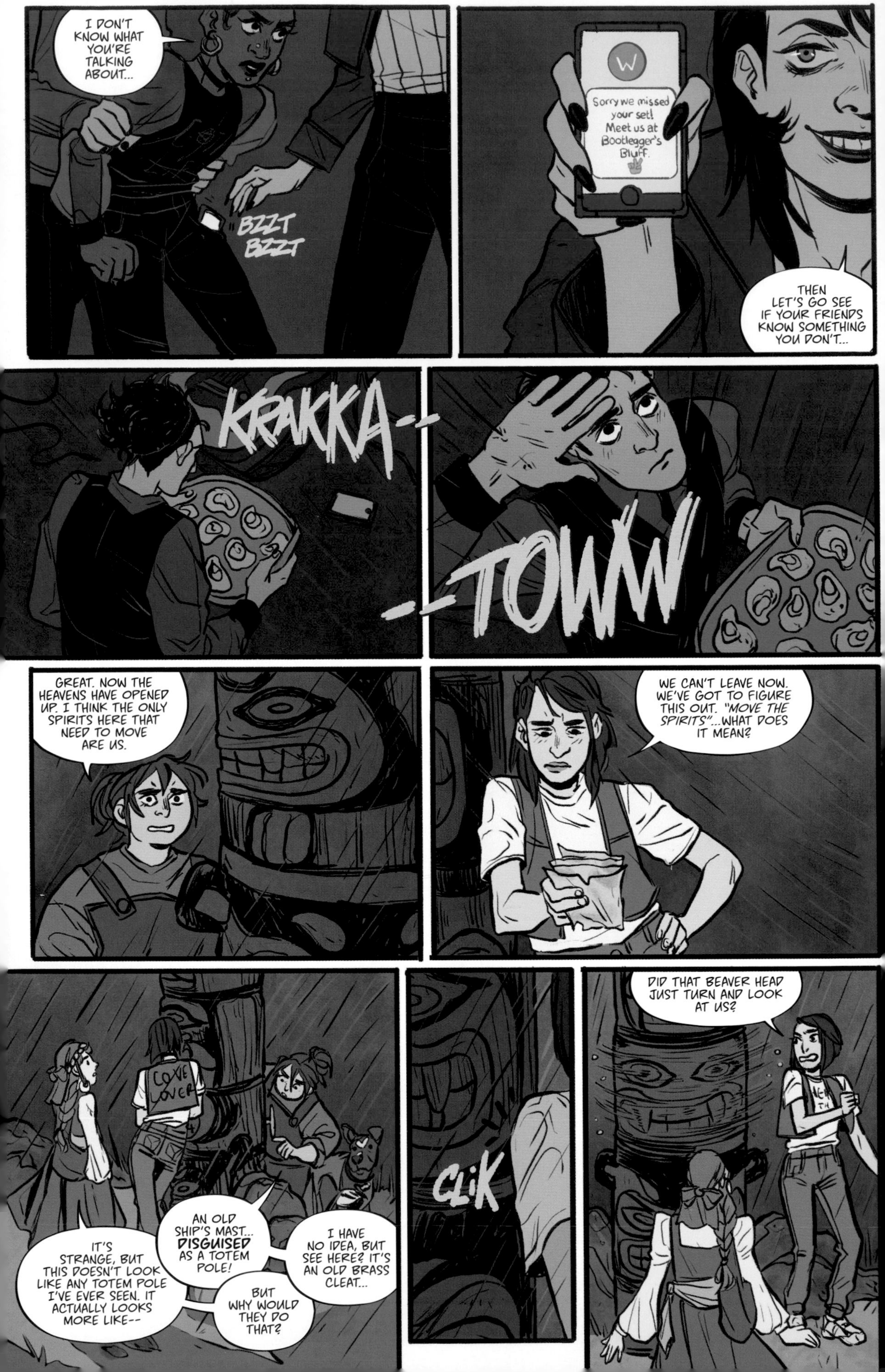
I DON'T KNOW WHAT YOU'RE TALKING ABOUT...
BZZT BZZT
W
Sorry we missed your set! Meet us at Bootlegger's Bluff.
THEN LET'S GO SEE IF YOUR FRIENDS KNOW SOMETHING YOU DON'T...
KRAKKA--
--TOWW
GREAT. NOW THE HEAVENS HAVE OPENED UP. I THINK THE ONLY SPIRITS HERE THAT NEED TO MOVE ARE US.
WE CAN'T LEAVE NOW. WE'VE GOT TO FIGURE THIS OUT. "MOVE THE SPIRITS"...WHAT DOES IT MEAN?
LOVE LOVER
IT'S STRANGE, BUT THIS DOESN'T LOOK LIKE ANY TOTEM POLE I'VE EVER SEEN. IT ACTUALLY LOOKS MORE LIKE--
AN OLD SHIP'S MAST... **DISGUISED** AS A TOTEM POLE!
BUT WHY WOULD THEY DO THAT?
I HAVE NO IDEA, BUT SEE HERE? IT'S AN OLD BRASS CLEAT...
CLIK
DID THAT BEAVER HEAD JUST TURN AND LOOK AT US?

THE ANIMAL CARVINGS...THEY MUST BE THE "SPIRITS" MARY WAS TALKING ABOUT! WE NEED TO MOVE THEM TO MATCH THE ONES ON THE MAP!

IS THAT IT?

I CAN'T REACH THE LAST ONE! WE NEED MACY...

KRAK-KA-KOWW

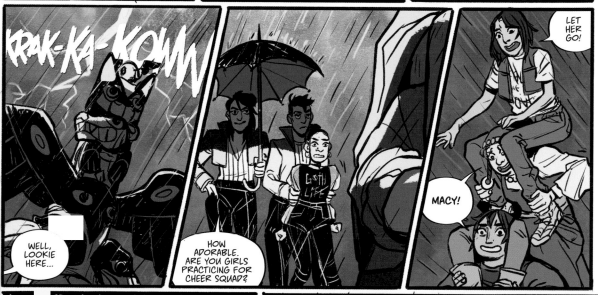

WELL, LOOKIE HERE...

HOW ADORABLE. ARE YOU GIRLS PRACTICING FOR CHEER SQUAD?

LET HER GO!

MACY!

SURE THING...JUST AS SOON AS YOU DROP THAT MAP IN YOUR HAND.

SNIK

NOT SO FAST...

THAT MAP IS MINE...

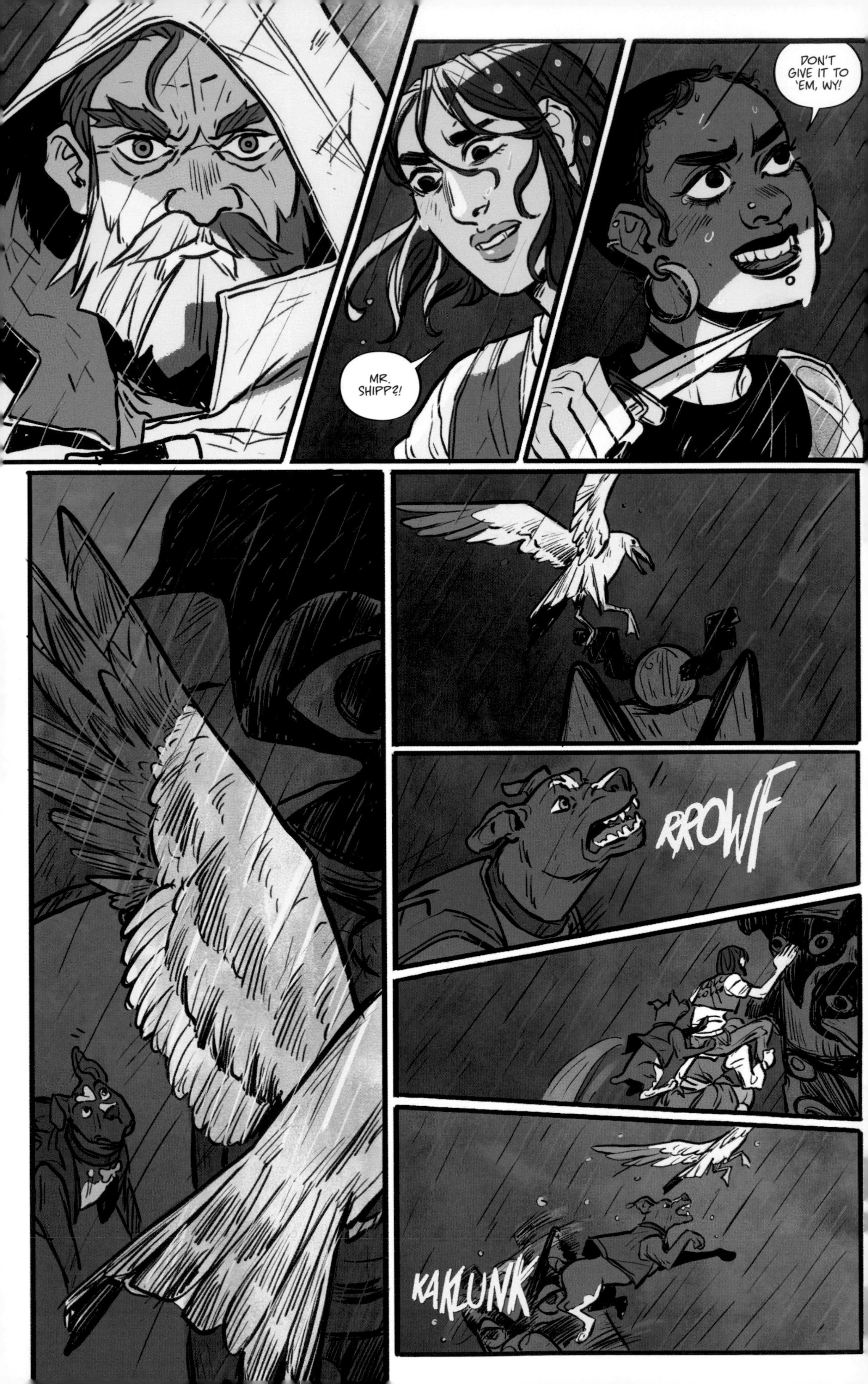
MR. SHIPP?!
DON'T GIVE IT TO 'EM, WY!
RROWF
KAKLUNK

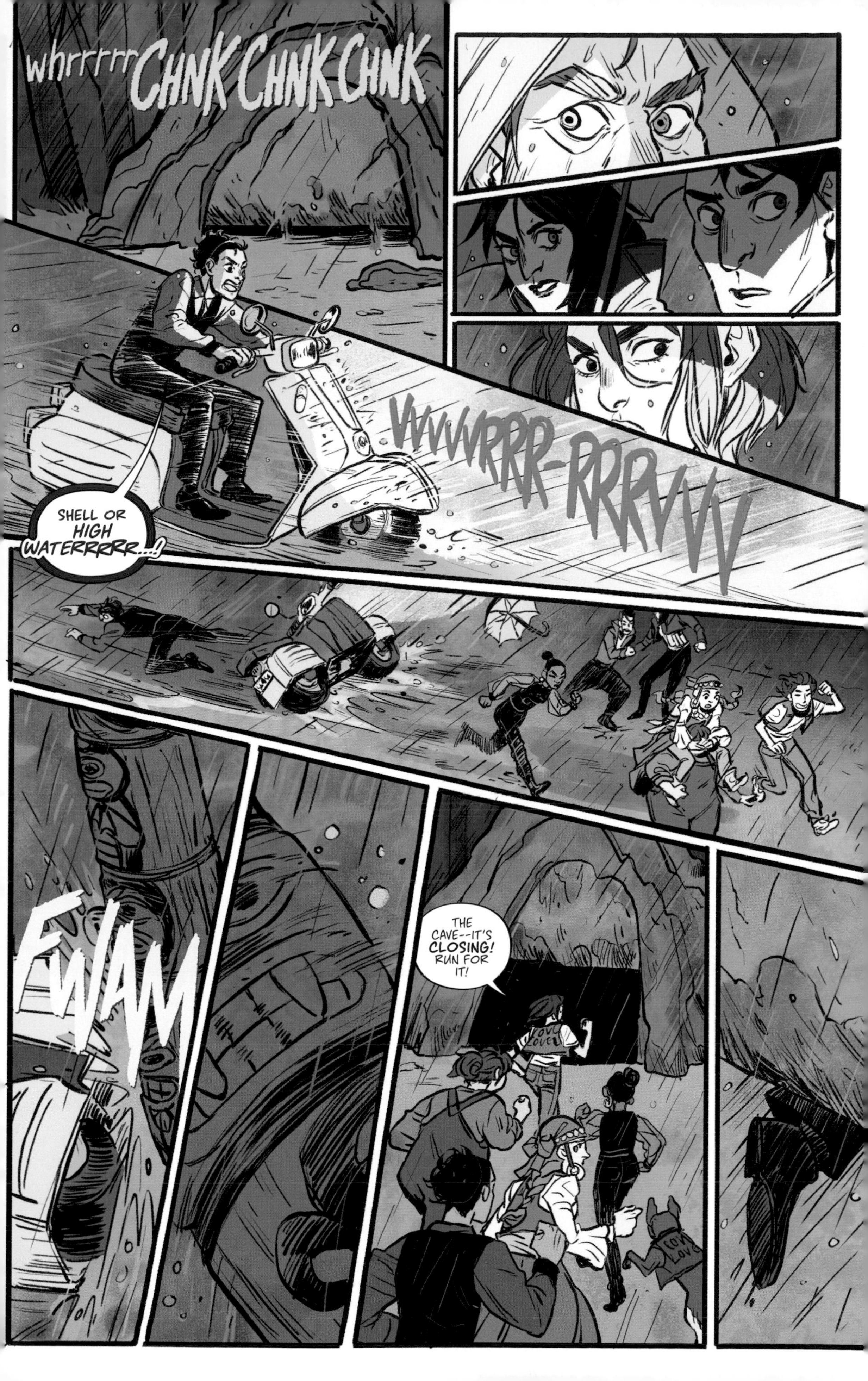
whrrrrr CHNK CHNK CHNK
SHELL OR HIGH WATERRRRR...!
VVVVVRRR-RRRVVVV
FWAM
THE CAVE--IT'S CLOSING! RUN FOR IT!

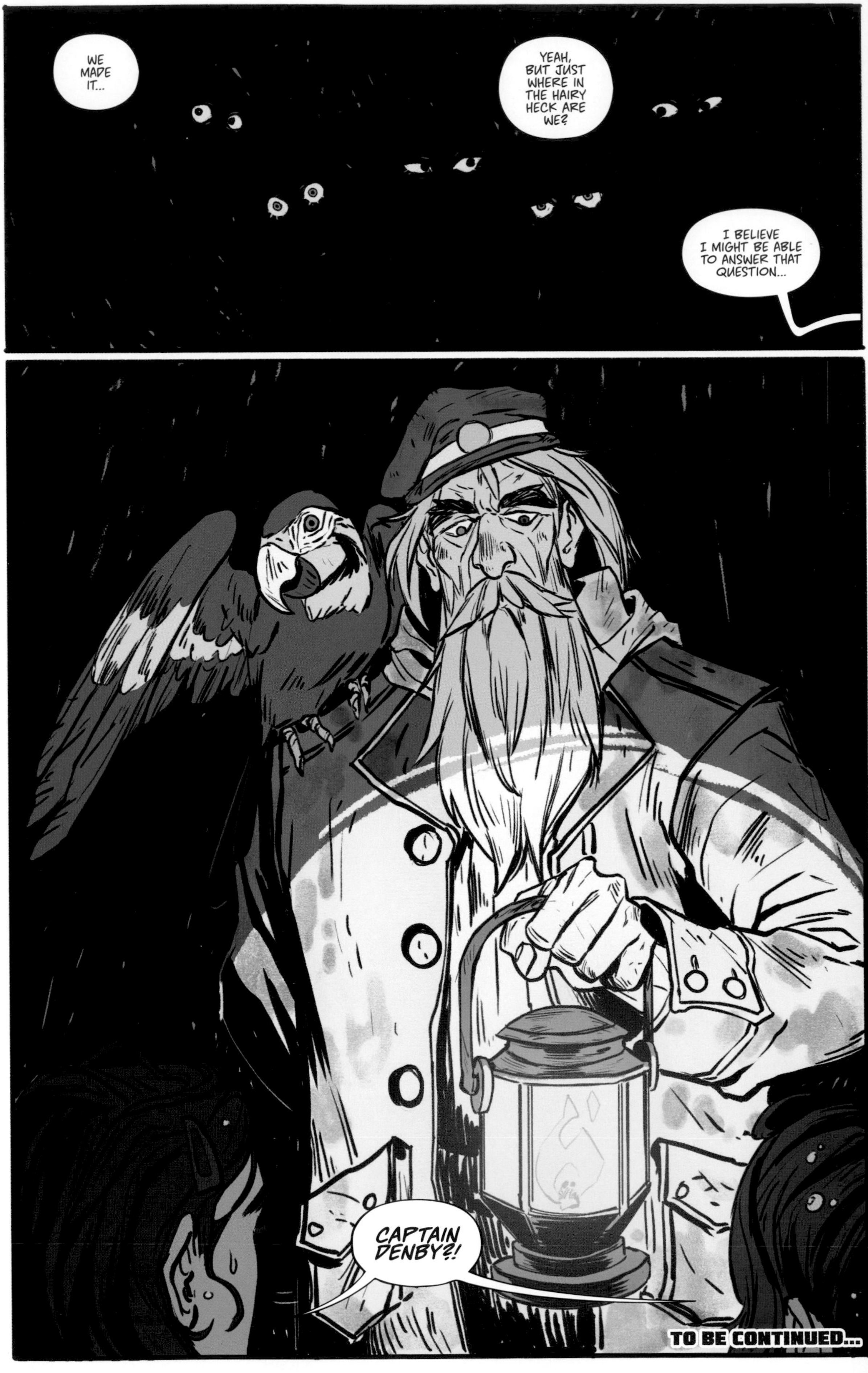
WE MADE IT...
YEAH, BUT JUST WHERE IN THE HAIRY HECK ARE WE?
I BELIEVE I MIGHT BE ABLE TO ANSWER THAT QUESTION...
CAPTAIN DENBY?!
TO BE CONTINUED...

COVER GALLERY

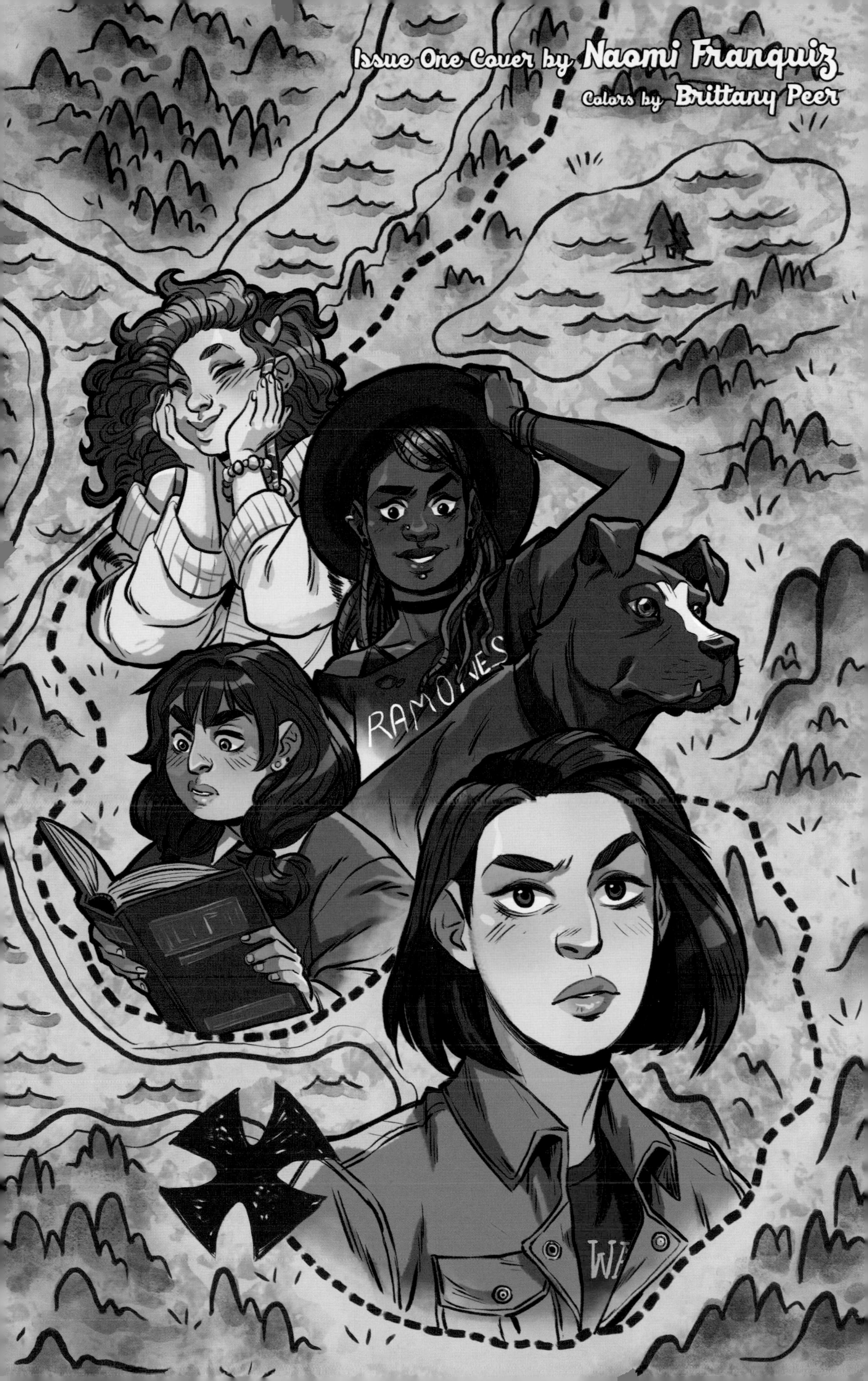
RAMONES

Issue One Cover by Naomi Franquiz
Colors by Brittany Peer

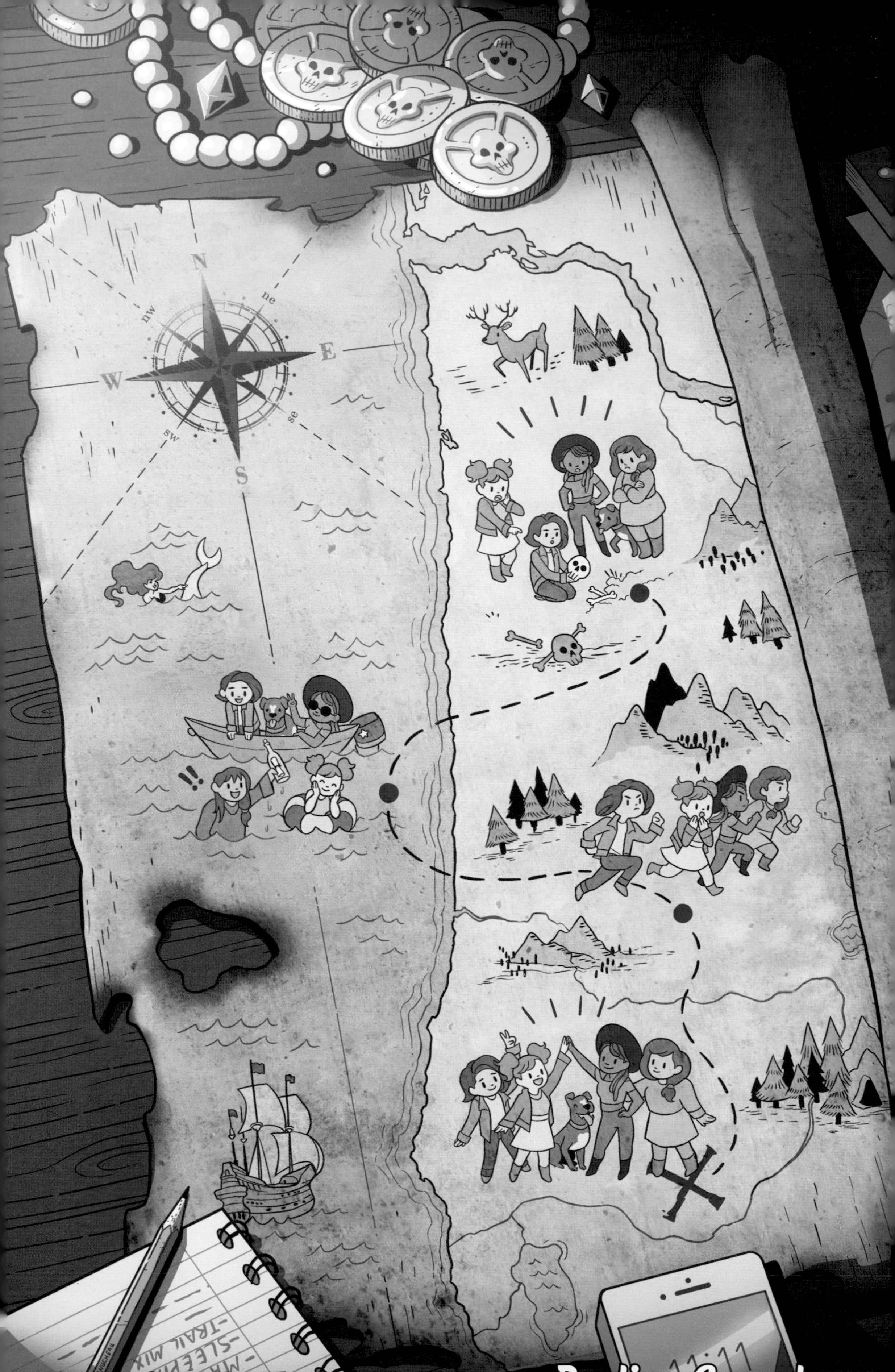
N
nw
ne
W
E
sw
se
S
-TRAIL MIX

Issue One Treasure Map Cover by Paulina Ganucheau

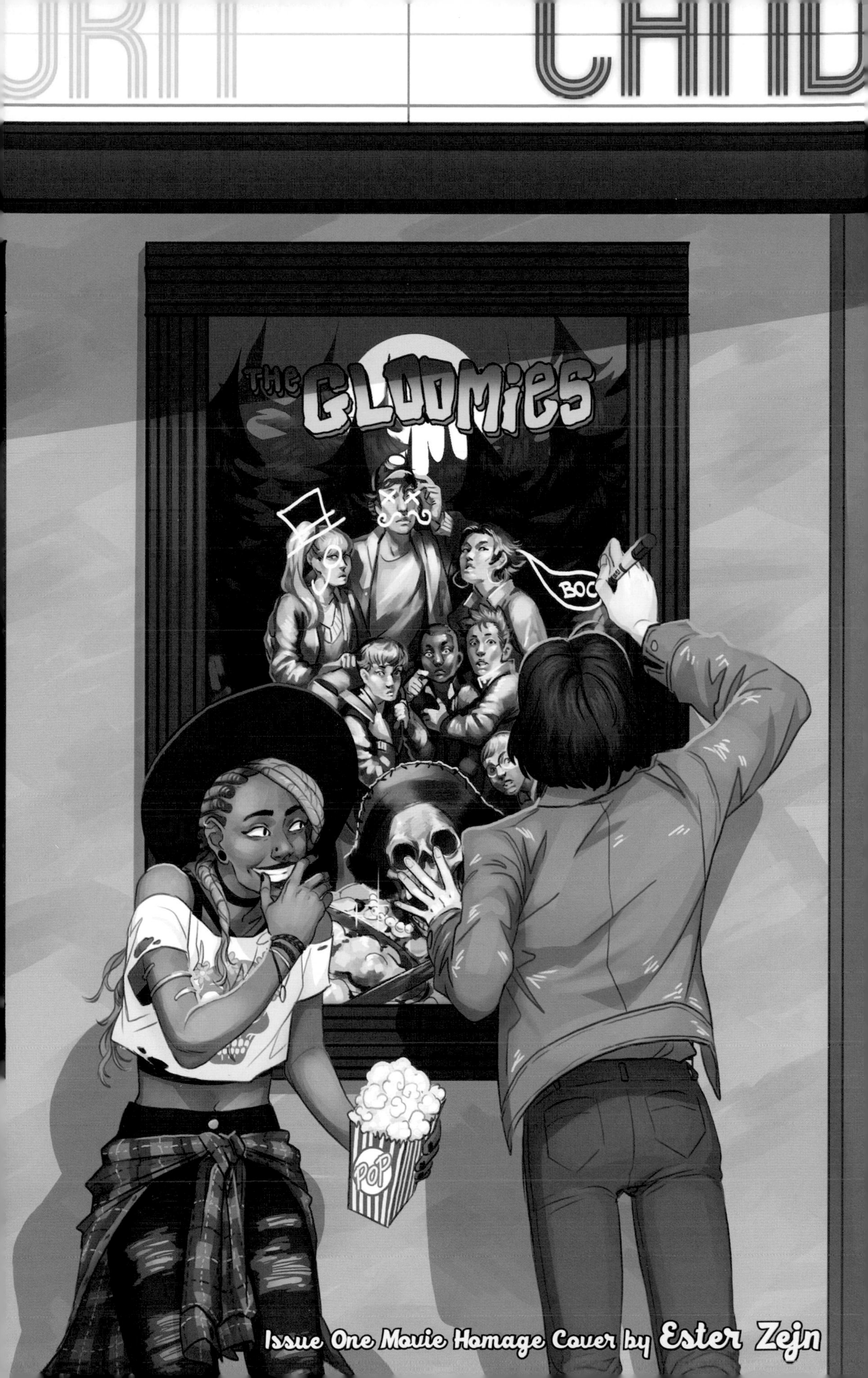
THE GLOOMIES
POP

Issue One Movie Homage Cover by Ester Zejn

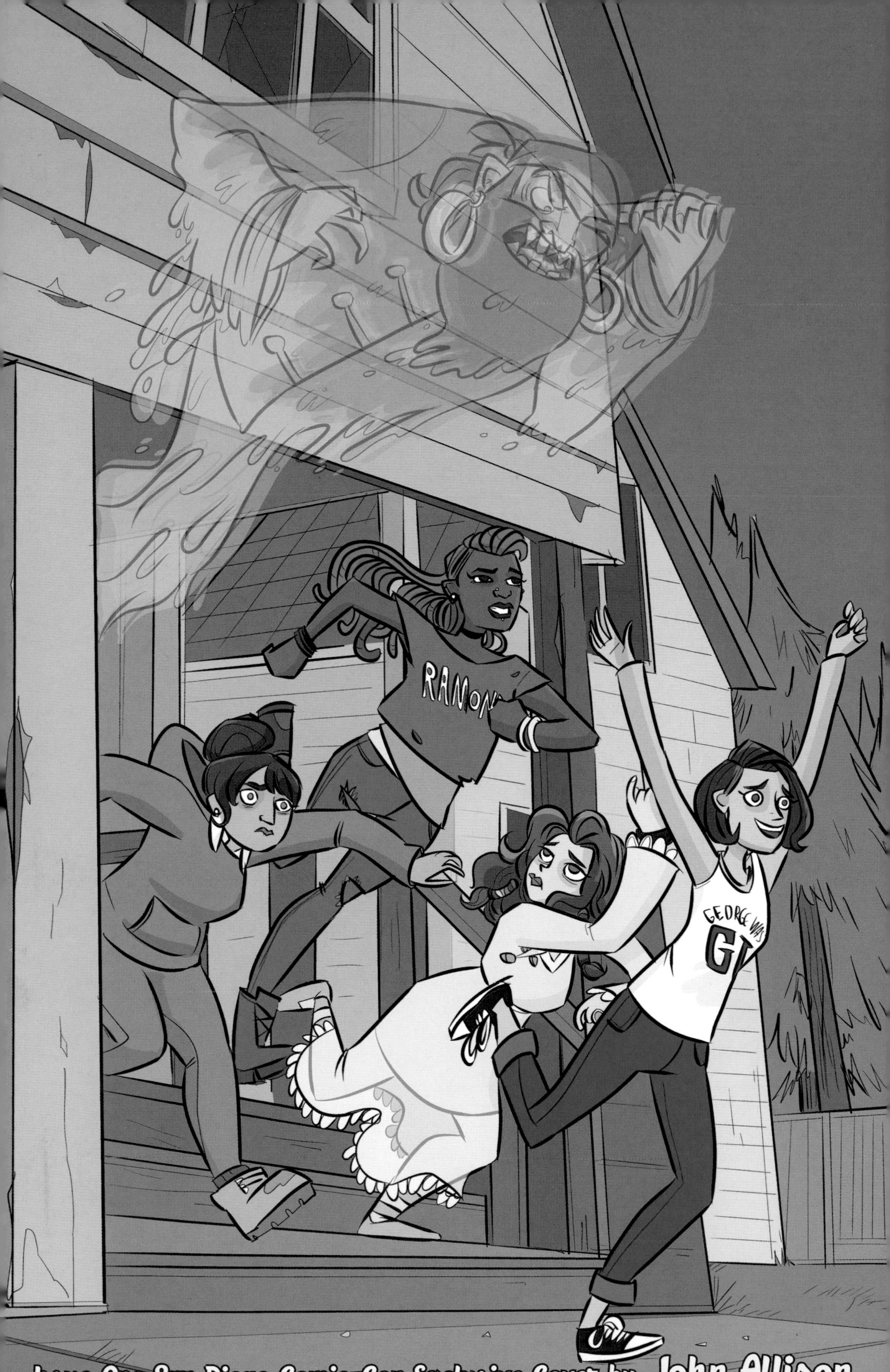
RAMONES
GEORGE WAS
GT

Issue One San Diego Comic-Con Exclusive Cover by John Allison

Issue Two Cover by **Naomi Franquiz**

Colors by **Brittany Peer**

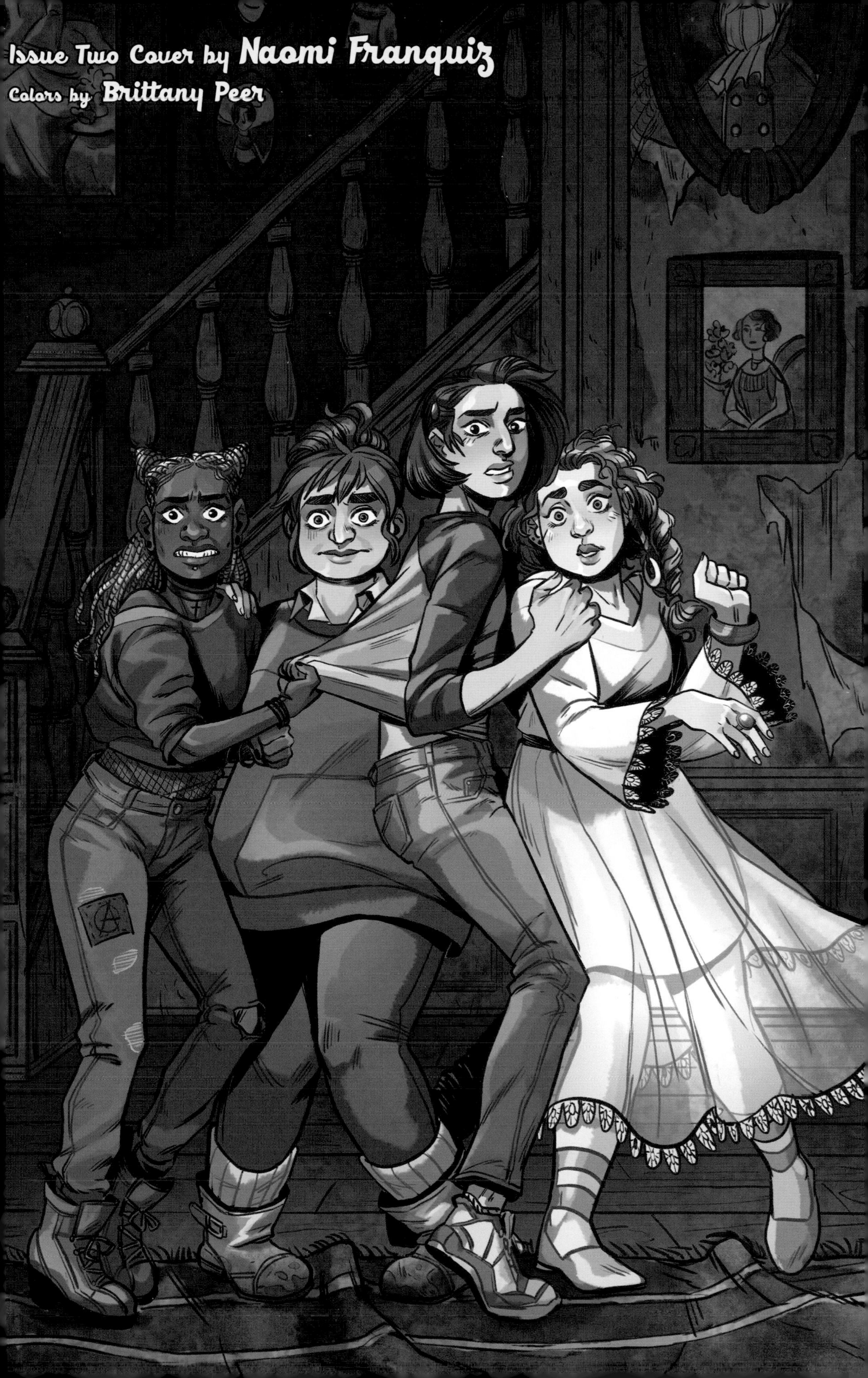

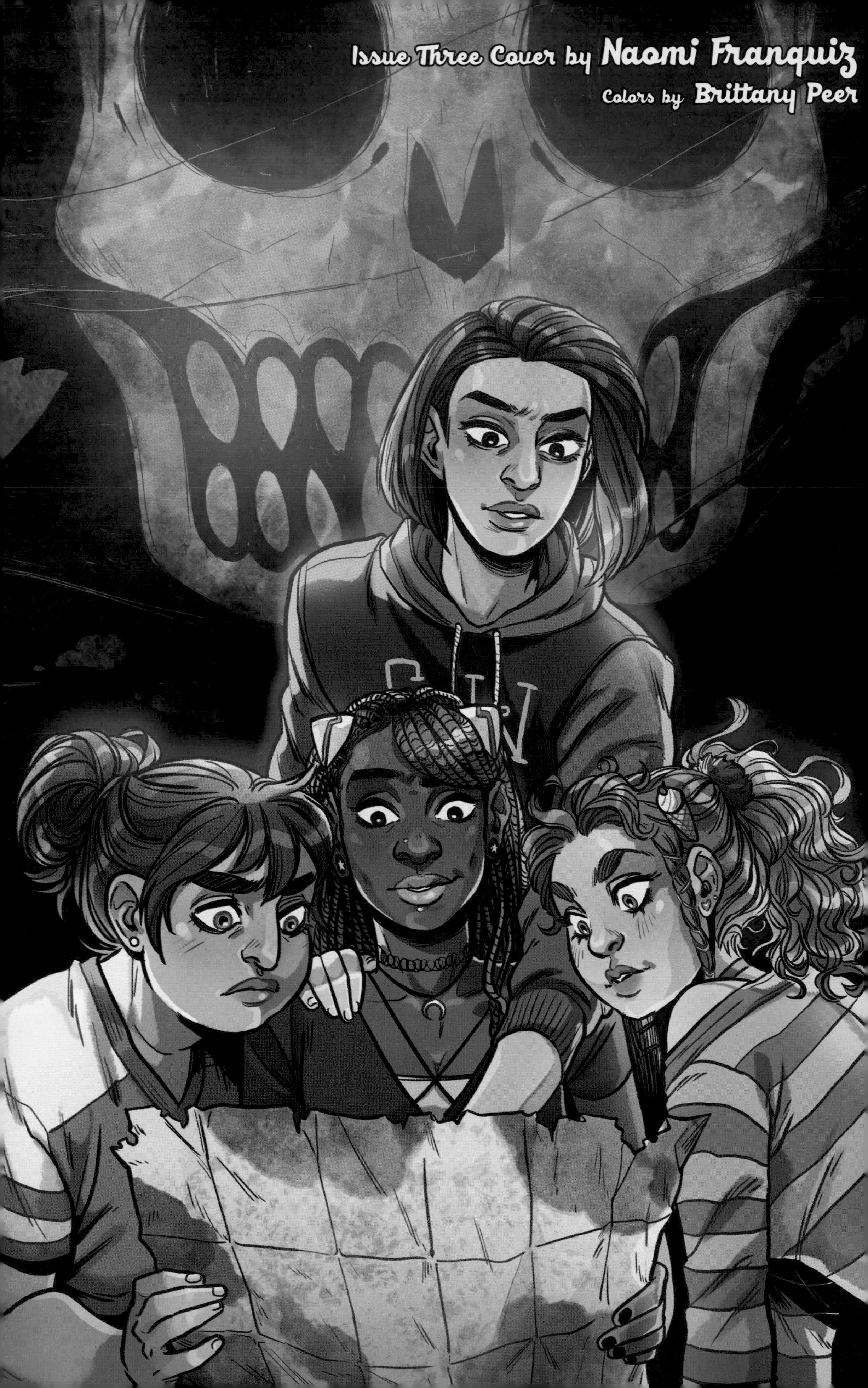

Issue Three Cover by Naomi Franquiz
Colors by Brittany Peer

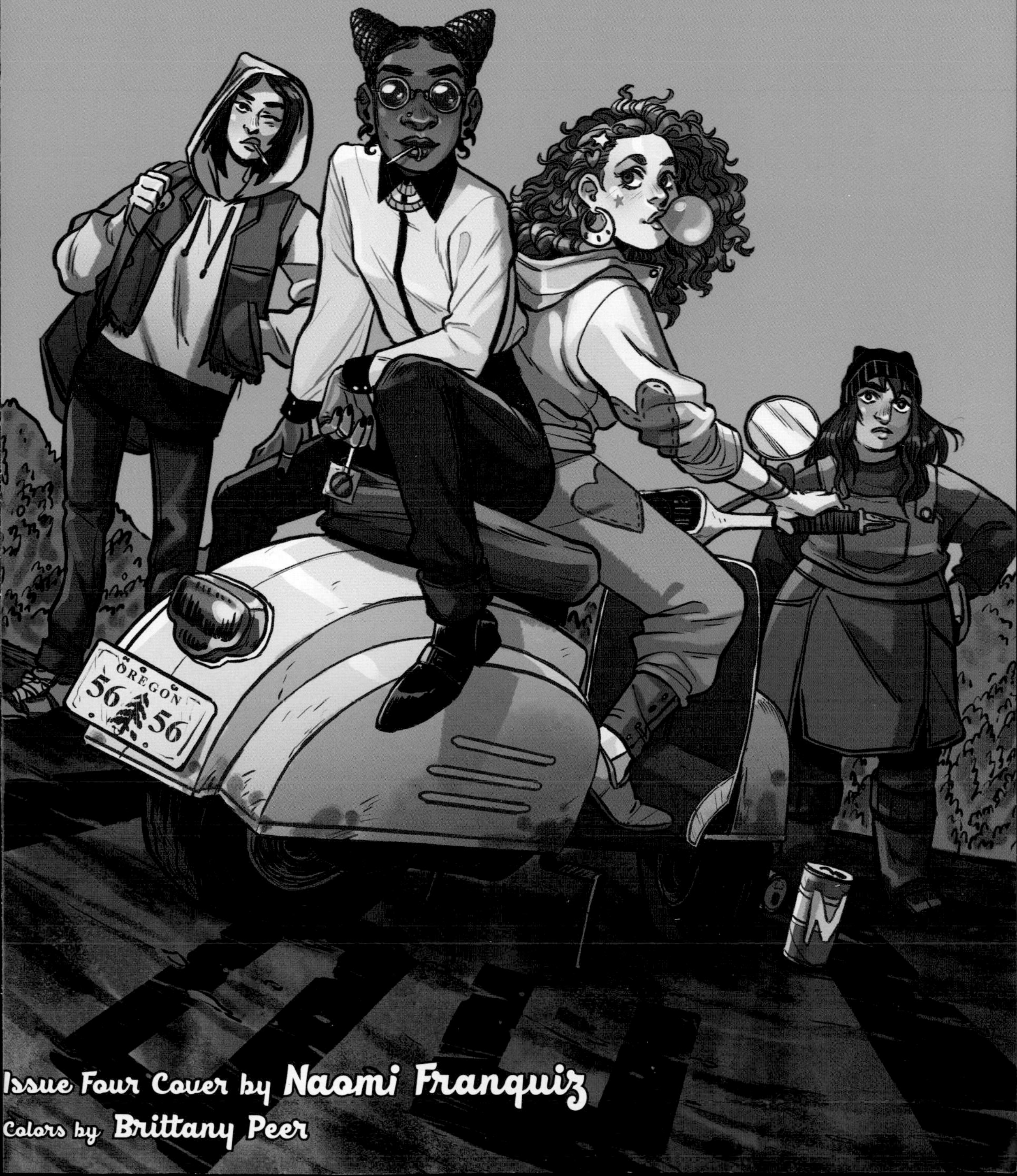
OREGON
56 56

Issue Four Cover by **Naomi Franquiz**

Colors by **Brittany Peer**

Character Design by
Naomi Franquiz

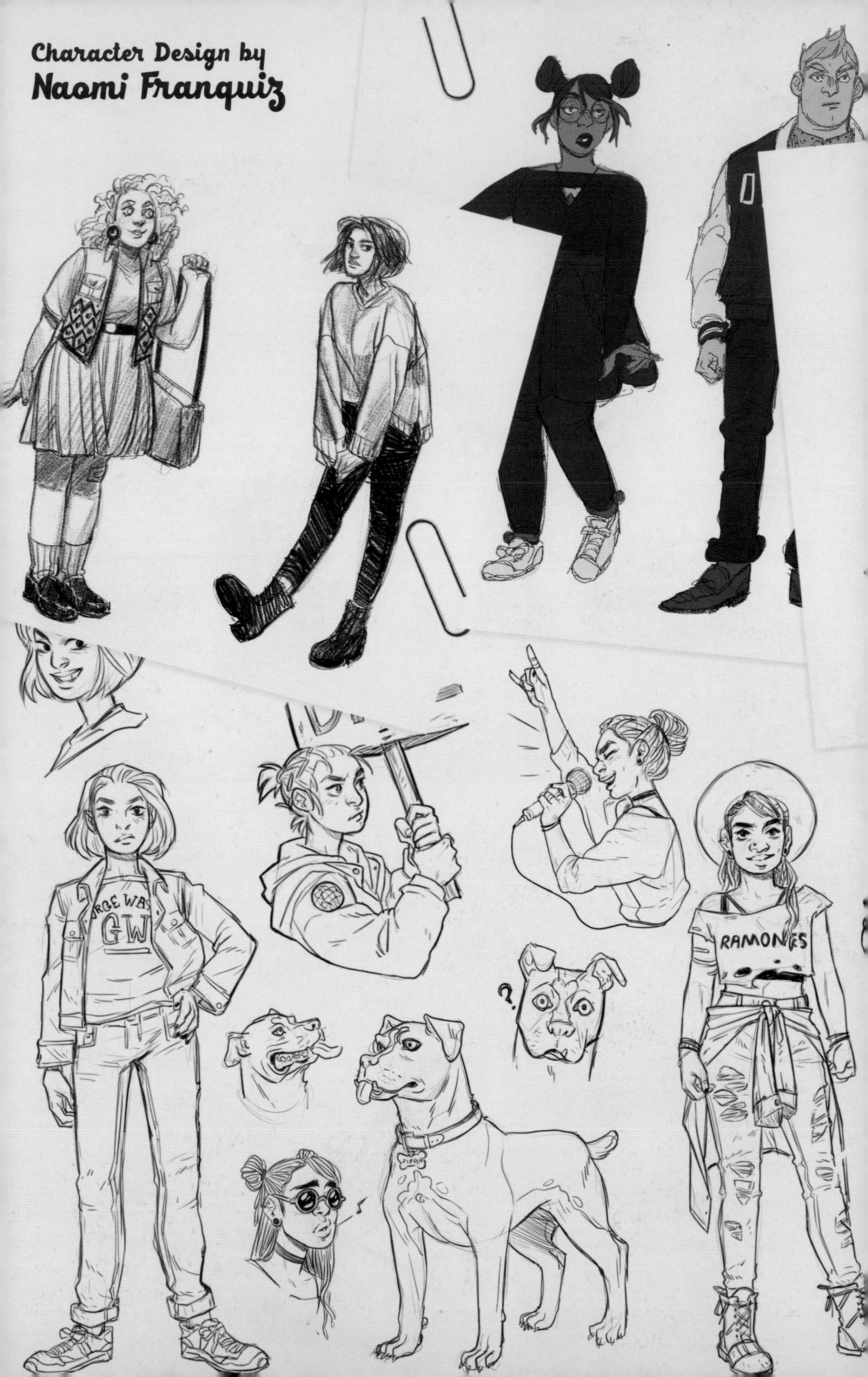

ORGE WAS
GW
RAMONES